Praise for *A Colder Kind of Death*:

"*A Colder Kind of Death* is a delightful blend of vicious murder, domestic interactions, and political infighting that is guaranteed to entertain." – John North, *Quill & Quire*

"A taut plot that moves along smartly with intriguing twists and surprises." – *Ottawa Citizen*

"A classic Bowen, engrossing and, finally, believable." – *Mystery Review*

"A denouement filled with enough curves to satisfy any mystery fan." – *Saskatoon Star-Phoenix*

"Gail Bowen writes terrifyingly clever thrillers." – *Horizons*

OTHER JOANNE KILBOURN MYSTERIES
BY GAIL BOWEN

Deadly Appearances (1990)
Murder at the Mendel (U.S.A. ed., *Love and Murder*) (1991)
The Wandering Soul Murders (1992)
A Killing Spring (1996)
Verdict in Blood (1998)
Burying Ariel (2000)

GAIL BOWEN

A Colder Kind of Death

A Joanne Kilbourn Mystery

M&S

This movie tie-in edition published January 2001
First M&S Paperback edition published September 19(
Cloth edition published 1994

Canadian Cataloguing in Publication Data

Bowen, Gail, 1942–
A colder kind of death

"A Joanne Kilbourn mystery"
ISBN 0-7710-1495-3

I. Title.

PS8553.O8995C6   C813'.54   C94-931733-0
PR9199.3.B68C6

We acknowledge the financial support of the Governm
of Canada through the Book Publishing Industry Develo
Program for our publishing activities.

Typeset in Trump Mediaeval by M&S, Toronto
Printed and bound in Canada

McClelland & Stewart Ltd.
The Canadian Publishers
481 University Avenue
Toronto, Ontario
M5G 2E9
www.mcclelland.com

1 2 3 4 5   05 04 03 02 01

For Ted, husband, lover, and friend

One

THREE minutes before the Hallowe'en edition of "Canada This Week" went on the air I learned that the man who murdered my husband had been shot to death. A technician was kneeling in front of me, adjusting my mike. Her hair was smoothed under a black skull-cap, and she was wearing a black leotard and black tights. Her name was Leslie Martin, and she was dressed as a bat.

"Check the Velcro on my wing, would you, Jo?" she asked, leaning towards me.

As I smoothed the Velcro on Leslie's shoulder, I glanced at the TV monitor behind her.

At first, I didn't recognize the face on the screen. The long blond hair and the pale goat-like eyes were familiar, but I couldn't place him. Then the still photograph was gone. In its place was the scene that had played endlessly in my head during the black months after Ian's death. But these pictures weren't in my head. The images on the TV were real. The desolate stretch of highway; the snow swirling in the air; the Volvo stationwagon with the door open on the driver's side; and on the highway beside the car, my husband's body with a dark and bloody spillage where his head should have been.

The sound was turned off. My hand tightened on Leslie's shoulder. "What happened there?" I asked.

Leslie turned towards the monitor. "I just heard part of it myself, but apparently that guy with the long hair was killed. He was out in the exercise yard at the penitentiary and someone drove past and shot him. He was dead before he hit the ground."

She stood and moved out of camera range. "Two minutes to showtime," she said. Through my earpiece, I heard the voice of the host of "Canada This Week."

"Happy Hallowe'en, Regina," he said. "What'll it be: 'Trick, or Treat'?"

Beside me, Senator Sam Spiegel laughed. "Trick," he said.

"Okay," the voice from Toronto said. "We'll start with NAFTA."

Sam groaned. "Why do we always have to talk about NAFTA?"

The host's voice was amiable. "Ours is not to wonder why, Sam. Now, I'll go to you first. Is the fact that environmental regulations aren't being equally enforced by our trading partners having an impact on investor confidence up here?"

Sam looked cherubic. "Beats me," he said.

Another voice, this one young and brusque, came through the earpiece. "This is Tom Brook in Toronto. Washington, is there any sign of Keith yet?"

I looked over at the monitor. The image of my husband's body had been replaced by images of Keith Harris, the third member of the "Canada This Week" panel. Keith was late, and as he slid into his chair and clipped on his lapel mike, he grinned apologetically. "I'm here. In the flesh, if not yet in the spirit. We're in the middle of a storm, and I couldn't get a taxi. Sorry, everybody."

The sight of Keith's private face, unguarded and gentle as his public face never was, stirred something in me. Until three weeks earlier, Keith had been the man in my life. At the outset, he had seemed an unlikely choice. We had both lived lives shaped by party politics; philosophically, we were as far apart as it is possible for reasonable people to be. Somehow, after the first hour we spent together, that hadn't mattered. Keith Harris was a good man, and until he had taken a job in Nationtv's Washington bureau at the beginning of summer, we had been happy. But distance had divided us in a way politics had not. Passion became friendship, and when Keith came to Regina for Thanksgiving he told me he had met someone else. I was still trying to sort out how I felt about that news.

The monitor switched to a picture of Sam and me. Through my earpiece, I could hear Keith's puzzlement. "Sam, what are you doing in Regina?"

"I came in with the prime minister yesterday and decided to stay over. I thought it would be fun to be with Jo in person for a change."

"Wise choice," Keith said. "I wish I was with you guys. It's colder than a witch's teat down here."

"Nice seasonal image, Keith," said the voice in my earpiece. "Okay, here we go."

In our studio, the man behind the camera, sleek in a spandex skeleton costume, held up five fingers, then four, three, two, one, and the red light came on. We were live to the East Coast.

I felt as if I had turned to wood. I missed my first question, and Sam Spiegel gave me a quick, worried look, then picked up the slack. When we broke for a commercial, he touched my arm. "Are you okay, Jo?"

"I think so," I said. "I just had a shock."

On the monitor, Keith was saying, "Come on, Jo. It's starting to sound like the Sam Spiegel show out there. The only reason I showed up tonight was to hear your voice."

"Five seconds," said the man in the spandex skeleton suit. He held up five fingers and started to drop them again.

Sam touched my arm. "I'll set you up. Tell about that screwup with the microphone when the P.M. was in town yesterday. It's a great story."

The red light went on. Sam turned the discussion to the

prime minister, and I told the story of the microphone that picked up some of the P.M.'s private and earthy musings about the U.S. president and broadcast them province-wide. My voice sounded odd to me, but Sam was right, it was a great story, and as I finished, the moderator's laughter rumbled reassuringly through my earpiece. We moved to other topics. I could hear my voice, remote but seemingly assured, suggesting, responding. Finally, the man in the skeleton suit held up his fingers again, and the red light on the camera in front of me went dark. It was over.

I turned to Sam. "Thanks," I said. "I was glad you were here tonight."

The producer, Jill Osiowy, came out of the control booth and said, "Good show, guys." Then she looked hard at me. "God, Jo, you look whipped. Is something wrong?"

I unclipped my microphone. "The monitor picked up the last few minutes of the news before we went on," I said. "Kevin Tarpley was shot today."

"And you were sitting here watching. Shit. Is there anything I can do?"

"Get them to run that tape with the sound, would you? All I saw was the pictures."

She looked at me dubiously. "Are you sure?"

"Yeah, I'm sure."

She sighed. "I'll get Leslie to set it up."

We went into an editing room and stood behind Leslie Martin as she brought the five o'clock news up on a monitor. It was a surreal moment. The woman in the bat suit conjuring up the image of my husband's killer.

When the boy with the goat's eyes appeared on the screen, I had trouble absorbing what the news anchor was saying. His words seemed to come at me in disconnected units. "Convicted murderer Kevin Tarpley . . . twenty-five . . . assailant unknown . . ."

He was twenty-five. He had been nineteen at the trial. When he stood up for sentencing, his hands were trembling, and I was filled with pity. Then I had remembered what those hands had done, and it hadn't mattered how young he was. I wanted him dead.

I had wanted him dead, and now he was.

More words came at me from the TV screen. "Police are baffled . . . model prisoner . . . born again . . . spent days and nights reading the Bible . . ."

The goat-eyed boy vanished, and the snowy highway filled the screen again. The polished voice of the news anchor continued, and I tried to make myself focus. He was talking about my husband. "Twenty-eight when he was named to Howard Dowhanuik's cabinet . . . the country's youngest attorney general . . . believed by many to be the man who would succeed Dowhanuik . . ." The anchor's handsome face filled the screen. Leslie Martin looked up. Jill nodded and the screen went blank.

"Come on," Jill said. "I'll buy you a drink."

"I can't," I said. "I've got to get home. Taylor's waiting to go Hallowe'ening."

Jill put her arm around my shoulder and gave it a squeeze. "I'll walk you to the door."

The lobby of Nationtv is a three-storey galleria with a soaring ceiling and glass walls. In the daytime, the area is filled with natural light, and the elm trees on the lawn outside make shadowy patterns on the terrazzo floor. But that night as Jill and I came upstairs from the TV studio, the sky was darkening, and the leafless trees were black against the cold October sky.

All Hallow's Eve. Reflexively, I shuddered. A man and two women came through the entrance doors into the lobby. I knew them; they had been in the Legislature with my husband. They were all out of politics now, but it was politics that brought them to Nationtv. Politics and auld lang syne.

The year before, after ten years in the wilderness, we had won the provincial election. People were feeling good about the party again, so it was time to raise money. The following Wednesday, we were holding a roast for the former

leader and one-time premier, Howard Dowhanuik. After he
resigned as leader, Howard had moved to Toronto to teach
constitutional law at Osgoode Hall. It was a long way
from the rough and tumble of Saskatchewan politics, but
Howard hadn't forgotten that even successful election
campaigns have to be paid for. Despite his loathing for testi-
monials, he was coming home. I was emceeing the dinner,
and I'd asked Jill to arrange for some of the members who'd
served in the Legislature with Howard to tape a segment of
a local show called "Happenings" to publicize the event.
The taping was that night.

For a beat, Howard's former colleagues stood in the doorway, unbuttoning jackets, accustoming their eyes to the
light. Then Craig Evanson spotted me and started across
the cavernous lobby. The others followed.

Craig was fifty years old, but he still moved with the
loose-limbed shamble of an adolescent. When he reached
out to take my hand, his fingers grazed my shoulder.

"You saw the news report," he said.

I nodded.

"Are you okay?" he asked.

"I will be," I said.

"This is all wrong, Jo," he said. "You and Ian were so
close. Julie always called you 'the legendary couple.'"

I didn't know what to say. Craig and his first wife, Julie,
had been a legendary couple, too. Craig was the most uxori-
ous of men, but Julie was poison. Before she had surprised
everyone by divorcing him two years earlier, she had come
close to destroying Craig's life. The day the divorce was
final, it was Craig's turn for surprises. He resigned his seat
in the Legislature and married one of his constituents, a
twenty-five-year-old midwife named Manda Traynor, who
had come to Craig's office asking him for help in organizing
a campaign to legalize midwifery. Now Manda was expect-
ing their first child, and as Craig stood holding my hand,
it was obvious that it was his new wife who filled his
thoughts.

"I'm just beginning to understand what you lost when you lost Ian," Craig said simply. "If anything were to happen to Manda . . ." His voice trailed off.

The woman standing behind Craig grunted with annoyance. Tess Malone looked exactly as she had on the day she'd been elected twenty years earlier: her hair was still a helmet of honey curls; the lines of her corsetted body were still bullet smooth. She looked impenetrable, like a woman who woke up every morning and prepared herself for combat. It was not a fanciful image. Tess's life was a battle.

She had run for office four times, and she had won four times. Her slogan was always the same: TRUST TESS. To an outsider, the words seemed sentimental and empty, but Tess's supporters knew the slogan was a covenant. The people who voted for Tess knew that they could trust her to be at their daughters' weddings, their babies' christenings, and their grandparents' funerals. They knew that Tess would be their champion if they needed to get their mother an appointment at the Chiropody Clinic, their son into drug rehabilitation, or their wife's resumé into the hands of a bureaucrat who might actually read it.

There was one other matter on which friend and foe alike knew they could trust Tess. Everyone who knew Tess Malone knew she would fight the right to an abortion till the day she drew her last breath. Ian had liked and admired her, but when he had been attorney general, he and Tess had fought bitterly about our government's policy on reproductive choice; after we lost, they still spent hours quarrelling over what he called Tess's life-long love affair with the foetus. The month after he died, Tess resigned her seat in the house to devote herself full time to a pro-life organization called Beating Heart. She said she quit politics because she was frustrated at our party's refusal to change its stand on abortion. I always thought she just missed her old sparring partner. As she stood looking up into Craig Evanson's face, speaking in the rasp of an unrepentant two-pack-a-day smoker, I felt a surge of affection.

"Don't be an ass, Craig," she said. "And don't chase trouble. As Jo can tell you, trouble finds you soon enough. You don't have to send up flares."

Tess turned to me. Rhinestone flowers bloomed on the frames of her glasses, but the eyes behind the thick lenses were clever and kind.

"What can I do to help, Jo? One thought . . . I'm sure you already have your talk for Howard's dinner organized, but if you don't feel like standing in front of a room full of people, I could be the emcee . . ."

Jane O'Keefe, the other woman in the group, raked her fingers through her short blond hair. "Not while I'm capable of rational thought," she said. Jane was an M.D., and the past summer she and three other doctors had opened a Women's Health Centre in which abortions were performed. There had been some ugly reactions in the community, and Tess had fanned the flames. She'd been on every talk show in town denouncing the Women's Centre and the women who staffed it.

"Gary can do it," Jane said. She turned and looked out the door towards the parking lot. "If he ever shows up, that is."

Tess moved towards her, "Jane, you yourself said . . ."

"I know what I said. I said I wanted a woman to emcee Howard's dinner, but if Jo backs out, you and I are the women, and I don't want you and you don't want me. That leaves Gary and Craig, and Craig is a lousy public speaker."

Craig made a little bow in Jane's direction. "Thank you, Jane."

Oblivious, Jane sailed on. "Don't be touchy, Craig. You're capable of keeping your pants zipped, which is more than I can say for my brother-in-law."

Right on cue, Jane O'Keefe's brother-in-law burst through the door of Nationtv.

In the women's magazines of the fifties there were love stories with heroes whose physical characteristics were as formulaic as those of a knight in medieval romance. With their rangy bodies and rugged features, they leapt off the pages into our female hearts. Gary Stephens had those kind of good looks, and once upon a time he had been a hero, at least to me. When I knew him first, Gary was a reformer out to transform the political landscape. Then, he changed.

It seemed to happen overnight. One day he just stopped fighting the good fight and became a jerk and a womanizer. The political world is fuelled by gossip, and for a while there was hot speculation about Gary, but the explanation most of us finally accepted was supplied by his sister-in-law. Jane O'Keefe said that, in her opinion, Gary simply lost his death struggle with the id. Whatever had happened, Gary Stephens wasn't a hero anymore, at least not in my books.

"Apologies for being late," he said. "I was . . ."

Jane smiled at him. "We understand, Gary. Everyone knows it takes a man longer after he hits forty."

Gary shrugged. "For the record, I was with a client." He turned towards me. "I heard about Kevin Tarpley on the radio coming over here. I'm sorry, babe. All those painful memories, and Ian was the best."

"I always thought so," I said, and I could hear the ice in my voice.

Jane O'Keefe looked at her watch. "We should get inside. Considering that not one of us was on time today, I don't think we should risk re-rescheduling." She touched my arm. "It was good to see you again, Jo. Hang in there."

Gary leaned forward, gave me a practised one-armed hug and kissed my cheek. The others said goodbye and headed towards the elevators. As the doors closed behind them, I reached up and brushed the place that Gary Stephens's lips had touched.

"Why would he kiss me?" I said to Jill.

She shrugged. "'Man sees the deed, but God sees the intention.'"

"That's a comforting thought," I said.

"Thomas Aquinas was a comforting kind of guy," Jill

said. "You'd know these things too, if you'd had the benefit of a Catholic education."

When we stepped through the big glass doors into the night, Jill breathed deeply. The air smelled of wet leaves and wood smoke.

"Hallowe'en," she said, hugging herself against the cold. "Good times."

She grinned at me, and the years melted away. She was the shining-eyed redhead I'd met twenty years before when she showed up unannounced at Ian's office the day she graduated from the School of Journalism. She had handed him her brand new diploma and said, "My name is Jill Osiowy, and I want to make a difference." Ian always said he hadn't known whether to hire her or have her committed.

"I'm glad Ian didn't have you committed," I said.

"What?"

"Nothing," I said. "You'd better get back inside. It's freezing out here. Call me if you hear anything more about Kevin Tarpley."

When I pulled up in front of my house on Regina Avenue, Taylor and Jess Stephens were on the front porch supervising as my friend, Hilda McCourt, lit the candle in our pumpkin. Jess was Gary's son, and he and Taylor had been friends since the first day of Grade 1 when they discovered they could both roll their eyes back in their heads so the pupils seemed to disappear.

Jess was dressed as a magician, Taylor was in her butterfly costume, and Hilda was wearing black tights, a black turtleneck, silver rings on every finger and, around her neck, a silver chain with a jewelled crescent moon pendant. Her brilliant red hair was frizzed out in a halo around her handsome face. Hilda was past eighty and counting, but she could still turn heads, and she knew it.

When she saw me coming up the walk, she called out. "Wait, I'll turn on the porch light for you. We had it off so the lighting of the pumpkin would be more dramatic."

"Don't spoil the effect," I said. "I don't need a light."

Jess waved at me.

"My mum's sick, and my dad's doing something. Taylor said I could come Hallowe'ening with you. Can I?"

"Sure," I said. "Go call your mum."

He grinned. I could see the space where his front teeth were missing. "I already did," he said. "My dad's gonna pick me up when we're through."

"Good enough," I said.

Taylor was looking at the face of the jack o'lantern, mesmerized. "Blissed out" her brother, Angus, would have said. I knelt down beside her. "T, I'm sorry I'm late," I said. "I got hung up with something at the station."

"I saw the news," Hilda said quietly.

I looked up at her. "Did the kids?"

Hilda shook her head. "No, Angus was in his room trying to decide what to wear to his dance, and tonight Taylor's concerns appear to stop at her wingtips." She leaned towards me. "How are you bearing up?"

"I think trailing along behind these guys with twenty pounds of candy in a pillowcase might be just what I need."

"In that case," said Hilda, "we'll continue with the ceremony here. I was just going to tell the magician and the butterfly the story of Jack O'Lantern."

I stood in the doorway and listened as Hilda told the kids the story of a man named Jack who was so mischievous that the devil wouldn't let him into hell because he was afraid Jack would trick him.

Hilda's voice was sombre as she finished. "And so, when Jack learned he'd have to roam the earth forever, he stole a burning coal from the underworld and placed it inside a turnip to light his way."

Jess looked puzzled. "Why didn't Jack use a pumpkin?" he asked.

"Because this was long ago, in Ireland, and they didn't have pumpkins," Hilda said.

Taylor shook her head. "Poor Jack. Carving that turnip must have taken him about twenty hours."

I touched Taylor's shoulder. "I'm going to go upstairs and check on your brother. You and Jess go in and have one last pee, and then we'll hit the streets. Okay?"

"Yeah," she said, "that'll be okay." She dropped to her knees and leaned forward so that her eyes were looking into the bright triangular eyes of the jack o'lantern. "How did Jack keep the coal lit?" she asked.

I went inside, glad it was Hilda who had to come up with an answer.

Angus was standing in the middle of his room. There were clothes thrown everywhere, but he wasn't wearing anything except a pair of boxer shorts with pigs on them. When he saw me, he exploded. "The guys are coming by in twenty minutes and I haven't figured out a costume. Everything I try makes me look totally stupid."

"I guess this isn't the time for me to suggest that you should have started planning your costume sooner," I said.

He looked exasperated. "Mum, just give me a little help here . . . Please."

At fifteen, Angus had Ian's dark good looks. He had grown about a foot in the last six months. I looked at him and remembered.

"I have an idea," I said.

I went down into the basement and pulled out a trunk in which, against all the advice in the books for widows, I had kept some of Ian's things. I'd filled the trunk a month to the day after Ian died, but until that Hallowe'en night I hadn't had the heart to open it.

Under a pile of sweaters, I found what I was looking for: an old herringbone cape with a matching Sherlock Holmes hat and a walking stick. I took them back upstairs and handed them to my son.

"Do you remember this outfit?" I asked. "Daddy wore it every Hallowe'en."

Angus had put on a pair of jeans and a turtleneck. He

threw the cape around his shoulders and pulled the cap over his dark hair. He looked so much like Ian I could feel my throat close.

"Well?" I said.

He looked at himself in the full-length mirror on his cupboard door.

"Pretty good," he said. Then his reflection in the mirror grinned at me. "Actually, Mum, the cape really rocks hard. Thanks." He started for the door.

"Hey," I said. "Aren't you going to clean up this mess?"

"Later," he said. "Chill out, Mum. It's a night to party."

When he left, the smell of the cape lingered, potent as memory. I swallowed hard and went downstairs to get my daughter and her friend.

It was a great night for Hallowe'ening. There was a three-quarter moon, and, for Taylor and Jess, every street held a surprise: doors opened by snaggle-toothed vampires and mummies swathed in white; stepladders with glowing pumpkins on every step; and on the corner of McCallum and Albert, a witch cackling in front of the cauldron that had smoked with dry ice every Hallowe'en since Angus was a baby.

When we turned onto Regina Avenue, Gary Stephens was pulling up in front of our house.

"Perfect timing," I said, as he got out of the car.

"Right," he said absently.

And then Jess ran to him, holding out his pillowcase. "Dad, look at all the stuff I got."

As he knelt beside his son, Gary's face was transformed. His charm with women might have been as false as the proverbial harlot's oath, but Gary Stephens's love for his son was the real thing. It wasn't hard to get warmth in my voice when I said goodnight.

Taylor went straight to the dining room and dumped all her candy on the table, checking for razor blades the way her Grade 1 teacher had instructed her to. She pulled up a chair and began to arrange the candy in categories: things she liked and things she didn't like. Then she tried new categories: chocolate bars, gum, candy kisses, gross stuff. Finally, she lay her head down on her arms.

"Okay," I said. "That's it. Time for this butterfly to fold her wings."

I took her upstairs, scrubbed off her butterfly makeup, and tucked her in. When I came back, Hilda was sitting in a rocker beside the fireplace. A fire was blazing in the grate, and on the low table in front of Hilda, there was a tray with two glasses, a bottle of Jameson's, and a round loaf of fruit bread.

"I thought you'd welcome a little sustenance," Hilda said, as she poured the Irish whiskey.

"Where did the bread come from?" I asked.

"Taylor and I made it this afternoon. It's called barm brack; it's traditional in Ireland at Hallowe'en."

I cut myself a slice and bit into it. It tasted of spice and candied peel and fruit. "Good," I said.

"The children didn't think so," Hilda said drily. "They were polite, but they didn't exactly wolf it down."

"All the more for us," I said and took another bite. My teeth hit something papery and hard. I raised my hand to my mouth and took the paper out.

Hilda laughed, "I should have warned you. The barm brack is full of little charms. Of course, you've already discovered that."

I looked at the waxed paper triangle in my hand.

"Open it," Hilda said. "The charm you get is supposed to foretell your future. Angus got the gold coin."

"Good," I said, "my old age is taken care of." I opened the paper in my hand. Inside was a baby doll, no larger than my thumbnail.

"I must have someone else's fortune," I said. "I'm forty-nine years old, Hilda. I think my child-bearing days are over."

"The barm brack is never wrong," Hilda said placidly.

"The baby in your future could belong to someone else, you know."

I thought of my older daughter and her husband. A grandchild. It was a nice thought. I lifted my glass of Jameson's to Hilda. "To Irish traditions," I said. "And to Irish stories. You know I'd forgotten that story about poor Jack O'Lantern with his turnip. My mother-in-law told it to me years ago."

Hilda looked thoughtful. "Your husband was Irish, wasn't he?"

"His family was. Ian was born here." I sipped my whisky. "And, as you saw on the news tonight, he died here."

"I remember the case, of course," she said. "It was before you and I met. It struck me as being a particularly brutal and senseless death."

"That about sums it up," I said. "At first, I thought the brutality was the hardest part to deal with. Isn't there a prayer where you ask God to grant you a good death?"

Hilda nodded.

"Well, Ian's death was not good. It was vicious and terrifying. He was beaten to death by a stranger. It was during the week between Christmas and New Year's. He was on the Trans-Canada, coming back from a funeral in Swift Current. There was a blizzard. A car had broken down by the side of the highway. When Ian stopped to help, Kevin Tarpley, that man who was killed today, asked Ian to take him and his girlfriend to a party. At the trial, Kevin Tarpley said that when Ian refused, he smashed Ian's head in with a crowbar."

The shadow shapes on the ceiling shifted. In the stillness I could hear the ticking of the hall clock, regular as a heartbeat.

"I had nightmares for months about what he must have gone through in those last minutes. But in the long run, it wasn't the brutality that drove me crazy; it was the lack of logic. It turned out that Kevin Tarpley's car hadn't broken down at all. When the police found it, it was fine. Kevin told them he got scared when the needle on the heat gauge went into the red zone." I leaned across the table. "Hilda, my husband died because a boy panicked. Isn't that crazy? But everything about Ian's death was senseless. Did you know he went to that funeral in Swift Current because he lost a coin toss?"

Hilda shook her head. "That particular cruelty didn't make the papers."

"We were at a Boxing Day party the Caucus Office had for families who'd stayed in town for the holidays. I guess everyone had had a couple of drinks when Howard remembered that somebody had to go to Charlie Heinbecker's funeral the next day. Charlie was . . ."

"Minister of Agriculture in Howard's first government. I remember him well," Hilda said. "He was a fine man."

"He was," I agreed, "but it's a long drive to Swift Current, and that time of year the roads can be treacherous. Nobody wanted to volunteer. Anyway, somebody decided all the M.L.A.s who knew Charlie should toss a coin. They did, and Ian lost. The next morning he drove off, and I never saw him again. Hilda, it could just as easily have been Howard or Jane or Gary or any of them on that road."

"But it wasn't."

"No," I said, "it wasn't."

The light from the fireplace struck the silver moon on Hilda's necklace and turned it to fire. When she spoke again, her voice was as old as time:

> ". . . this invites the occult mind,
> Cancels our physics with a sneer,
> And spatters all we knew of denouement
> Across the expedient and wicked stones."

Suddenly, I was so tired I could barely move.

"Hilda, how can we live if the only answer is that there are no answers?"

She leaned across the table. Her eyes were as impenetrable as agate. "That's not what the poem says, Joanne. It says there always are answers. They may sicken us and they may terrify us, but that doesn't make them any less true, and it doesn't make them any less powerful."

She picked up a knife and sliced into the barm brack. "Now, let's have some bread and a little more whisky before the fire dies."

After Hilda went up to bed, I walked through the darkened house, checking, making sure we were safe. As I locked the front door, I glanced through the glass and saw our jack o'lantern on the porch, its candle guttering in the October darkness.

I opened the door and, hugging myself against the cold, I blew out the candle, picked up the pumpkin, and brought it back into the kitchen. When I moved Angus's schoolbooks along the counter to make a place for the jack o'lantern, I uncovered a small stack of mail. There wasn't much: a new *Owl* magazine for Taylor, a bill from Columbia House addressed to Angus, a pretty postcard inviting me to the opening of a visiting show of Impressionist landscapes at the Mackenzie Gallery, and an envelope, standard size, nine by twelve. My students had had essays due the day before, and my first thought was that the envelope held an essay from one of them, trying to limit the penalty for a late paper. But when I glanced at the envelope, I noticed that the letters of my name and address were oddly formed, as if the writer couldn't decide between printing and writing. I opened the envelope. There was a letter in the same curiously unformed hand.

Dear Mrs. Kilbourn,

I must be the last one you thought you'd here from but this is important. WE MUST ALL APPEAR BEFORE THE

JUDGEMENT SEAT OF CHRIST, THAT EVERY ONE MAY
RECEIVE THE THINGS DONE IN HIS BODY, ACCORDING
TO THAT HE HATH DONE, WHETHER IT BE GOOD OR
BAD. (2 CORINTHIANS, 5) But the Rev. Paschal Temple
says I must try to atone on this side of the grave for the
wrongs I did. I'm sorry for what happened to your husband, but things are not what they seem. You may hate
me, but pay attention to what I wrote on the picture
because it is not My Truth. It is God's Truth.

                                          Kevin Tarpley

Attached to the letter with a paperclip was a newspaper clipping. It was the publicity photo for Howard
Dowhanuik's dinner. I was in the middle, looking slightly
dazed as I always seem to in photos. On my left was Craig
Evanson, and beside him was Tess Malone. On my right
were Jane O'Keefe and Gary Stephens. Jane was holding the
whimsical ceramic statue of Howard that the party was
going to present to him the night of the roast. Kevin Tarpley
had cut off the original caption of the photo and taped on a
piece of scribbler paper. There was a quotation printed in
block letters on the paper: "PUT NOT YOUR TRUST IN
RULERS, PSALM 146."

I was standing in my own kitchen. The air was pungent
with the smells of burned pumpkin meat and candle wax –
good familiar smells. Upstairs my children and my friend
were sleeping, safe and happy. In the hall, the clock struck
twelve, and I could feel my nerves twang. Hallowe'en was
over. It was All Saints' Day, the day to remember "our
brethren departed," and I had just received a warning from a
dead man.

Two

WHEN I looked out my bedroom window at 7:00 a.m. on All Saints' Day, the world was grey, the colour of half-mourning the Victorians wore when the first black-edged grief was over. Fog blanketed everything. Rose, our golden retriever, came over to the window and nudged me hopefully.

"I don't suppose you'd forgo the walk this morning," I said. She looked anxious. "I withdraw the suggestion," I said. I pulled on my jogging pants and a sweatshirt and found my running shoes under the bed. When I was ready, I went into Angus's room. Our collie was sleeping in her usual place at the end of his bed.

"Come on, Sadie," I said, "no rest for the wicked." As I walked through the kitchen, I plugged in the coffee and took a coffee cake and a pound of bacon out of the freezer. On Sundays, I declared all the food in our house cholesterol-free.

As the dogs and I ran down the steps from Albert Street to the north shore of Wascana Lake, I was chilled by the wind off the water. It was an ugly morning. Usually, when I stood on the lakeshore, I could see the graceful lines of the Legislature that had been the focal point of so much of my adult life, but today the legislative building was just a shape, dark and foreboding in the fog, and the lake where

19

Ian and I had canoed in summer and taught our children to skate in winter was bleak. Around the shoreline, ice was starting to form, and it pressed, swollen with garbage, against the shore. The geese in the middle of the lake seemed frozen, lifeless as decoys. Every spring Ian and I had taken the kids to the park to feed the new goslings; by mid-summer the birds, wise in the ways of the park, would run at us if we forgot to bring them bread. Ian used to call them the goose-punks.

As I crossed the bridge along the parkway, Nabokov's description of a room of his childhood floated to the top of my consciousness. "Everything is as it should be. Nothing will ever change. Nobody will ever die." Numb with cold and the pain of memory, I turned south and headed for home.

I could hear Taylor the minute I walked through the door. She was in the kitchen talking on the telephone. She was still in her pajamas, and there was a half-eaten candy apple in her hand. When she saw me, she grinned and waved it. As I took the dogs off their leashes and set the table, Taylor's flutey little-girl voice was telling the person on the other end of the phone about Hallowe'en.

"At the house on the corner by the bridge, there was a Count Dracula giving out candy, and he had pointed teeth and blood on his chin, but Jess said it was fake, and next door to Count Dracula there was just an ordinary man but he gave out UNICEF money and McDonald's coupons, and then there was . . ."

I turned on the oven, put in a pan of bacon and the coffee cake, then started upstairs. Angus and Hilda were in the living room, drinking orange juice and talking about Shakespeare. Hilda had taught high-school English for forty-five years, and Angus had an essay on *Othello* due the next day. I gave them the thumbs-up sign and tiptoed by. When I had showered and came back downstairs, the kitchen smelled of bacon and cinnamon, and Taylor was in mid-sentence. "Sixteen packets of Chiclets," she was saying, "thirty-two little candy bars, a lot of candy kisses, seven bags of peanuts . . ."

"Okay, T," I said, "that's enough. Time to get off the phone."

She smiled and held out the receiver. "It's for you," she said. "Long distance."

Keith Harris was on the other end of the line.

"Tell me you didn't reverse the charges," I said.

"I didn't reverse the charges," he said, "and it was worth every penny. Taylor has a nice narrative style – very thorough. It was almost like being there."

"I'll bet it was," I said, as I watched her disappear into the living room with her candy apple.

When Keith spoke again, his voice was serious. "Jo, one of the Canadian press guys just told me about Kevin Tarpley. He didn't know much. Just that Tarpley was shot, and the police were investigating."

"That's all I know too, except . . . Keith, I got a letter from Kevin Tarpley last night."

Keith swore softly.

"Apparently," I said, "when he was in prison, he was born again. Just as well, considering the events of the past twenty-four hours. Anyway, he wrote me a letter full of scriptural warnings and advice about how I should live my life."

"Is there anything I can do?"

"There's nothing anybody can do." I could hear the petulance in my voice. It was as unappealing as petulance usually is. I took a deep breath and started again. "Keith, I'm sorry. It's just that that whole time was so terrible, not just Ian dying, but the trial and our lives splashed all over the papers. I didn't want to think about any of it ever again. And now . . ."

"And now you have a chance to put an end to it once and for all." Keith's voice was strong and certain. "Jo, has it occurred to you that maybe that poor bastard Tarpley has done you a favour? Maybe now that he's dead, you really can close the door. You've got a lot to look forward to, you know: the kids, your job, the show."

"But not you, anymore," I said. "How's the lady lobby-ist?"

"She's fine. Jo, I thought we'd agreed to keep her out of it."

"Sorry," I said. "Being dumped isn't any easier at forty-nine than it was at fourteen."

"You weren't dumped," he said. "It was a joint deci-sion."

"Yes, but you made the joint decision first. Look, let's change the subject. What's happening in Washington today?"

"I'm having lunch with some Texas bankers."

"Three fingers of Jack Daniel's and a platter of ribs. You lucky duck."

"Actually, we're eating at a place in Georgetown that specializes in braised zucchini."

"Good," I said. "Being dumped is one thing. But knowing you're having great barbecue while I'm eating Spaghetti-O's would just be too much."

He laughed. "The day you eat Spaghetti-O's . . ."

"Listen, I'd better let you get rolling," I said. "The cost for this phone call must be into four digits."

"Money well spent," he said. "Take care of yourself, Jo."

"You too," I said.

The next phone call wasn't as heartening. It was a reporter from one of our local radio stations. He told me his name was Troy Smith-Windsor, and he asked me how I felt about Kevin Tarpley's death.

"Relieved," I said, and hung up.

He must have speed-dialled me back. This time his voice was low and confiding. "I know this is hard for you," he murmured. "Believe it or not, it's hard for me, too. Sometimes I hate my job, Mrs. Kilbourn, but as much as you and I value your privacy, people have a right to know. You're a well-known member of this community. People want to hear about how you're dealing with this tragic reminder of your husband's murder. Give me something to share with them."

When I answered, I tried to match Troy Smith-Windsor's tone. Unction has never been my strong suit, but I did my earnest best. "I guess I hadn't thought of it that way, Troy," I said. "But now that I have, could you tell your listeners that I appreciate their concern. And Troy, could you please tell them that, while I regret Kevin Tarpley's death as I would regret the death of any human being, I welcome the chance to put this tragedy behind me and get on with my life. Have you got that?"

"I've got it, Mrs. Kilbourn," Troy Smith-Windsor said huskily. "And thank you."

"Thank you, Troy," I said, and I hung up, proud of myself.

My self-esteem was short-lived. When I turned, Angus was standing in the kitchen doorway. He was still wearing his pig shorts; his eyes were puffy and his dark hair was tangled from sleep.

"Someone shot the man who killed Dad," he said. "The woman on the radio said it happened yesterday. You knew." A statement, not a question.

I nodded. "Angus, you've been through so much already. Last night you were excited about your party. I thought the news about Kevin Tarpley would keep till morning."

"You should have told me," he said.

I reached my arms out to embrace him. He twisted away from me.

"I'm not a kid, Mum. Last summer I went down to the library and looked up the stories about Dad. They have them on microfiche."

I closed my eyes and the scene was there: my son in the dimly lit microfiche room, surrounded by strangers as he watched the images of his father's death flicker on a screen.

"Angus, if you wanted to hear about what happened, you should have come to me."

His voice was exasperated. "Mum, don't you remember what you were like then? You weren't like you. You were like a zombie or something. I didn't want that to happen again."

"It's not going to," I said. I put my hands on his shoulders. "Now, what do you want to know?"

"Everything," he said.

He was six-foot-one, but his body was still lithe with a child's vulnerability.

"You're sure about this, Angus."

He looked at me steadily. "I'm sure, Mum."

"Okay," I said, "I'll call Jill and get her to dig out the files."

Five minutes later, it was all arranged. After church, Angus and I would go to Nationtv and look at everything the network had on the Ian Kilbourn case. Hilda had already planned to take Taylor to the art gallery, so the afternoon was free. There were no obstacles. As I poured the eggs into the frying pan, I wavered between dread and anticipation. Pandora must have been unsure, too, in that split second when her hand lingered at the edge of the box.

Few places are deader than a television station on a Sunday afternoon. A security guard watching a Mr. Fix-it show on TV waved us past the front desk. We met Jill in the corridor outside her office. She was wearing jeans and an Amnesty International sweatshirt, and she was pulling a little red wagon full of Beta tapes.

"I hope you two know you're taking a chance with these," she said. "I just brought them up from the library, and I haven't screened any of them. There may be things you'd rather not see."

"I'll be okay," Angus said. "Mum. . .?"

"Let's go," I said.

Jill started towards the elevator. "The boardroom upstairs is free. We can screen the tapes there. It's got a fridge, Angus. They usually keep it pretty well stocked."

As the elevator doors closed, I turned to Jill. "Have you heard anything more about what happened at the penitentiary?"

"Not much," she said. "The prison officials are mortified, of course. It doesn't do to have a prisoner killed inside a federal penitentiary, but the warden says their job is to make sure their inmates don't get a shot at John Q. Public; they're not set up to keep John Q. Public from getting a shot at one of their inmates. And, you know, the man has a point. Prince Albert, Saskatchewan, isn't Detroit. No one could have predicted a drive-by shooting."

"Especially not of a model prisoner," I said.

Jill looked at me sharply. "Right," she said. "And he was a model prisoner. Until six months ago, the warden said all he did was work out in the gym, watch television, and count the days till his next conjugal visit."

The elevator doors opened, and we stepped out. "With Maureen Gault," I said, remembering. "The girl who was in the car with him that night. They got married during the trial, didn't they?"

"In unseemly haste, some thought." Jill raised her eyebrows.

"That's when he changed his story." Angus's voice was tense. "I read that in the paper. After they got married, he said she tried to stop him from . . . doing what he did. That's why her fingerprints were on the . . ." For a moment he faltered again. Then he said firmly, "on the weapon."

"The Crown dropped the charges against her that afternoon," Jill said. "Just like in the movies." She stopped and pulled a key-ring out of her jeans pocket. "Here we are," she said. "Corporate heaven."

The boardroom was handsome: walls the colour of bittersweet, an oversized rectangular oak table surrounded by comfortable chairs, a big-screen TV, and, in the far corner, a refrigerator with fake wood finish. Jill opened the fridge and handed a Coke to Angus.

"Pick a chair, any chair," she said. She took out a bottle of beer, opened it, and positioned it carefully on the table. "Heads up, Jo," she said, then she slid the beer along the polished surface of the table towards me. As I caught it, she grinned. "I've always wanted to do that," she said. "Okay, it's your show. Where do you want to start?"

I bent over and took a tape out of the wagon. The label on the spine said "Kilbourn/Tarpley/Gault." The names had the resonance of the familiar, like the names of partners in a law firm or of baseball players who had executed a historic triple play. I handed the tape to Jill. When she put it in the VCR and switched off the lights, my pulse began to race. I wasn't looking forward to the show.

But the first images that filled the screen weren't of death but of life at its best. Ian was standing on the steps of the Legislature being sworn in as Attorney General. It was a sun-splashed June day; the wind tousled his dark hair and, sensitive even then about how his hair was thinning, Ian reached up quickly to smooth it. As he took the oath of office, the camera moved in for a closeup; at the sight of his father, Angus leaned forward in his chair.

And then I was there on the screen, beside Ian. My hair was shoulder-length and straight; I was wearing a flowered granny dress and holding our oldest child, Mieka, in my arms. She was three weeks old, and I was twenty-eight.

"You were so young," Angus said softly.

I felt a catch in my throat. Jill's voice from the end of the table was caustic. "And her hair was so brown, Angus. Check it out . . ."

A smile started at the corners of Angus's mouth.

"How come your hair didn't turn blond till you were forty, Jo?" Jill continued.

Angus's smile grew broader. Relieved that we'd gotten through the moment, I said. "I don't know. It seems to have happened to a lot of women my age."

"Maybe it had something to do with living through the sixties," Angus said innocently, and we all laughed.

Then the next image was on the screen, and we stopped laughing. It was the scene on the highway. Jill jabbed at the remote control and fast-forwarded the tape until the snowy highway gave way to scenes outside the Regina Courthouse. Police cars pulled up. Officers ran out of the building, then ran back in. Television people jostled one another for position. One young woman with a camera was knocked back into a snowbank. The sequences were as mindlessly predictable as a bad movie of the week.

"This is where the RCMP brought Kevin Tarpley and Maureen Gault in," I said to Angus. He seemed frozen in front of the screen. "Their luck ran out. You know that stretch of the Trans-Canada, where it happened, Angus. Normally, during a blizzard they could have counted on those hills south of Chaplin being deserted. There wasn't anything to connect the two of them to your dad, so they might have gotten away. But there was a car from Regina going back from the funeral. The driver spotted the Volvo by the side of the road and pulled over; she called the RCMP on her CB radio. Kevin and Maureen had started back to where they'd left their car on the grid road just south of the highway. The RCMP didn't have any trouble catching them."

"Good," he said.

I took a long swallow of beer. Kevin and Maureen had finally appeared on screen; the officer taking Kevin from the car put his hand on top of Kevin's head to keep him from hitting it on the doorframe. It was an oddly tender gesture. I remembered the bloody mess of my husband's head and swallowed hard. Kevin and Little Mo were wearing matching jackets from their high school; I could see their names on their sleeves. He was wearing her jacket, and she was wearing his. Kevin and Little Mo, cross-dressing killers. They disappeared inside the courthouse, and the screen went black.

"More?" asked Jill

"I have to go to the bathroom," Angus said.

"Are you okay?" I asked. He caught the anxiety in my voice, and his eyes flashed with anger.

"I'm fifteen years old, Mum," he called over his shoulder as he walked out of the room.

"Fifteen," Jill said, "capable of handling life."

"He seems to be doing a better job of it than I am at the moment," I said. "When I saw those faces, I wanted to smash in the screen."

"I'm glad you restrained yourself," Jill said. "Smashing this set would pretty well have put an end to my rise up the Nationtv corporate ladder."

"I'm serious, Jill. I don't want to be here. I don't want to be dredging up the past. I don't know why Angus is convinced he has do this. And something else . . . I have a letter from Kevin Tarpley."

Jill's body was tense with interest. "Can I see the letter?"

"Be my guest," I said. "Come over to the house after we're through here. You can take it with you and put it in your memory book. It gives me the creeps."

"Jo, I think you'd better hold on to that letter. I have a feeling the cops are going to want to see it."

"They'd be wasting their time," I said. "There's nothing there but a warning to listen to God's truth and not to put my trust in rulers."

Jill looked thoughtful. "It could be worse," she said. "I wasn't going to mention this, but your letter wasn't the only one Kevin Tarpley sent out before he died. Apparently, there were two more. The inmate in the cell across from Tarpley's says that Kevin spent most of the last week of his life writing those letters. It was slow going for him because he was barely literate, but – get this, Jo – Kevin told his fellow inmate that he had to get the letters out to save the innocent and punish the guilty."

Suddenly, I felt cold. "Who else got letters?"

"The prison people don't know."

"Don't they keep records of the mail the inmates send out?"

"They do," Jill said, "but it seems these letters went out with a man they call 'the prison pastor.'"

"Kevin mentioned him," I said. "His name is Paschal Temple."

"Right," said Jill. "And he doesn't know who they were addressed to. He was doing God's work, Jo. He just dropped the letters in the mailbox and trusted the Lord."

Angus came back into the room. He'd been crying. His eyes were red and his hair was slicked back, wet from where he'd splashed water on his face.

"Why don't you get yourself another Coke," I said. It was as close as he would let me come at that moment, and he got the message.

He gave me a weak smile. "Thanks, Mum," he said.

Jill held up another tape. "Ready?"

Angus snapped open the tab on the pop can. "Ready."

"This is the trial," Jill said.

There were establishing shots of the street outside the courthouse. The sky was blue, and the trees on the courthouse lawn were leafing out into their first green. Two police cars pulled up: Maureen was in the first; Kevin in the second. As they stood, blinking in the pale spring sunlight, Maureen and Kevin were almost unrecognizable. She was in a navy dress with a white Peter Pan collar, and her explosion of platinum hair had been tamed into a ponytail. His long blond hair had been trimmed, and he was wearing a dark suit. Miss Chatelaine and her Saturday night date.

Spectators hurried into the courthouse. I recognized some of them: Mieka's English teacher; Tess Malone; our next-door neighbours; our minister; Gary Stephens and his wife, Sylvie; Jane O'Keefe with Andy Boychuk, who was dead now too; our dear old friend Dave Micklejohn; Craig and Julie Evanson. Then Howard Dowhanuik with his arm protectively draped around the shoulders of the woman beside him. As they started up the steps, the woman shook off his arm and turned to face the camera. Her mouth was slack and her eyes were as blank as a newborn's. I shuddered. The woman with the unseeing eyes was me. Angus was right. I had been a zombie.

I turned to Jill. "Is there another beer?" I asked.

"Help yourself," Jill said, and I did.

The reporting of the trial had its own rhythm. For four days there were shots of the key players arriving at the courthouse, then courtroom sketches of the experts as they gave their testimony. Police officers, forensic specialists, pathologists, two psychiatrists. The faces of these witnesses, skilfully drawn but static, were the perfect counterpoint to the reporter's voice droning through the endless technical details of expert testimony.

Then on the fifth day of the trial, there was real news. Kevin Tarpley had confessed he acted alone. No time now for careful sketches; just file footage of Kevin and Maureen as the news anchor's voice, high-pitched with excitement, relayed the breaking story. Kevin had lied. It hadn't been Maureen who used the crowbar. She had pleaded with him not to harm Ian Kilbourn. Her fingerprints were on the crowbar because she had tried to tear it from Kevin's hands. He was guilty; she was innocent.

The Friday before Mother's Day, Maureen Gault walked out of the courtroom for the last time, and the cameras went wild. Maureen's mother, a mountain of a woman who had been a media star from the moment of her daughter's arrest, bore down on the press.

"She's vindicated," Shirley Gault said. "Little Mo is vindicated. What more Mother's Day present could I ask?" Beside her, Maureen stood silent, smirking, her fair hair as insubstantial as dandelion fluff in the May sunshine. As her mother droned on about lawsuits and mental suffering and Little Mo's good name, Maureen looked off in the distance. Finally she'd had enough. She grabbed her mother's doughy arm, and headed down the courthouse steps. Before she got into her mother's car, she flashed the cameras a V-for-victory sign. The screen went dark.

"And so justice was done," I said.

Jill flicked off the console and turned on the lights. "Isn't it always?" she said mildly.

She picked up the tapes. "I'll leave a note with our library that you can requisition these. That way, if you want to come over some night, you can. There's a lot of stuff you and Angus might feel more comfortable looking at on your own."

"Like what?" Angus asked.

"Like the footage from the Heinbecker funeral, the one your father went to in Swift Current that last day." Jill turned to me. "Charlie's widow sent it to me last year. She's getting on, and she wanted me to have it for our archives. I almost pitched it, then I remembered that your dad had given the eulogy, Angus. People said it was terrific."

"I guess I'd like to hear that," he said. "And Jill, if you have a tape of Dad's funeral . . ." The sentence trailed off. When he spoke again, his voice was small and sad. "I'd kind of like to hear what people thought about my dad."

We went back to Jill's office and got our coats. My son and I were silent as we walked to the parking lot. There didn't seem to be much left to say.

Three

Taylor wouldn't let me throw out the pumpkin. When she saw me heading out to the alley with it Monday morning, she burst into tears. Normally she was easygoing, but the jack o'lantern meant a lot to her. I put it back on the picnic table. When I headed for the university the next day, I noticed that Jack's eyeholes were beginning to pucker and his smile was drooping. Apparently, when it came to aging, pumpkins weren't any luckier than humans.

In the park, city workers were putting snow fences around the broad, sloping lawns of the art gallery. Above me, the last of the migrating geese formed themselves into ragged V's and headed south. Winter was coming, and I climbed the stairs to the political science department buoyed by the energy that comes with the onset of a new season.

My nerves jangled the minute I opened the door to my office. Like Miss Clavel in Taylor's favourite book, I knew that something was not right. But, at first, it was hard to put my finger on what was wrong. My desk was as I had left it: clear except for a jar full of pencils, a notepad, and a folder of notes labelled "Populist Politics and the Saskatchewan Election of 1982."

It was never my favourite part of the course. At the top of the first page I had written "Why the Dowhanuik

Government was Defeated." There were three single-spaced pages of reasons, but the explanation I liked best was the one Ian gave a reporter on election night. All of the Regina candidates and campaign workers had met at the Romanian Club for the victory party. By the time the evening was over, we had lost fifty-seven of the sixty-four seats, the temperature in the hall had climbed past thirty degrees Celsius, and everybody was either drunk or trying to get there. When the reporter doing the TV remote asked my husband if he could isolate the reason for the government's loss, Ian had looked at the man with amazement. "When you lose this badly," he said, "it pretty much means that from the day the writ was dropped, everybody everywhere fucked up everything."

Even with the expletives deleted, it had been a memorable sound bite. I leafed through the notes in the folder. A few pages in, I found a newspaper clipping: it was a picture of the survivors of the '82 election: Howard Dowhanuik, Ian, Craig Evanson, Andy Boychuk, Tess Malone, Gary Stephens, and Jane O'Keefe. The premier-elect, who considered himself the consummate cracker-barrel comic, had announced that he would call them the Seven Dwarfs.

I never thought the joke was very funny, and I didn't think what had happened to the picture on my desk was funny either. Someone had taken a felt pen and drawn X's over the faces of my husband and Andy Boychuk. I could feel my muscles tighten. Reflexively, I took a deep breath. It was then that I noticed the smell in my office, musky and sweet: perfume, not mine.

I went back out into the hall. It was empty. I walked down to the political science office. The departmental secretary was putting mail in our boxes. Rosalie Norman was a small and prickly woman, grudging with students and contemptuous of faculty.

"Did you let someone into my office this morning?" I asked.

She clenched her jaw and took a step towards me.

"Hardly," she said. Then, certain the balance of power had been restored, she went back to her mail.

"I'm sorry," I said. "I didn't mean to suggest you'd been careless. It's just someone's been in there, and I need to know how they got in."

"Look in a mirror," she said. "None of you ever remember to lock your doors." Then, for the first time that morning she smiled. "Here," she said, handing me an envelope. "It's from Physical Plant. Looks like you forgot to pay a parking ticket."

The day went downhill from there. Two students told me they were going to the department head to complain that the mid-term test was too hard, and one young woman in my senior class cornered me to tell me I was the best prof she'd ever had and could she have an extension on her essay because she'd had to go to a bridal shower the night before her paper was due. She said she knew I would understand. I didn't.

It got worse. When I went to the Faculty Club to grab a quick sandwich for lunch, the first person I ran into was Craig Evanson's ex-wife, Julie. The population of Regina is 180,000, and I had managed to avoid Julie for almost four years, but, as my grandmother used to say, the bad penny always turns up, and Julie Evanson was one very bad penny.

She was standing in front of a painting of flame-red gladioli that set off her silver-blond hair and her black silk suit so brilliantly that, for a moment, even I enjoyed looking at her. Age had not withered Julie, nor, as it turned out, had time staled the infinite variety of ways in which she could upset the equilibrium of anyone who crossed her path.

When she spotted me, she smiled her enchanting dimpled smile. "Jo, I hoped I'd run into you here. It saves me a trip to your office. I'm working on the Christmas fashion show the Alumni Association is putting on, and I wanted to see if I could put you down for a table."

"I don't think so, Julie. Those events are always a bit pricey for me. Good luck with it, though." I started to move past her towards the dining room. She moved with me, blocking my escape.

"You've never concerned yourself much with fashion, have you?" she asked brightly.

"No," I said, "I guess I always thought there were other things . . ."

She looked me over with the deliberation of a professional assessor. "Of course, your life has always been so full of things," she said. Then she reached over and brushed chalk dust from the shoulder of my sweater. "I wonder why it is that some people seem to lead such messy lives? And now Kevin Tarpley's murder. Another mess for you."

"It's not a mess for me, Julie. It has nothing to do with me."

She shrugged. "I ran into a very interesting little birdy today who told me differently."

I remembered the defaced newspaper pictures in my file. "Who were you talking to?" I asked.

When she heard the tension in my voice, Julie's eyes lit up. "Oh, no, you don't," she said. "I have to protect my sources. You know about that, Joanne, now that you're such a big TV star." She looked at her watch. "I've got to fly," she said. Then she lowered her voice. "But there is one thing I feel I really do have to tell you."

I moved closer to her. "What?" I asked.

"You have a noticeable run in your panty hose," she said, and she smiled her dimpled smile and headed for the buffet.

By the time I got home, the milk of human kindness had curdled in my veins.

Taylor met me at the door. One of her braids had come undone, and her eyes were bright with conspiratorial excitement. "There's a lady here," she whispered. "She said she knew you from a long time ago. I let her in. Angus is upstairs, so it was okay."

I swore under my breath. I was certain it was Julie Evanson, back for a rematch. It took every ounce of resolve I had to walk into the living room.

The woman was standing by the fireplace; in her hands was the framed photograph of Ian that I kept on the mantel. She was dressed in black: black angora pullover, elaborately beaded; black skirt, tight and very short; black hose. When she heard my step, she looked up slowly. She wasn't disconcerted. It was as if I was the interloper.

"Hello, Joanne," Maureen Gault said. Her voice was low and husky. "I just came back from Kevin's memorial service, and I figured it was only right to bring you and your family a memento of this sad day."

She put Ian's photograph back on the mantel. "Looks like we have even more in common now," she said.

Dumbfounded, I stared at her.

"You know, both of us widows and all," she added helpfully. Little Mo had control of the scene, and she knew it. "I wish I'd had a portrait done of Kevin, so our son could remember his dad."

When I didn't respond, she shrugged, walked over to my coffee table and picked up her purse. "We couldn't have a real funeral on account of the cops haven't released the body. Anyway, Kevin's mum wants to donate his remains to science for the good of mankind. Lame, eh? But I thought there wasn't much point in waiting around." She opened her purse and took out a funeral-home program. "This has the service on it," she said, "and there's a celebration of Kevin's life. I guess all of us are a mix of bad and good. I thought your kids might want this for historical reasons. Set the record straight."

Finally, I came up with a line. It wasn't much. "Get out," I said. "Get out of my house."

She shook her head sadly. "Loss is supposed to put everybody on common ground, Joanne," she said. "I thought you would know that by now."

She took a compact and a lipstick out of her purse. She opened the lipstick and drew a careful mouth on top of her own thin lips.

"Cherries in the Snow," she said. "I love this colour." Her platinum hair had been arranged in an elaborate crown of curls. One of the curls had come loose, and she slid it back into place before she picked up her coat.

"I forgive you," she said, and her smile, sly and knowing, was the smile of the girl who had stood triumphant on the courthouse steps the day Kevin Tarpley's confession set her free. "My boy's father would want me to forgive you. He found Jesus at the end. He was saved."

"I know," I said. "He wrote to me." I felt the rush that comes with meanness. I thought my words would wound her, suggest that she wasn't the sole custodian of Kevin Tarpley's last moments on earth. But when Maureen Gault looked at me, she didn't look wounded. She looked victorious, as if I'd just handed her exactly what she'd come to my house for.

"What did he say?" she asked lazily.

"It was a private letter," I said.

"Suit yourself, Joanne," she said. She dropped the memorial-service program on the coffee table and started for the door. As she came parallel with me, she reached up and touched the scarf I was wearing. It was my favourite: an antique silk, bright as a parrot. My son-in-law, Greg, had given it to me for my forty-ninth birthday.

"I like this," she said, fingering the silk. "It just kills me how women like you always know how to wear these things. What do you do? Go to scarf school?"

She laughed at her joke and walked out of the room. I heard the front door close. She was gone, but the scent of her perfume lingered: musky and sweet. I didn't like the smell any better than I had liked it that morning in my office.

I grabbed the program from the coffee table and headed

towards the back door. Out on the deck, the air was fresh and cold. I tore the program celebrating Kevin Tarpley's life into a dozen pieces and dropped them in the garbage. As I went back into the house, the jack o'lantern smirked at me from the picnic table.

Four

WHEN I checked the back yard the night of Howard Dowhanuik's dinner, the pumpkin's smirk had sagged into a leer. I thought about my daughter. She was a resolute child. In the summer one of her friends had found a kitten; every day since, Taylor had asked if she could have a cat. And now we had the pumpkin. I looked at him, plumped on the picnic table, King of the Back Yard. "I'll bet you'll still be here on St. Patrick's Day, Jack," I said.

Hilda McCourt came into the kitchen as I was knotting the scarf Greg had given me. She bent to look at its intricate swirls of colour.

"Amazing," she said. "A silk for the seraglio."

She was wearing a black and gold velvet evening coat, and jewelled starbursts flashed in her ears. With her deep russet hair, the effect was stunning.

"You look as if you could be in a seraglio yourself," I said.

"I don't think I'd last," Hilda said. "I've never found it agreeable to dance on command." She smiled serenely. "I must admit, though, that the idea of having young men dance at my bidding is not without appeal."

The snow started as we turned off Albert Street onto College Avenue. By the time I drove into the parking lot behind Sacred Heart Cathedral it was coming down so hard I could barely make out the hotel across the road.

I pulled up next to an old Buick. A man was leaning over the car, brushing the snow off its windshield. I couldn't see his face, but I would have recognized the familiar bulk of his body anywhere. Howard Dowhanuik had paid his way through law school with the money he earned as a professional boxer. Age had thickened his body, but you could still sense his physical power.

I got out of the car and walked over to him. The former premier of Saskatchewan was peering so intently into the front seat of the Buick that he didn't hear me.

"Angus tells me these vintage cars are a snap to hot-wire," I said. "Want to go for a joy-ride before the big event?"

He didn't look up. "Sure," he said. "It'd bring back a lot of memories. The first time I ever got laid was in a car like this."

"When was that?" I said.

"In 1953," Hilda said. "This is a 1953 Buick Skylark, Joanne."

Howard straightened and faced us.

"And you're sixty now," I said. "That would make you twenty-one. Good for you for waiting, Howard. I'll bet not many boys in law school did."

He laughed and threw an arm around my shoulder. "Same old Jo," he said. "Still a pain in the ass." He held out his other arm to Hilda. "Come on, Hilda. Let's get in there. I'll buy you a Glenfiddich before the agony begins. Did you come down from Saskatoon just to watch me squirm?"

"I'd come farther than that for a tribute to you," Hilda said simply.

Howard's old fighter's face softened. "Allow me to make that Glenfiddich a double," he said.

When we saw what was waiting for us outside the hotel, we were ready for a double. The Saskatchewan is a graceful dowager of a hotel, but that night the dowager was confronting the politics of the nineties. Demonstrators spilled from the entrance and onto the sidewalk. There seemed to be about forty of them, but they were silent and well-behaved. Around the neck of each protestor, a photograph of a foetus was suspended, locket-like, from a piece of cord. Two boys who didn't look as old as Angus were holding a scroll with the words BEATING HEART written in foot-high letters.

Beating Heart was Tess Malone's organization. The media potential of Howard's dinner must have been too tempting for her to resist. The new premier and half his cabinet were coming, and they all supported the Women's Health Centre. When the demonstrators saw Howard, there was a stir. Howard might have been only an ex-premier, but he was still the enemy. Oblivious, he took my arm and Hilda's and started up the stairs. The Beating Heart people moved closer together. Beneath the heavy material of his overcoat, I could feel Howard's body tense.

"Hang on," he said. I shuddered, remembering other demonstrations I'd had to wade through since the Women's Health Centre had opened in late summer. They were never any fun. I braced myself and moved forward. Then Hilda was in front of me, so close to the demonstrators that her trim body seemed pressed against the body of the man in front of her.

In the silence, I heard Hilda's voice, as civil and unworried as it would have sounded in the classroom. "Gerald Parker, that is you, isn't it?"

The man in front of her smiled.

"Yes, Miss McCourt," he said.

"I hear you've done well for yourself," Hilda said. "Real estate, isn't it?"

"Last year I made the Million Dollar Club for the third straight year." he said.

"Splendid," said Hilda. "You always were a hard worker. Now, Gerald, I wonder if you could let us pass. You've made your point. Nothing's to be gained by keeping us out here in the snow."

Without a word, Gerald broke his connection with the woman next to him, and Hilda walked between them. It wasn't Moses parting the Red Sea, but it was close. Before Gerald changed his mind, I followed. Then Howard. We had just reached the top of the stairs when I heard a man's voice: "She's here."

I turned. Jane O'Keefe was getting out of a taxi at the front of the hotel. Her sister, Sylvie, was with her. They glanced at the crowd, and then they turned towards one another. Their profiles were almost identical: cleanly marked jawlines, generous mouths, short strong noses, carefully arched brows. The two women had the scrubbed blond good looks you could see on the golf course of the best club in any city in North America. In fact, the O'Keefe sisters had grown up in the pleasant world of private schools and summers at the lake. As the crowd began to surge towards them, that idyllic existence must have seemed a lifetime away. The lights in front of the hotel leached the sisters' faces of colour, but Jane and Sylvie didn't hesitate. They started towards the stairs. Sylvie was carrying a camera and she hunched her body around it, protecting it the way a mother would protect a child.

The crowd surrounded the two women, cutting them off. No one moved. The only noise was the muted sound of traffic on the snowy streets. Then Howard came down the stairs towards them. This time there was force. He used his powerful shoulders as a wedge to break through the line. When he got to Jane and Sylvie, he linked hands with them and started back up the steps.

"Proverbs 11:21." A woman's voice, husky and self-important, cut through the silent night. "Though hand join in hand the wicked shall not be unpunished but the seed of the righteous shall be delivered."

I turned towards the voice. So did a lot of other people. When she saw that she was centre-stage, a smile lit Maureen Gault's thin face, and she gave me a mocking wave.

The demonstrators on the front steps had broken ranks during Little Mo's outburst, and Howard took advantage of the situation to get Sylvie and Jane into the hotel. Seconds later, the five of us were safe in the lobby, our shaken selves reflected a dozen times in the mirrors that lined the walls.

Hilda took command of the situation. She turned to Sylvie and Jane. "We were planning to have a drink before the festivities started. Will you join us?"

Jane O'Keefe smiled wearily. "As my grandfather used to say, 'Does a bear shit in the woods?' Let's go."

The Saskatchewan Lounge is a bar for genteel drinkers: the floral wallpaper is expensive; the restored woodwork gleams; the chairs, upholstered in peony-pink silk, are deep and comfortable; and the waiters don't smirk when they ask if you'll have your usual. We found a large table in the corner as far away as possible from the singing piano player. When the waiter came, I asked for a glass of vermouth, then, remembering the menace in Maureen Gault's smile, I changed my order to bourbon.

Howard raised his eyebrows. "Trying to keep pace with the guest of honour, Jo?" he asked.

"No," I said, "but Howard, didn't you see . . ."

He'd been smiling, but, as he leaned towards me, the smile vanished, and I changed my mind about telling him Maureen Gault had been in the crowd. Howard had always been there when I needed him, and this was his night.

"Nothing," I said. "Just a case of mistaken identity."

"Sure you're okay?" he asked.

"Yeah," I said, "I'm sure."

"Fair enough," he said. Then he turned to Jane O'Keefe. "So, are you having second thoughts about the Women's Centre?"

"Not a one," she said. "And I've waded through crowds a lot loonier than that bunch out there."

Sylvie started to speak, but Jane cut her off. "My sister doesn't agree with me on this issue. But my sister hasn't had to try to salvage women who've been worked over by

butchers. If you'd seen what I'd seen, Sylvie, you'd know I
didn't have a choice."

"No," Hilda said, "you didn't. For sixty-five years, I've
known that an enlightened society can't drive women into
back alleys."

I was surprised. There were some subjects I never discussed with Hilda. The drinks came and, with them, another surprise. Hilda had never been forthcoming about her
private life. She sipped her Glenfiddich and turned to Jane
O'Keefe. "My sister died from a botched abortion," she
said. "By the time I'd convinced her to let me take her to
the hospital, she was, to use your word, Jane, unsalvage-
able. It's vital that women are never driven to that again."
Hilda's eyes were bright with anger.

On the other side of the bar, the piano player had started
to sing "Miss Otis Regrets." Jane reached over and touched
Hilda's hand. "Thanks," she said. "There are times when I
need a little affirmation."

Howard snorted. "Janey, you never needed affirmation.
You always had bigger balls than any of us."

Jane looked at him, deadpan. "What a graceful compliment," she said, and everybody laughed.

Everybody, that is, except her sister. For as long as I'd
known her Sylvie O'Keefe had been an outsider. As I
watched her blue eyes sweep the table, I wondered, not for
the first time, what that level gaze took in.

She had always been unknowable and, for much of her
life, enviable. She was rich, she was talented, and she was
beautiful. She and Gary had been a golden couple. Physically, they were both so perfect, it had been a pleasure simply to watch them as they came into a room. In the days
when we were all having babies, we joked about the glori-
ous gene pool Sylvie and Gary's child would draw from. But
there was no baby, and as the months, then years, went by,
Gary and Sylvie stopped being a golden couple. By the time
Jess came, Gary and Sylvie had stopped being any sort of
couple at all.

Jess was a miracle, but he didn't bring his parents together. Gary continued his headlong rush towards wherever he was going, and Sylvie became even more absorbed in her career. She was a gifted photographer, and her son soon became her favourite subject. Her luminous black and white photographs of him, by turns sensual and savage, were collected in a book, *The Boy in the Lens's Eye.* The collection established Sylvie's reputation in the places that counted. She was a success.

As I watched her assessing the people drifting into the hotel bar, I wondered if the time would ever come when Sylvie O'Keefe and I would be friends. Somehow, it seemed unlikely, but one thing was certain: after twenty years, fate – or the vagaries of small-city living – had brought our lives to a point of convergence again.

"Kismet," I said.

Sylvie turned reluctantly from the partygoers to me. "I don't understand."

"Sorry," I said, "just thinking out loud about how the kids' discovering each other has brought our lives together."

"Actually, I'm glad we were brought together tonight," she said. "I was going to call you about taking some pictures of Taylor. Have you ever watched her when she draws? She's so focussed and so . . . I don't know . . . tender. She has a great face."

"She looks like her mother," I said.

Sylvie looked at me quizzically.

"You know Taylor is adopted," I said. "Her mother was Sally Love."

Sylvie's eyes widened. "Of course. I'd forgotten. Sally's work was brilliant," she said.

"It was," I agreed. "That's one reason I'm happy Taylor's spending some time around you. I think being with another artist can give Taylor a link with her real mother."

Sylvie leaned towards me. "And that doesn't bother you?"

Before I had a chance to answer, there was an explosion of laughter at the other end of the table. Howard was in the middle of a story about a rancher he'd acted for in a lawsuit against a manufacturer of pressurized cylinders. The rancher's semen tank had sprung a leak. Like Onan, his seed had been wasted on the ground, but the rancher wasn't waiting for God's judgement. He hired Howard and took the case to court.

As I turned to listen, Howard was recounting his summation for the jury. It was funny, but it was crude, and at the next table a smartly dressed man with silver hair and a disapproving mouth turned to glare at him. Howard smiled at the man, then, still smiling, leaned towards me. "I make it a policy never to get into a fight with a guy whose mouth is smaller than a chicken's asshole."

The pianist segued into "Thanks for the Memories," and I stood up. Howard looked at me questioningly. "It's time to get out of here," I said. "Some cracks are starting to appear in your guest of honour persona."

We finished our drinks, and headed for the lobby. Gary Stephens was just coming up the steps from the side door, and he joined us.

"Sorry I'm late, babe," he said to Sylvie. She looked at him without interest, and I wondered how often she'd heard that entrance line. But Jane O'Keefe was interested. Her grey eyes burned the space between herself and her brother-in-law. "You're a real bastard, Gary," she said. Then she turned her back to him and started towards the cloakroom. We followed her and dropped off our coats, then we took the elevator upstairs to the ballroom.

The crowd in the upstairs hall was surprisingly young. Many of the men and women who were now deputy ministers or People on Significant Career Paths had been having their retainers adjusted and watching "The Brady Bunch" when Howard Dowhanuik became premier, but tonight that didn't seem to matter. Our party's first year back in government was going well, and there seemed to be a consensus that we had something to celebrate. In the ballroom, a string quartet played Beatles tunes, the crystal chandelier blazed with light, and silvery helium-filled balloons drifted above every table set for eight. It was party time.

Hilda looked around the room happily. "It's everything Howard deserves," she said. "Now I'd better find my place." She lowered her voice. "Joanne, I'm sitting with a man I met at the art gallery last Sunday. If we continue to enjoy one another's company, I might not go home with you. My new friend tells me he has an original Harold Town in his apartment."

"But you hate Harold Town."

Hilda raised an eyebrow. "Well, there was no need to tell my friend that."

I laughed. "Let me know if you need a ride."

"I will," she said. "Now, you'd better get over to the head table. Howard likes people to be punctual."

Manda and Craig Evanson were already in their places. Manda was wearing a blue Mexican wedding dress, scoop-necked and loose fitting to accommodate the swell of her pregnancy. Her dark hair, parted in the middle, fell loose to her shoulders. She was very beautiful.

Sylvie stopped in front of Manda, took out her camera, and began checking the light with a gauge. As always, Sylvie seemed to have dressed with no thought for what other women might be wearing, and as always she seemed to have chosen just the right thing. Tonight, it was a pin-striped suit the colour of café au lait, and a creamy silk shirt. As she moved around the table, adjusting her camera, I noticed more than one woman in iridescent sequins taking note.

"I don't usually walk around like the inquiring photographer," Sylvie said, "but I thought Howard might like some pictures of his party."

Manda smoothed the material of her dress over her

stomach. "He'll be thrilled. Having Sylvie O'Keefe take your party pictures is like having Pavarotti sing 'For He's a Jolly Good Fellow' right to you."

Sylvie smiled. "Thanks," she said, "but Howard has it coming. He's a good guy." She knelt so that Manda Evanson was in her lens. "Stay exactly as you are, Manda. Don't smile. Just be. If Frida Kahlo had ever painted a Madonna, she would have looked like you."

Face glowing with love, Craig Evanson looked down at his wife. The happiest man in the world.

When Tess Malone came in, the temperature at the head table dipped ten degrees. We all knew she'd orchestrated the demonstration outside. She went straight to where Howard was sitting. That was like her: confront the problem, no matter how painful. She was wearing a satin dress in a pewter shade that made her tightly corsetted little body look more bullet-like than ever.

She sat in the empty chair beside him, lit a cigarette, inhaled deeply, and began. "I know how angry you must be, Howard, but I won't apologize. I like you and I respect you, but this dinner was a good chance for us. Never miss a chance. That's what you taught me when we were in government. If the shoe was on the other foot, you wouldn't have passed up this evening, and you know it."

For a moment, he stared at her. Then he started to laugh. "You're right," he said. "I wouldn't have passed up a chance like this. Anyway, for once, your God Squad doesn't seem to have done any harm."

Tess looked at him levelly. "In the spirit of the evening, I'll ignore that."

"Good," Howard said. "Now let me get you an ashtray before you ignite the tablecloth."

We all relaxed, and for a while it was a nice evening. The hip of beef was tender, and the wine was plentiful. Just as dessert was being served, Tess's protesters began pounding their drums in a heartbeat rhythm, and she went out and told them they'd done a terrific job and they could call it a night.

By the time the last dish was cleared away, and I stood to announce that the speeches were starting, the room was warmed by a sense of community and shared purpose. The new premier's remarks about Howard were witty and mercifully brief, and the other speakers followed his lead. Sanity all around.

And then Maureen Gault joined the party. The speeches had just finished, and there had been a spontaneous singing of "Auld Lang Syne." People were getting up from their tables to visit or to head to the bar for drinks. Our table was breaking up too. The new premier and his wife had another function to attend, and they were already headed towards the doors that would take them out of the ballroom. Manda and Craig Evanson were standing, saying their goodbyes to Tess. Howard was talking to a group that had driven in from Stewart Valley. Jane O'Keefe was leaning across her brother-in-law, saying something to her sister. I couldn't hear her words, but she didn't look as if she'd cooled off much. A waiter came with a note in Hilda's bold hand: "I think it's time to revisit Harold Town. Don't wait up. H." It seemed like a good time to do some visiting myself. I was standing, looking for familiar faces in the crowd, when I felt a hand on my shoulder. I turned and Maureen Gault was behind me. She was smiling.

"I thought I'd give you a chance to apologize," she said.

"For what?" I said.

"For being rude when I came to your house." She moved towards me. Close up, her perfume was overpowering. "Apologize, Joanne."

"Are you crazy?" I said.

People at the tables closest to us fell silent, and my words rang out, bell clear.

Maureen Gault's pale eyes seemed to grow even lighter. "You'll be sorry you said that, Joanne," she said. "I'm not crazy. But I'm powerful. I can make things happen. Just ask them," she said, and her hand swept in a half-circle that included everyone at the head table.

She leaned towards me. "Ask them," she hissed. "Ask your friends what Little Mo can do." Her spittle sprayed my mouth.

I rubbed my lips with the back of my hand. I was furious. "Get out," I said. "This is a private party. Nobody wants you here."

She drew her hand back as if she was about to hit me. Then she seemed to change her mind. She looked thoughtfully at the head-table guests. "Tell Joanne I have every right to be here," she said. Her eyes were so pale they were almost colourless. "I thought it was nice the way you sang when I came in. 'Should old acquaintance be forgot,'" she laughed. "Nobody better forget me."

It was a good exit line, but she couldn't leave it alone. When she had walked the length of the dais, Maureen Gault turned towards us. "I haven't forgotten any of you, you know."

I could still feel her spittle on my lips. I took a step towards her. "I told you to leave us alone. You're not the only one who can make things happen, Maureen. If you're not out of here in thirty seconds, I'll get somebody from hotel security to throw you out."

She smiled, then left.

Howard's group from Stewart Valley were wide-eyed. Life in the big city was every bit as exciting as it was cracked up to be. Craig tightened his grip on his wife's shoulder. Sylvie looked impassively at the spot where Maureen had stood. Gary Stephens, who by all accounts should have been accustomed to strange women making public scenes, seemed thrown off base by Maureen Gault's outburst. White-faced, he poured the heel of the wine into his glass and drained it in a gulp. Jane O'Keefe left the table. Tess Malone was lighting a cigarette with shaking hands. Only Manda Evanson was immune.

"That's one flaky lady," she said mildly.

We did our best to restore the mood. But after a few nervous jokes, it was apparent the party was over. I picked up my bag and headed for the door. I wanted to go home, have a hot shower, and fall apart in peace.

There was a lineup outside the cloakroom. Regina is a government town, and the next morning was a work day. By the time I'd waded through the crush and found my coat, I was hot and irritable. My temper wasn't improved when, after I'd tied my belt, I noticed my scarf was missing. I tried to check the coat-rack and the floor, but I kept getting jostled, and after I got an elbow in the eye, I gave up and went into the hall to wait till the crowd thinned. When, finally, I went back into the cloakroom, the scarf wasn't there.

I decided to call it a night. I was tired and dispirited, and scarves were, after all, replaceable. I'd already started down the steps which lead to the side door when I remembered Greg's shy delight as he'd handed me the scarf at my birthday party. I couldn't leave without checking out all the possibilities. It was possible the scarf had fallen out when I'd taken my coat off in the bar. However, when I went back to the Saskatchewan Lounge, the scarf wasn't at our table, and the discreet waiter said no one had turned it in.

I took the elevator upstairs to the dining room. The waiters were stripping the tables, stacking the chairs. The head table had already been dismantled. It was as if the party had never been. I remembered Maureen's pale eyes and her brilliant mouth. Maybe my luck would change, and the whole evening would turn out to be a dream. I took the elevator down to the lobby. As I stepped out, I noticed the reservations clerk talking on the phone at the front desk. I went over to her and waited, but she ignored me. When I didn't go away, she put her hand over the mouthpiece. "Is there a problem?" she asked.

"Has anyone turned in a silk scarf, sort of a swirling pattern on a dark green background?"

She made a cursory pass through the paper in front of her.

"Nothing about a scarf," she said, and went back to her phone call.

I took a piece of paper from my purse, wrote my name and address on it, and shoved it across the desk towards her.

"Call me, please, if it turns up."

"Right," she said, and she waved me off.

I left through the side door. The snow had stopped, but it had been a substantial fall. Across Lorne Street, Blessed Sacrament, fresh with snow, glowed in the moonlight. The parking lot had pretty much cleared out. Only a few cars were left. The old Buick was still there, and as I walked towards my car, I thought of Howard's prolonged virginity and smiled. I stopped smiling when I saw the body.

She was lying on her back, close to the right rear wheel of the Buick. I thought at first that someone had run her down. Then I saw the scarf. Bright as a parrot. I had always loved the way the material draped itself in a swirl of colours over the shoulder of my coat. But tonight the scarf wasn't tied right. It had been pulled so tight around Maureen Gault's neck that her head angled oddly and her eyes bulged from her head.

I felt my knees go weak. Then I took a deep breath and stumbled back through the snow towards the hotel. When I saw the cruiser turning down Lorne Street, I shouted for it to stop. The officer who jumped out of the car seemed too young to be out this late, but he knew his job. He followed me across the parking lot, but when he saw the body, he grabbed me.

"Don't go any further," he said. "Leave the area alone till the crime scene people get here. I'll call for backups." But he didn't start for his car immediately. Instead, he took a step towards the body, and looked down.

"Do you know her?" he asked.

"Her name was Maureen Gault," I said. "Little Mo," I added idiotically. The security lights glinted yellow in

Maureen Gault's unseeing eyes. The crimson mouth drawn over her own thin lips seemed like a wound in her milky skin.

"Do you know of anybody who'd want her dead?" he asked.

I stared down at Little Mo's inert body and shivered. My voice seemed to come from somewhere far away. "Me," I said. "I wanted her dead."

Five

HALF an hour later, I was sitting in police headquarters on Osler Street studying the medicine wheel on the wall behind the desk of Inspector Alex Kequahtooway. A Cree elder had told me once that the medicine wheel is a mirror that helps a person see what cannot be seen with the eyes. "Travel the four directions of the circle," she said. "Seek understanding in the four great ways."

I stared hard at the markings on the medicine wheel. At that moment, I would have given a lot to see what could not be seen with the eyes, but all I saw was cowhide and beadwork. I knew the fault was with me. A seeker must be calm and receptive. I was scared to death.

Inspector Kequahtooway was from Standing Buffalo Reserve, about a hundred kilometres east of the city. I knew this because I knew his brother. Perry Kequahtooway had been the RCMP officer in charge of investigating a tragedy which had threatened my family. During the investigation, I had counted on Perry's calm determination to discover the truth; afterwards, I had come to know his kindness, and we had become friends. But that night, in police headquarters, it didn't take Alex Kequahtooway long to let me know that my relationship with his brother didn't cut any ice with him. When he led me through the litany of what I had done and whom I had been with that evening, his face was impassive.

As I talked, he made notes in a scribbler that looked like the kind my kids used in grade school. When I'd finished, he read his notes over unhurriedly. I stared at the medicine wheel, and tried to remember the four great ways to understanding: wisdom, illumination, innocence, and something else.

Finally, satisfied that the first part of the interrogation was in order, Inspector Alex Kequahtooway turned the pad to a fresh page and looked up at me.

"Just a few more questions, Mrs. Kilbourn. You seem tired."

"I am tired," I said.

"Then let's get started. When was the last time you saw your scarf that night?"

"I left it with my coat."

"In the downstairs cloakroom. There's a coat check upstairs near the ballroom. Why didn't you use it?"

"None of us did. I came in with five other people, and we all left our coats in the cloakroom on the main floor. You have to pay to check your coat upstairs."

"Too bad you didn't pay," he said, and there was an edge to his voice. "Nobody can touch the coats upstairs without dealing with the people who work there, whereas your coat . . ."

". . . was unguarded right out there where anyone could get at it."

"Right," he sighed. "Now the next question presents even more of a problem." He looked at his notes. "Before you came in, I had a few moments to talk with Constable Andrechuk. He was the first officer on the scene after you discovered Maureen Gault's body. Constable Andrechuk tells me he pointed to the deceased and asked you, and I quote: 'Do you know of anybody who'd want her dead?' Is that an accurate quote, Mrs. Kilbourn?"

"Yes," I said, "it is."

Inspector Kequahtooway made a check mark in the margin beside the question. "Now, listen carefully, Mrs. Kilbourn. Constable Andrechuk says that, when he asked you that question, you answered, 'Me. I wanted her dead.' Is that accurate?"

"Yes," I said, "it is."

"Why did you want her dead, Mrs. Kilbourn?"

I was silent. Images of Little Mo flashed through my mind.

Inspector Kequahtooway leaned towards me. His obsidian eyes seemed to take everything in. "Did you hate her because Kevin Tarpley had killed your husband?"

"No," I said, "I was afraid of her."

"You were afraid of her all these years?"

"No," I said. "I wasn't afraid of her after Ian died. When you see the files on his murder, you'll know that there wasn't anything . . . personal . . . about his murder."

"That's an odd word to use, Mrs. Kilbourn."

"It's the right word. Ian was killed because he was in the wrong place at the wrong time. It was Fate, like being hit by a bolt of lightning on the golf course."

Alex Kequahtooway's voice was so low I had to strain to hear it. "Something changed," he said.

"For the six years after the trial I never saw Maureen Gault. Then the day of Kevin Tarpley's memorial service, November 3, she came to my office at the university and she came to my house."

"Did she threaten you?"

"Not verbally. But, Inspector Kequahtooway, something had come loose in her. She seemed to feel she had to pursue me. I don't know why. Last night at the hotel, she told me that she could make things happen, and I'd better remember her."

"Some people who were sitting near the head table say they heard you call her crazy."

"She was crazy," I said, "and dangerous."

"And you're glad she's dead."

I looked at him. He was older than his brother, and harder. I remember Perry telling me his brother was the first Indian to make inspector on the Regina police force. I guess he'd had to be tough, but there was something about him that invited trust. I took a deep breath.

"Yes," I said. "I'm glad she's dead. But Inspector Kequahtooway, I didn't kill her."

He made a final note in his scribbler, and capped his pen. "That's good news," he said. He stood and motioned towards me. "You can go now, Mrs. Kilbourn. I guess I don't have to tell you that we'll expect you to keep us aware of any travel plans."

When I stood up, my legs were so heavy I knew I'd be lucky to make it across the room. "Travel won't be a problem," I said. "Goodnight, Inspector."

It was a little after 2:00 a.m. when I got home. I checked on Angus and Taylor, showered, put on my most comforting flannelette nightie, and climbed into bed. I was bone-tired, but I couldn't sleep. Every time I shut my eyes, I saw the red wound in Maureen Gault's white face: Cherries in the Snow.

Finally, I gave up and went down to the kitchen. Hilda was sitting at the table, drinking tea and reading a book titled *Varieties of Visual Experience*.

"Boning up on Abstract Expressionism?" I asked, and then, I began to sob.

Hilda leaped up and put her arms around me. "Good God, Joanne, what's the matter? It's not one of the children . . . ?"

"No, it's not the children," I said. "It's me. Hilda, I'm in trouble . . ."

I started to tell her about Maureen, but I guess I wasn't making much sense, because she stopped me.

"Let me get you some tea," she said. "Then you can start again. This time, tell me what happened in chronological order. Nothing calms the nerves more effectively than logic."

Hilda poured half a mug of steaming tea, then she went into the dining room and came back with a bottle of Metaxa. She added a generous shot of brandy to the tea and handed the mug to me. "Drink your tea," she said, "then we'll talk."

An hour later, when I went to bed, I slept. It was a good thing I did, because the next morning when I picked up the paper, I knew it was going to be a long day. The paper was filled with stories about Maureen Gault's murder and, whatever their starting point, by the final paragraph they all had an arrow pointing at me.

I could feel the panic rising, and when the phone rang, I froze. "Whoever you are, you'd better have good news," I said as I picked up the receiver. I was in luck. It was my daughter, Mieka, sounding as exuberant as a woman should when she was on a holiday with her new husband.

"Mum, guess where I am."

"Some place sunny and warm, I hope."

"I'm sitting at a table in a courtyard at the Richelieu Hotel in New Orleans, and I just had grits for the first time in my life."

"And you phoned to tell me," I said.

"No, I phoned to tell you that Greg and I got the same room you and Daddy had when you stayed here on your honeymoon."

A flash of memory. Lying in each other's arms, watching the overhead fan stir the soupy Louisiana air, listening to the sounds of the French Quarter drift through the open doors to our balcony.

"I hope that room's as magical for you as it was for us."

"It is," she said softly.

I could feel the lump in my throat. "I'd better let you get back to your grits while they're still hot," I said. "As I remember it, grits need all the help they can get. And, Mieka, tell Greg thanks."

"For what?

"For making you so happy."

"I will," she said. "And you tell everybody there hello from us. We'll call on Taylor's birthday."

I'd just hung up when my oldest son, Peter, called from Saskatoon. He tried to be reassuring, but I could tell from his voice that the stories in the Saskatoon paper must have been pretty bleak.

"You know, Mum, I think I'd better come home for a while," he said.

"In the middle of term?" I said. "Don't be crazy. You know the kind of marks you need to get into veterinary medicine. Besides, by the time you get down here, this will have blown over."

"Do you really think so, Mum?"

"No, but I really do think you're better off there. Pete, if I need you, I know you can be in Regina in three hours. At the moment, that makes me feel a lot better than having you jeopardize your term by coming here to hold my hand."

"Are you sure?"

"Absolutely. Now let me tell you about what your sister and Greg are doing."

"Eating everything that's not nailed down, I'll bet," he said.

"You got it," I said. By the time I finished telling Peter about New Orleans, he sounded less scared and I felt better. When I heard Hilda and the kids coming downstairs, I took the paper outside and shoved it into the middle of the stack in our Blue Box. Out of sight, out of mind. I made porridge and, for the next half hour, life was normal. The night before, Hilda had volunteered to stay a few days to keep my spirits up during what she called "this trying time." I turned her down flat, but as I watched her help Taylor braid her hair, I was glad Hilda had overruled me.

When Angus came to the table, it was apparent he hadn't been listening to the radio. He knocked over the juice, and, as he mopped up, he grumbled about a bill that showed he owed Columbia House $72.50 plus handling charges for cassettes and CDs.

Taylor, who was turning six on Remembrance Day, chirped away about plans for her birthday. "What I want," she said, "is a cake like the one Jess had. His mum made it in a flowerpot and there were worms in it."

Angus emptied about a quarter of a bag of chocolate chips onto his porridge. "You know, T, that's really gross," he said.

I took the chocolate chip bag from him. "Speaking of gross . . . ," I said.

Taylor grinned at her brother. "They're not real worms. They're jelly-bellies. On top, Jess's mum had brown icing and flowers made out of marshmallows. Jo, do you think you could ask her how she did it?"

"Consider it done," I said.

"Probably we'll need to make two," Taylor said thoughtfully. "I have a lot of friends."

"I'll ask Jess's mum to copy out the recipe twice," I said.

Taylor shook her head. "That's another one of your jokes, isn't it, Jo?" She took her cereal bowl to the sink and trotted off upstairs.

Angus leaned towards me. "Am I supposed to be at this party?"

"Only if you expect help paying that $72.50. I hear Columbia House has goons who specialize in shattering kneecaps."

He flinched. "I'll be there," he said, and he stood up and started for the door.

"Hang on a minute," I said. "Angus, something happened last night. I think you should take a look at the paper before you go to school."

I brought the paper in, and as he read it, his eyes widened with concern. "They don't think you did it, do they?"

"I don't know what they think," I said. "But I know I didn't kill Maureen Gault." I put my arm around his shoulder. "Angus, this is going to work out. But you'd better prepare yourself for a little weirdness at school."

"I don't get it, Mum. Maureen Gault just shows up out of nowhere and all of a sudden she's dead and they think it's you. It doesn't make any sense."

"It doesn't make sense to me, either," I said. "But Angus, there isn't any logic here. Whatever else happens, hang on to that. 'This invites the occult mind,/ Cancels our physics with a sneer.'"

He furrowed his brow. "What?"

"Chill out," I said.

He gave me a small smile. "Yeah," he said. "And you stay cool, Mum. There's going to be weirdness coming at you, too."

He was right. I could hear my 10:30 class buzzing as I came down the hall, but as soon as I stepped into the classroom, there was silence. They seemed to have trouble looking at me, and I remembered a lawyer on TV saying he always knew the verdict was guilty if the jury couldn't make eye contact with the defendant. Some of my colleagues seemed to have a problem with eye contact too. As I passed them in the hall going back to my office after class, they muttered hello and hurried by.

When I opened my office door, I was glad to see Howard Dowhanuik sitting at my desk. He had shaved and he was wearing a fresh shirt, but he looked like a man who had been up all night. When he saw me, he smiled.

"First friendly face I've seen since I got here," I said.

"That bad?"

"That bad," I said. "This is a city that reads its morning paper."

"That's why they keep the morning paper at a Grade 6 reading level," Howard said.

"Whatever happened to your reverence for the common man?" I said.

"Man and woman, Jo. I'm surprised at you. And the answer is I don't have to revere them any more. I'm out of politics."

"Right," I said.

Howard looked weary. "Have you got coffee or something?"

"We can go to the Faculty Club," I said. Then, remembering the ice in the greetings I'd gotten on my way back from class, I said, "On second thought, maybe I'd better make us a pot here."

I made the coffee and plugged it in. "Howard, before we talk, let me call Taylor's school. I want to make sure someone's keeping an eye on how she's dealing with all this."

After I talked to Taylor's principal, I felt better. Taylor was the fourth of my children to go to Lakeview School, and over the years Ian MacDonald and I had come to know each other. He knew that none of the Kilbourns would ever be a Rhodes Scholar, but he also knew that my kids were decent enough, and that he could count on me when he needed an extra driver for a field trip. He said he'd talk to Taylor's teacher, then he cleared his throat and told me he knew I wasn't a murderer and he would make sure that other people knew that, too.

I'd often thought Ian MacDonald was a bit of a taskmaster with the kids, but at the moment he was a hero, and my eyes filled with tears. The tissue box in my desk drawer was empty. All I could find in my purse was a paper napkin with the Dairy Queen logo. I mopped my eyes on it. "Dammit," I said, "I'm so tired I feel like I'm going to throw up. Howard, how bad is this?"

He sipped his coffee. "At the moment it's not great, Jo. I was down at the police station after you were there. Gave them my statement, then I just kind of nosed around. I go back a long way with some of those guys."

"And . . .?" I said.

"They've got a window for the time of death. You found Maureen Gault's body at 11:15, and the woman who works in the hotel smoke shop remembers seeing Maureen just before 11:00. She was just closing the till when Maureen came in to buy a package of LifeSavers. She said they were for her son."

For the first time since Maureen died, I felt a pang. "I'd forgotten about him," I said.

"You had a few things on your mind," Howard said drily. "You still do, Jo. The cops are still checking people's stories. Logically enough, I guess, they're starting with the head table. There are only two of us who haven't got even a sniff of an alibi. I'm one of them and you're the other."

"We should have gotten together," I said, "told the cops that we spent the hour in Blessed Sacrament praying for the justice system."

He didn't laugh. "I wish we had. Gary's okay. He went over to Tess Malone's for a nightcap. Jane and Sylvie ended up at Tess's too."

"Talk about strange bedfellows," I said.

Howard shrugged. "Apparently, Sylvie and Tess are tight as ticks. Have been for years. Anyway, the four of them were together until midnight. Craig and Manda went straight home. Their neighbour was out shovelling snow, and they talked to him at about 10:30. Around 11:00 Manda ordered pizza. It was delivered at 11:29. The pizza place they got it from is one of those 'if we're late, it's free' operations, so they keep pretty good records. Anyway there are some holes in Craig and Manda's story, but it's better than . . ."

"What I have," I said. "Howard, I don't understand this. I saw a hundred people when I was looking for Hilda. Doesn't anybody remember seeing me?"

"Lots of people remember seeing you, but nobody is willing to swear it was between 11:00 and 11:15. Jo, that's only fifteen minutes. Most people at the dinner had had a couple of drinks by then and, you know how it is, time gets kind of fuzzy." He looked as tired as I felt. "Do you want me to hang around for a couple of days? My plane leaves in an hour, but I don't have to be on it. I can get somebody to cover my classes."

"I don't need a babysitter, Howard. I just need the police to find something. And they will. They have to. For one thing, there has to be a connection with Kevin Tarpley's murder, and I'm in the clear there."

"No handgun with your initials on it at the crime scene?" Howard asked.

"No. And I wasn't anywhere near Prince Albert that day. I have witnesses, too. There was a Hallowe'en party at the art gallery. Taylor and I went to it after her lesson. There must have been thirty-five people there. After that, we picked up Angus and took him downtown to get new basketball shoes. I'll bet we went to six stores and I'm sure the sales people would remember us. Angus is a difficult customer. Howard, I could find fifty people to verify that I was in Regina Saturday. That's probably a world record. Now come on, if we make tracks, I can get you to the airport and still get back for my next class."

As we drove along the expressway, it was like old times. We talked about politics and Howard's ongoing courtship of his ex-wife, Marty. Reassuringly ordinary conversation, but when Howard turned to say goodbye to me at the airport, I lost my nerve, and Howard, who had known me for years, saw it happen.

He reached across and covered my hand with his. "Jo, I think you're right about this thing resolving itself pretty quickly, but until it does, promise me you'll stay out of it. Whatever's going on here is ugly. This isn't a case for Nancy Drew. Go home. Enjoy your family. Teach your classes. Be safe. Trust the cops."

"I'll try," I said.

He shook his head and opened the car door. "Not good enough," he said, "but a start. I'll be in touch."

As I drove off I could feel the tension in my body. All the brave words in the world couldn't change the reality.

For the time being at least, I was the prime suspect. And Howard was right. Something really ugly was happening. The only thing to do was steer a prudent course and pray that police would work their magic.

I headed back to the university. Filled with resolve, I went down to the political science office to check my mail.

Rosalie Norman was there waiting for me. "In the morning paper there was a picture of that woman who was murdered. I recognized her. She was in the hall outside your office the day you accused me of leaving your door open." Her blackberry eyes were gleaming with excitement. "What do you think I should do?"

I leaned across the desk and picked up her phone. "I think you should tell the police, Rosalie. Here, I'll dial the number for you. Put a little excitement in that life of yours."

The adrenalin was still pumping when I walked into class. I ignored the whispers and the averted eyes, and the class went well. "Don't let the bastards grind you down," I muttered as I put the keys in the ignition and started home. As I drove past Gary and Sylvie's big grey clapboard house on Albert Street, I remembered the worm cake and, on impulse, I pulled up in front of their house.

Jess answered the door. He was wearing blue jeans, a Blue Jays T-shirt, and a fireman's hat. He looked past me expectantly.

"Where's Taylor?" he said.

"At our house, I guess. I haven't been home yet, but Miss McCourt's there. I just stopped by to ask your mum if I could get the recipe for your birthday cake."

"Sure," he said. "She's out back in her darkroom. I'll go get her. You can come in."

I stepped into the entrance hall. It was a handsome area. The hardwood floor gleamed, and the patchwork quilt draped over the carpenter's bench by the door was welcoming. But my eyes were drawn to the walls. They were lined with blowups of black and white photographs. When I moved closer, I saw that the subject in all of them was the same: Jess.

I had seen Sylvie's book, *The Boy in the Lens's Eye*, and I'd been moved by the way in which she had captured the vulnerability and the toughness of her son. But nothing in the book prepared me for the power of the originals. Jess, at four, an otherworldly child, swinging naked on a tree branch, his small body surrounded by a cloud of light. Jess at two, laughing as he is engulfed by a field of sunflowers. All the fugitive moments of Jess Stephens's childhood were rivetting, but one in which he seems to swagger as he holds a brace of dead gophers out to the person behind the camera was a knockout. I was leaning close to the photograph, marvelling at the contrast between the black stiff bodies of the animals and the soft radiance of little-boy flesh, when the real Jess came up behind me.

I felt as if he had caught me trespassing, but he was nonchalant. "You can look at those anytime. Come in the living room, I've got tropical fish."

We looked at the fish, then Jess drifted off the way my kids always did when they'd fulfilled what they considered their social duty. Alone in the room, I looked around. More prints, not Sylvie's. Two Robert Mapplethorpe prints of flowers, a Diane Arbus, some I didn't recognize. Over the mantle above the fireplace was a photograph of Ansel Adams. Handwritten in its corner was a quotation, "Not everybody trusts paintings, but people believe photographs," and the signature, "Ansel Adams."

I walked over to a bookcase looking for *The Boy in the Lens's Eye*. I wanted to see if the gopher picture was there. But the book I found was Sylvie's first book, *Prairiegirl*. It had come out ten years before, and its publication had dealt a serious blow to Gary's political career. *Prairiegirl* was a collection of photographs of small-town girls from the southeast of the province. The girls were very young, mostly prepubescent, and their parents, not versed in the aesthetics of Mapplethorpe and Sally Mann, had been out-raged when, instead of freezing their daughter's innocence in time, Sylvie's photographs had explored their burgeon-ing sexuality. I had just begun to look at the book when Sylvie came into the room.

Without a word, she strode over and took *Prairiegirl* from my hands. Her gesture was so rude that I was taken aback.

"Jess invited me in," I said. "He was a very good host till he lost interest. His social skills seem about on a level with my kids'."

She didn't respond. She was wearing blue jeans and an oversized white shirt. Her face was scrubbed free of makeup and her blond hair was brushed back. She looked weary and hostile.

"Sylvie. I just came for a recipe. Taylor's birthday is next week and she wanted me to make the same cake you made for Jess . . . He really did ask me in," I added.

She was holding *Prairiegirl* tight against her chest as if, given the chance, I would rip it from her hands. Her fear didn't make sense. Then, like Paul on the road to Damascus, the scales fell from my eyes. Sylvie thought she had a murderer in her living room. There didn't seem much point in prolonging the agony.

I walked to the entranceway. Sylvie followed me, and as I sat on the carpenter's bench pulling on my boots, she watched in silence. I put on my coat and headed for the door. When I opened it, Sylvie said, "I'll send Gary over with the recipe. I wouldn't want to spoil Taylor's birthday."

I turned. Sylvie had positioned herself in the centre of the hall, and her stance was aggressive. Behind her, Jess peeked out from the living room. "I wouldn't let you," I said, and I closed the door behind me.

When I pulled up in front of our house, there was more good news. A van from Nationtv was parked in my drive-way, and there was a young woman on my front lawn talking to Taylor while the camera whirred. This time I was the one who did the grabbing. I took my daughter's hand and turned to the young woman. "Beat it," I said. "If I ever catch you bugging my kids again, I'll break your camera."

She started to argue, but I was past listening. "Count on it," I said, and I was pleased to see that she backed away.

Hilda opened the door just as Taylor and I hit the front porch. She took in the situation as soon as she saw the Nationtv van.

"Damn them," she said, her eyes flashing with anger. "I've been fending off media people on the telephone and here they were in the driveway." She looked at me. "Did they talk to . . ."

I nodded.

"No ethical sense," she said. "Ruled by expediency and the imperative to exploit."

When I picked up the telephone, my hands were shaking so badly I could barely dial Jill Osiowy's number. As the phone in her office rang, I could hear the call-waiting beep on my line. I looked out my front window. The red, white, and blue truck of another TV network was pulling up in front of my house.

Jill had to bear the brunt of my anger. "Whose decision would it be to send a news team out here to ask a six-year-old child if her mother was a murderer?"

For a moment, Jill was silent. Then she said, "It's news, Jo. I'm sorry. I know that's not the answer you want, but that's the answer there is. You're news."

"And that makes my kids fair game," I said.

"In some people's minds, yes," she said.

On the notepad beside the telephone, Hilda had carefully written the telephone numbers of all the media people who had phoned. Most had called more than once, but Troy Smith-Windsor had gone for the gold and called five times. Suddenly I was so exhausted I couldn't move.

"How long will this go on, Jill?" I asked.

"Till they find someone else."

"I'm not going to wait that long," I said.

There was silence on the other end of the line. Finally, Jill said. "What can I do to help?"

"See what you can find out about Kevin Tarpley's murder. There has to be a connection, and I'm in the clear there."

"I'll check our police sources, and I'll ask Terry Norlander from the Prince Albert affiliate to go talk to that guy in the cell across from Kevin's. The one who helped Kevin with his letters."

"Ah, yes, the letters," I said. "You know that minister – Paschal Temple – Kevin might have told him something. Jill, see if you can track him down, will you? If it sounds like he'll talk to me, I can drive up there this weekend. Hilda said she'll stay a few days, so the kids will be okay."

"You got it," Jill said. Then she laughed, "Hey, Nancy Drew, it's good to hear that you're back in business."

I winced, relieved that Howard Dowhanuik was snarled somewhere in Toronto rush-hour traffic, safely out of earshot.

Dinner was, given the circumstances, a cheerful affair. After I'd talked to Jill, I ran through the options for dinner and ordered in pizza, extra large, loaded. The kids ate like people with nothing more serious on their minds than double cheese and pepperoni. I relaxed and listened as Taylor ran through the guest list for her birthday party and Angus talked about a girl named Brie who had just moved to Regina from Los Angeles. "Talk about culture shock, eh, Mum?"

"Yeah," I said, as I opened bottles of Great Western beer for Hilda and me. "Brie's going to find it hard to keep up with the scene here in Regina."

Jill called at 6:30. "I just got off the phone with Terry Norlander. The police up there have zip on the shooting. Their ballistic people say the bullets came from a handgun. Kevin was with that inmate from the cell across from him. According to Terry, this guy is something else. Apparently, he's embraced our prison system so wholeheartedly that he prefers to be known as 49041 Rudzik. Anyway, Kevin and 49041 were shooting baskets in the exercise yard. When Kevin went down, 49041 thought he'd tripped. Then he saw the blood. Apparently the car and the driver just disappeared. Terry is going to try to see 49041 again tomorrow, but I wouldn't hold your breath about any revelations there. Speaking of revelations, we've had some luck with Paschal Temple. I called his house and got his wife. Paschal's in Regina. One of the brethren had a heart attack, and he's taken over the church down here till the guy recovers. It's Bread of Life on 13th Avenue. His wife told me they have a 7:00 service tonight, so if you hustle, you can still make it."

"I'll hustle," I said. I could hear the grimness in my voice.

Apparently, Jill did too. "Hey, Jo, guess what Mrs. Paschal Temple's name is?"

"Hepzibah," I said.

"Wrong by a country mile," said Jill. "It's Lolita."

An hour later, I was sitting in Bread of Life Tabernacle waiting for Lolita Temple's husband to begin his sermon. Bread of Life had the cheerless utilitarian look of a building that had been constructed on the cheap, but the pews were filled, and the air was electric with emotion. I sat next to a man who seemed to be about my age, but most of the congregation was in its teens. A Christian rock group with the name Joyful Noise spray-painted on its bass drum began to play.

As the music soared, some kids near the front stood up, raised their hands towards heaven, closed their eyes, and began to sway. The man beside me smiled and shook his head. I smiled back. Two middle-aged people commiserating about the excesses of youth. The music grew more intense, and the kids who were swaying began to whirl up the centre aisle towards the altar. I was absorbed in their progress when the man who had smiled at me began to howl and speak in tongues.

It was a relief when a small, sensible-looking man who appeared to be in his mid-sixties walked to the front and stood behind the lectern. He was wearing trousers, an open-necked shirt, and a red cardigan. He thanked the members of Joyful Noise and smiled with real affection at the kids who had danced in the aisle and who had collapsed, sweaty and depleted, on the floor to the left of him.

He looked out over the congregation. "I'm Paschal Temple," he said, "and I'm glad to be here." His voice was a prairie voice, flat, gentle, unhurried. He began to speak about what St. Paul had said about the gifts of the spirit in his letter to the Corinthians. I had heard the words a dozen times, but that night they struck a nerve. "Now we see only puzzling reflections in a mirror, but then we shall see face to face. My knowledge now is partial, then it will be whole . . ."

I hadn't any plan about how I would approach Paschal Temple, but he took care of the problem for me. As soon as the service was over, he came down to where I was sitting.

"Can I help, Mrs. Kilbourn?" he said.

"You know my name," I said.

He looked down, abashed. "It's been in the papers lately," he said.

"That's why I'm here," I said.

"Would you like to come to the office and talk awhile?" he asked.

The office was a small room, cheery with children's drawings of Jesus. There was a photograph on the desk of a woman holding a strawberry shortcake up to the camera. I pointed to it. "Your wife?" I asked.

"My heart," he said.

Lucky Lolita. Paschal Temple motioned me to sit down. Up close I could see the fine network of lines around his eyes. He sat back in his chair and smiled at me, patient, encouraging. I thought he had the kindest face I'd ever seen.

"I don't know where to begin," I said. "That text you used for your sermon, that's my life right now. Partial knowledge and puzzling reflections."

"That's the human condition, Mrs. Kilbourn."

"I know," I said. "But if you've been reading the papers, you know I haven't got the time to muddle through. I have to clear up some things pretty quickly. I thought one place to start was with Kevin Tarpley."

"You know about my connection with him," Paschal Temple said.

"He wrote to me." I opened my bag, took out Kevin's letter and slid it across the desk. "This came the day he died."

He read the letter and then handed it back to me. "Kevin was a very simple boy," he said sadly.

"He was a murderer," I said.

Paschal Temple touched his fingertips together and, for a few moments, he looked at them with great concentration. Then he raised his eyes to mine. "No," he said, "I don't believe Kevin was a murderer."

The room was so quiet I could hear the ticking of the wall clock. On the desk in front of me, Lolita Temple held her strawberry shortcake up to the camera. I felt as if I had turned to glass.

The Reverend Temple's voice was filled with concern. "Can I get you something Mrs. Kilbourn? Tea? Water?"

I shook my head.

"Then I'll explain myself," he said. "I guess I should start by telling you that if you hadn't come to me, I would have come to you. Until this week, I had looked upon Kevin's conversations with me as confidential, 'under the seal' as the Roman Catholics say."

"Two people are dead, and I'm in serious trouble," I said. "Surely that changes things."

"It does," he agreed. "That's why I'm talking to you now. But Mrs. Kilbourn, you mustn't get your hopes up. Kevin Tarpley never gave me a full and frank confession of wrongdoing. He was a troubled young man with some persistent questions. That's all we have to go on."

"It's better than what I have now," I said.

Paschal Temple looked at me closely. "As they say here at Bread of Life, 'Half a loaf is better than none.'"

"That's a terrible joke," I said.

"I know, but it made you smile, and that makes me feel hopeful. Let's begin at the beginning, Mrs. Kilbourn. The first time I met Kevin Tarpley was after my weekly prayer service at the penitentiary. I asked Kevin why he'd come, hoping, as you can imagine, for some indication of searching or need. But do you know what he said?"

I shook my head.

"He said, 'Some guy told me if I come to chapel, they'll parole me earlier.' That was Kevin. He had been in jail for six years without inquiring about the avenue to parole, but when someone he barely knew told him that going to chapel was the route to follow, he went to chapel. It would never have occurred to him to question the validity of the argument or the reliability of the source. He was very limited intellectually, Mrs. Kilbourn. I had counselling sessions with him twice a week for six weeks, and I was constantly surprised that a fellow like that had been allowed to live on his own. He was one of those sad cases that our society allows to slip through the cracks: not so severely limited that social services could step in, but certainly not capable of making decisions for himself."

I closed my eyes, and Maureen Gault was there, derisive, boasting. "I can make people do things." That's what she'd said the night of Howard Dowhanuik's dinner. I thought of the scene on the highway. What had she made Kevin Tarpley do?

My heart was pounding. "What did he talk about in your sessions?"

"Lies," said Paschal Temple. "He agonized over a lie he had told. He asked me repeatedly how bad it was to tell a lie. And I told him repeatedly that he should ask God's forgiveness and then he should tell the truth. It wasn't enough. Finally, not long before he died, he told me what was troubling him. 'What do you do,' he asked, 'if one person is hurt by the lie, but another person is hurt by the truth?' I told him he would have to work out who was being hurt more, and then I showed him that passage about responsibility and judgement that he quoted in his letter to you. That seemed to turn the tide for him. He accepted Christ as his Saviour that night, and he told me he knew now that he had to tell the truth."

"And then he was murdered," I said. "Did he tell you the name of the person who would be hurt by the truth?"

"No," he said. "But as I remember it, there was only one other person with him on the highway the night your husband was killed."

Kevin Tarpley's letter lay on the table in front of me. The anguish even the physical act of printing had cost him was apparent in every carefully formed word.

"This wasn't the only letter," I said. "The prisoner in the cell across from him said there were two more."

Paschal Temple nodded. "Kevin told me he had three letters to write."

I pointed to the words Kevin had so laboriously printed on the bottom of the publicity picture for Howard Dowhanuik's roast.

"Did he ask you about this quote? From what you've said about Kevin Tarpley's intellectual capacity, it doesn't seem likely he would have found it on his own."

Paschal Temple read the words aloud. "'Put not your trust in rulers. Psalm 146,'" he said. "I didn't tell him about that passage, at least not directly."

There was a battered briefcase on the floor beside him. He reached into it, pulled out a piece of paper and handed it to me. It was a photocopied sheet labelled "Biblical Character Building Chart." Beneath the title were two neat columns. The first was headed "Character Building Qualities," the second, "Character Destroying Qualities." Under

"Character Building Qualities," words like "Abstinence" and "Morality" and "Thrift" were followed by a biblical reference, chapter and verse.

Paschal Temple leaned across and pointed to an entry in the column labelled "Character Destroying Qualities." "Wilful Blindness. Psalm 146." "There's your quote, Mrs. Kilbourn, and Kevin did have a copy of this sheet. I gave it to him. I give copies of this to a lot of the fellows at the penitentiary."

Unexpectedly, he grinned. "Mrs. Kilbourn, you have the same look on your face you had when the man beside you began speaking in tongues."

"I'm sorry," I said, "I guess I'm uncomfortable with this kind of thing."

"We don't all come to God in the same way," he said gently. "And whatever you may think of these little spiritual shortcuts, for some people they're just the ticket. The Reinhold Niebuhrs of this world are few and far between, you know."

"You read Reinhold Niebuhr?" I asked.

"A cat can look at a king," he said kindly, and I could feel myself redden with embarrassment.

"Well, that's neither here nor there," he said. "That passage I used as a text for the sermon tonight tells us that knowledge will 'vanish away.' It also tells us that there are three things that last forever: faith, hope, and love; but the greatest of them all is love. Maybe that passage will lead you to an understanding of what Kevin Tarpley did. And Mrs. Kilbourn, perhaps if you come to understand Kevin, you'll be able to forgive him."

I stood up. "Thank you," I said.

"I'm afraid I wasn't really very helpful," he said as he walked me to the door.

I turned and faced him. "You were," I said. "More than you know."

As I drove south on Albert Street, I tried to do what Paschal Temple had urged me to do. I tried to think about faith and hope and love. I tried to make myself understand that Kevin Tarpley had lied because he loved Maureen Gault. I tried to picture the love he felt for her. But try as I might, the only image I could summon was the image of Maureen Gault killing my husband. It blocked out everything else. Those pale eyes had looked into Ian's eyes as she raised her arm and then brought the crowbar down on the side of his skull.

I was still seeing through a glass, darkly.

Six

I SLEPT badly and woke up with a headache and a sense of foreboding so acute that it took an act of will just to put on my sweats and sneakers. The run along the lakeshore with the dogs seemed endless, and by the time I got into the Volvo to drive Angus to his basketball practice and Taylor to her art class, I felt as if my nerve ends were exposed. The scene inside the car didn't help. The radio was blasting something loud and dissonant, and in the back seat Taylor was tormenting her brother about Brie, the girl who'd moved from L.A.

I turned down the sound, punched the button to change stations, then angled around towards Taylor.

"Stop it, T," I said. "I mean it."

Angus leaned over to his sister. "She means it. I can tell by her voice."

"Thank you, Angus," I said, and I snapped on my seat-belt and pulled out of the driveway.

"Top of the hour on your Rock and Roll Heaven Week-end," said the man on the radio. "Here's a celestial six-pack: Karen Carpenter, Ritchie Valens, Buddy Holly, Louis Armstrong, Bobby Darin, and Marvin Gaye, Six Greats Whose Stars Shine Bright Even After Death!"

"I hate that station," said T.

"You can borrow my Discman," Angus said; then he hissed, "but listen, if you even breathe wrong, I'm taking it back."

At College Avenue, we had to stop for a funeral procession. As I sat and watched the hearse and the mourners go by, Karen Carpenter sang about how love had put her on the top of the world.

We dropped Angus at the Y, and Taylor hopped in the front seat with me. As we drove to the Mackenzie Gallery, she filled me in on her new art teacher.

"His name is Fil with an *F*," she said. "He wears a sleeve on his head, and he says if you understand planes, you can draw anything."

"Planes?" I said. "Planes like at the airport?"

Taylor shook her head. "Is that another one of your jokes, Jo?"

"No," I said, "it's not. I really don't understand."

"Planes like on your face." She looked at me thoughtfully. "Except," she said, "you're like me. No planes. Just chipmunk cheeks."

"Thanks, T," I said. "I needed cheering up."

She undid her seatbelt and slid across the seat towards me. "I love you, Jo."

I looked at her worried face. She'd only been with me two years, not secure yet.

"I love you, too, Taylor," I said. "Now get your seatbelt back on."

"We're almost there."

"Doesn't matter," I said. "Snap!"

Most Saturdays I used the two hours when Taylor was at her art lesson to run errands, but that morning I didn't feel like braving the eyes of the curious in the mall. I remembered the visiting exhibition of Impressionist landscapes at the gallery. I decided I could use an infusion of incandescent light and pastoral peace.

It helped. As I walked through the still rooms, I could

feel my pulse slow and my mind clear. Paschal Temple's revelation had shaken me. For six years I had lived with the fact that Ian's death had been random, a chance occurrence in a fatalist's tragedy. But if Maureen Gault had killed Ian, the character of the tragedy changed. In the months after Ian's murder I had tormented myself imagining what his death must have been like. But as frightening as the movie in my head was, it lacked specifics. Darkness. Shadows. A spill of blood on the snow. I could never bring Kevin Tarpley into focus. Maureen Gault was another matter. When I closed my eyes, she was there, pale eyes flat with menace, thin mouth curled in triumph, as she ended Ian's life. Oh, I could see Maureen all right. But try as I might, what I couldn't see was why she had killed my husband.

I checked my watch as I came out of the exhibit. Taylor would be in her lesson for another hour. I wandered through the lobby. In the corner was a rack of brochures for tourists. I rejected the ones for other galleries and museums in our city, and chose one entitled "Tips for Healthy Living." It was full of robust good sense:

> Nutrition – Eat Right
> Physical Fitness – Exercise Regularly
> Stress – Learn to Cope
> Accident Prevention – Practise Safety
> Communicable Diseases – Practise Prevention

I put it back in the rack. Now that I had the key, Healthy Living would be easy. I checked my watch again. I still had almost an hour. Time enough to fight stress by coping. Jill had left me a pass for the video library at Nationtv; I could go over the tapes of Ian's death and the trial and see if there was anything I'd missed.

When I pulled into the parking lot behind the station, Janis Joplin was singing "Me and Bobby McGee." I was still humming the tune as I crossed the lobby and took the elevator upstairs. The young woman working in the video library was wearing Doc Martens, and she had a small diamond in her nose. When I asked for the Ian Kilbourn file she said, "You mean the whole thing?"

"Freedom's just another word for nothin' left to lose," I said.

She chewed her gum thoughtfully. "Is that a yes?"

I nodded. "That's a yes."

As I headed out of the library with my armload of tapes, she called me back.

"This one goes with the file, too," she said, and she balanced another tape carefully on the pile I was holding.

I looked at the name on the spine: "Heinbecker Funeral." It was the tape Jill had mentioned the afternoon Angus and I had come to Nationtv. She had said then that the eulogy Ian had given for Charlie Heinbecker had been terrific.

As soon as I got into the editing suite, I put the Heinbecker tape in the VCR. I was in the mood for something terrific.

I fast-forwarded past scenes of the mourners arriving, the choir processing, and the minister praying. Before I had a chance to prepare myself for it, Ian's image was on the screen. As I watched my husband deliver Charlie Heinbecker's eulogy, I think I stopped breathing.

It was apparent that the video had been shot by an amateur. Periodically, the camera would jerk away from Ian to focus on the members of Charlie's family in the front pews. The transitions were too abrupt, and often the images the camera captured were out of focus. None of that mattered to me. Jill had been right. Ian was terrific that day. He quoted Tennyson ("I am a part of all that I have met . . . /How dull it is to pause, to make an end/To rust unburnished, not to shine in use"), and he talked about stewardship and our obligation to others.

Good words, but it was Ian's face, not his words, that drew me closer to the screen. He had less than three hours to live, and he didn't know it. He didn't know that today was the day the dragon waited at the side of the road. In a gesture I had seen ten thousand times, Ian brushed back his hair with his hand, and I felt something inside me break. Tired of holding the pieces together, I closed the door to the editing suite and gave in.

Crying helped. By the time the monitor showed the mourners leaving the church, I had distanced myself from what was happening on the screen. As I watched for Ian, I was in control again. Finally, he came out, and the camera zoomed in for a closeup. For a moment, he stood blinking as the December light bounced off the snow. Then he started down the church steps, and the camera arced away from him and began to follow another cluster of mourners as they moved from the church to the street. I was leaning forward to punch the stop button when Ian stepped into camera range again. Blurred but recognizable, he began walking down the street. He didn't get far before a slight figure in a dark jacket came up behind him, reached out, and touched his shoulder. Ian turned. Then the camera made another of its convulsive transitions, and I was looking at the pallbearers carrying Charlie's casket out of the church.

I hit the rewind button. The first time, I rewound too far. Then I fast-forwarded past the sequence I needed to see. It took awhile, but finally my husband and his murderer were on screen. I pressed stop.

Maureen's back was to the camera, but her white-blond bouffant was unmistakable, and the baseball jacket she was wearing was the one she would be arrested in a few hours later. Ian was looking straight into her face. What did he see there?

I touched the rewind button. Ian turned from Maureen and, in the robotic walk of an actor in a silent movie, my husband and the woman who was about to kill him moved away from one another. If I kept rewinding, I could change the outcome. I could defeat death. But as I watched the mourners at Charlie's funeral walking backwards up the steps of the church, I knew I couldn't rewind the tape forever. I flicked on the lights in the editing suite. It was time to push the button marked "forward." I blew my nose, threw the Heinbecker tape into my handbag, and collected the others to take back to the library.

When Taylor and I pulled up in front of our house, Jess Stephens was standing at the front door. He handed me the worm-cake recipe.

"That's from my mum," he said.

There was no note with the recipe, but at least Sylvie had let him come over. That was a start.

"Can he stay for lunch?" Taylor asked.

"It's okay with me," I said, "but he'd better check at home."

Taylor stepped closer to Jess. She was looking at his face appraisingly. "Great planes," she said.

Jess looked baffled.

"Taylor's learning how to draw faces in her art class," I said.

"You'd be good to draw, Jess," Taylor said.

"No, thanks," he said.

I looked at him. Taylor was right. Jess would be good to draw. His cheekbones were high and well defined, and his eyes had the slightly upward tilt you sometimes see in Slovenes. Somewhere along the line, an ancestor of the O'Keefes or the Stephenses must have spent some quality time in Eastern Europe.

Taylor grabbed Jess's hand. "Go call your mum. Then we can look at Jack."

I followed them down the hall and watched through the kitchen window as they went out on the deck. Taylor immediately pressed her face against the pumpkin, peering into his right eye hole. Then she moved back to let Jess look. As I turned from the window, I thought that November had been kinder to Jack than it had to me. His rate of disintegration had slowed in the chill.

When Hilda came in, she gave me a sharp look. "I'd say 'Penny for your thoughts,' but from the look on your face, I don't think I'd be pleased with my purchase."

"I'm thinking about death and decay," I said.

Hilda picked up a knife and began buttering bread. "Not elegiacally, I take it."

"I had a lousy morning," I said. I went to the fridge and took out a block of cheddar. Everybody liked grilled cheese. As I sliced the cheddar, I told Hilda about the funeral tape. When I finished, her face was grim.

"What are you going to do?" she said.

"Take the tape to the police," I said.

"Wouldn't they have seen it already?"

"I don't think so, Hilda. It was a private taping of a family event. Old Mrs. Heinbecker had it until last year when she gave it to Jill, and Jill put it straight in the archives."

Hilda looked thoughtful. "The police have to see it, of course. That's the only ethical option you have, but, Joanne, that tape isn't going to help your case."

I shuddered. The resonance of the phrase "your case" was not pleasant.

"I don't seem to know how to help my case," I said.

"Follow the strands back to the place where they meet," Hilda said. "Find out everything you can about Kevin Tarpley and Maureen Gault." Her voice dropped. "And, Joanne, I think you're going to have to scrutinize your husband's life as well."

I could feel the rush of anger. "You're not suggesting there was a relationship between Ian and Maureen Gault, are you?"

Hilda's voice was patient, but firm. "There was a relationship. You saw it yourself on that tape. In all likelihood, the relationship was that of stalker and victim, but, if that was the case, you still need to know what it was about Ian that made Maureen hunt him down. And you need to know how long she pursued him and whether he knew about the pursuit. There are a dozen questions, Joanne."

As I plugged the parking meter outside police headquarters, I was heavy with discouragement. *A dozen questions.* I looked at the tape in my handbag. When Inspector Alex Kequahtooway saw it, a dozen questions would be just the beginning.

As I opened his office door, the first thing I noticed was that there was a Beethoven violin sonata playing softly on the CD player in the corner; the second was that Alex Kequahtooway had had his hair cut. His brother, Perry, wore his hair traditionally, in braids, but Alex's hair was very short. A "cop-cut" Angus would have called it. The night of the murder Inspector Kequahtooway had been dressed casually, but today he was wearing a navy suit, a striped shirt, and a floral silk tie.

"I like your tie," I said.

"Thanks," he said. "I was in court all morning. What can I do for you, Mrs. Kilbourn?"

He listened to my account of the tape carefully, and as I finished, he smiled thinly.

"I have to hand it to you for bringing the tape in. I can't say for certain until I see it, but it sounds as if that tape may be helpful."

"I hope it is," I said.

He nodded. "Me too," he said. Then he leaned towards me. "Mrs. Kilbourn, what were you looking for at Nationtv?"

"Answers," I said.

"Leave that to us, Mrs. Kilbourn. Don't involve yourself in this."

"I am involved. Haven't you read the papers or turned on your TV? I'm the number-one suspect."

He raised his eyebrows. "Do you believe everything you hear from the media?"

For the first time since Maureen Gault's murder, I felt a glimmer of hope.

"If you don't think I killed her, why aren't you telling the press?"

Unexpectedly, he smiled. "First, because, at least to my knowledge, there has been no flat-out assertion that you're guilty. The press has been very careful to imply rather than state. And second, because, at the moment, there are certain advantages to having the focus on you."

"Because the real killer might relax and make himself vulnerable?"

"Him or her self, Mrs. Kilbourn. And yes, that's what I'm hoping for. A lot of police work is just waiting around, you know. When I was a kid, I owned an old retriever – best squirrel dog on the reserve. He never seemed to do anything but lie in the sun. All the other dogs, soon as they spotted a squirrel, they'd start running around, yapping, going crazy till they got that squirrel into a tree. Nine times out of ten that was the end of it. The dogs would get tired and bugger off, and the squirrel would go on about his business. But that old retriever of mine would just sit and wait, and as soon as the squirrel thought it was a lovely day for a walk . . . bingo!" He smiled. "That old dog would have made a good cop."

"So you're just waiting?"

He shook his head. "No," he said.

"Then what are you doing?"

"Checking and re-checking stories," he said.

"To see if someone's lying?"

"No, just to see how everybody within earshot of the head table remembers the evening's events. People see things differently, Mrs. Kilbourn."

"Depending on where they were sitting," I said.

"Yeah, and depending on what happened to them in their lives before they walked into that room. What I'm trying to do right now is find out everything I can about the people who were sitting at the head table that night."

"Know the truth about the teller and you'll know the truth about his tale," I said.

Inspector Alex Kequahtooway's dark eyes widened with interest. "Something an elder told you?" he asked.

"Something my grandmother told me," I said.

His round face creased in a grin. "She must have been an Ojibwa."

We both laughed.

"Finding the truth about the tellers and the tales is what I'm trying to do now," he said.

"Are you getting anywhere?" I asked.

"At the moment, no. All I'm doing is mouse work." He gestured towards the medicine wheel on the wall behind him. "The other day you mentioned the Four Great Ways of Seeking Understanding. You know how Brother Mouse understands his world?"

"By sniffing things out with his nose, seeing what's up close, touching what he can with his whiskers."

He smiled. "Did your grandmother teach you that, Mrs. Kilbourn?"

"No," I said, "I learned that from my instructor in Indian Studies 232."

"Then you know that when I've got my treasure trove of facts and information, I'll try to stop seeing like a mouse and start seeing like an eagle. The big picture, Mrs. Kilbourn. That's what I'm going for."

He extended his hand to me. "Thank you for coming, Mrs. Kilbourn.

I took his hand. "You're welcome," I said. "And, Inspector, I enjoyed the Beethoven."

When I got home, Hilda was sitting at the kitchen table with the morning paper spread out in front of her and a pad and pencil beside her.

She gestured to the window when she saw me. "The

children are building a snow fort. They've been remarkably persistent. It's quite impressive."

I looked into the back yard. Taylor and Jess were installing the jack o'lantern in a place of honour at the top of the snow fort. I watched as they packed snow around his base to secure him. Shrivelled but menacing, Jack surveyed the back yard. The fort and those within it were safe.

"Any word from Angus?" I asked Hilda.

"He came by with a group of friends. They admired my earrings, I admired theirs, and they left. He says he'll be home at the regular time for supper."

"Good," I said. I poured a cup of coffee and sat down opposite her. The paper was open to a story about Maureen Gault. "Anything new?" I asked.

"There might be," Hilda said. "I decided to read through all the stories about Maureen and note the significant points."

"Mouse work," I said.

She looked puzzled. When I explained, she laughed. "I like that," she said. She picked up her notepad. "Now, here's my pile of nuts and berries: Maureen Gault was born on Valentine's Day, 1968, in Chaplin."

"Kevin Tarpley was from there, too," I said. "And that's where Ian died. Funny, isn't it? For years, Chaplin was just a place I drove past on the highway, but it always gave me the creeps. It wasn't the town so much as the sodium sulphate plant on the outskirts. There were always these huge mounds of salt on the ground there. They made me think of the Valley of Ashes in *The Great Gatsby*."

Hilda raised her eyebrows. "That's certainly an ominous association."

I nodded. "It's lucky we don't know what's ahead of us, isn't it?" I said.

"Very lucky," Hilda said. She picked up her notepad again. "Maureen's father was killed in a farming accident five months after she was born. Now this next is a quotation from an interview with Maureen's mother, Shirley.

'When my husband died, I decided to devote my life to my girl. She had it all: tap, jazz, ballet, ringette. Little Mo always knew exactly what she wanted, and she knew how to get it from me. I don't know how things could have turned out so bad for her.'"

"Poor woman," I said. "Maureen was her life. I remember Shirley Gault from the time after the arrest. I think she was on the news every night, If there was a cabinet minister coming to town, she'd be at the airport, demanding justice. If there was a public meeting, she was at it, handing out leaflets, trying to get herself in front of the cameras."

"She sounds unbalanced," Hilda said.

"I thought so," I said, "but I was pretty unbalanced myself at the time, so I was no judge."

Hilda looked at me sharply. "Are you sure you want to pursue this, Joanne?"

"In for a penny, in for a pound, as my grandmother used to say."

Hilda smiled. "My grandmother used to say that, too." She took a deep breath. "Now, for Maureen's career, which to put it charitably seems somewhat chequered. She never finished high school, but in 1989 Maureen graduated from Vogue Beauty School with a degree in Cosmetology and Depilatory Esthetics. I presume that means she was licensed to apply makeup and remove body hair. At any rate, according to the paper, at the time of her death she was working at a beauty salon called Ray-elle's."

"That's not far from here," I said. "It's in the basement of that strip mall on Montague. I've seen their sign, but I've never been in there."

Hilda raised an eyebrow. "Ray-elle's may be worth looking into," she said. Then she closed her notepad. "Joanne, the most promising information I gathered isn't written down anywhere. It's just a feeling. The paper printed a number of comments about Maureen from girls she knew at school. Not much there, except a certain agreement about the fact that Maureen was a loner who always seemed to know how to get what she wanted. But the reporter from the paper also called the principal of Maureen's old high school in Chaplin for a comment."

"And . . . ?" I said.

"And the woman refused to talk to him."

"That is interesting," I said.

"There's more," Hilda said. "They printed the woman's name; it's Carolyn Atcheson. I know her. Not well, but, before she was a principal, Carolyn was an English teacher. We served on a curriculum committee together. So I called her this morning. And . . . and it was very puzzling. She was delighted to hear from me, very welcoming, full of questions about what I was doing now. But as soon as I mentioned Maureen Gault's name, there was a chill."

"Maybe she thought you were just satisfying your curiosity," I said.

Hilda shook her head. "No, I explained at the outset that my interest in Maureen Gault was not whimsical, and that a dear friend's life had been thrown into turmoil because of Maureen. Carolyn reacted oddly to that. She laughed, not a nice laugh. Then she said, 'I wonder how many lives were thrown into turmoil by that girl?'

"I thought I would press my advantage then. I asked Carolyn straight out if she believed Maureen Gault was capable of murder. There was such a long silence on the line, I wondered if she'd hung up on me. But finally Carolyn said, 'Maureen Gault was capable of anything. She was pathological.'"

"It sounds as if Carolyn's worth talking to," I said.

Hilda said, "It won't be easy. Joanne. From the minute I mentioned Maureen's name, Carolyn Atcheson sounded as if she was terrified."

"But Maureen's dead," I said. "What could Carolyn Atcheson be frightened of?"

Hilda stood up. "That's what I'm going to find out. First thing tomorrow morning, I'm driving down to Chaplin."

"What about church?" I asked. "I've never known you to miss."

Hilda folded the newspaper carefully. "I think sometimes God likes action from his foot-soldiers."

I looked at my watch. "Speaking of action, I'd better get supper started. How does spaghetti sound to you?"

"Splendid," Hilda said.

"Good," I said. For the next hour, I chopped, sautéed, stirred, simmered, and thought about the best way of finding out the truth. "Follow the strands back to the place where they meet." That's what Hilda had said. Jill was looking into Kevin's life; Hilda had taken on Maureen. That left Ian, and no one was going to follow that strand back but me.

Just as I moved the spaghetti sauce to the back burner, Jess and Taylor came in from outdoors, cheeks rosy with cold and excitement.

"It smells like Geno's in here," Taylor said.

Jess turned to her. "Do you ever go there on Kids' Night?"

Taylor shook her head. "Jo says she'd rather be pecked to death by a duck. We just go regular nights."

Jess smiled at me. I could see the edge of a permanent tooth pushing through. I bent down and looked more closely.

"Nice tooth, Jess."

"Thanks. Mrs. Kilbourn, do you have hot chocolate here?"

"Yes," I said, "I think we do."

Five minutes later, we were all sitting around the kitchen table, drinking hot chocolate and listening to Taylor talk about how, if she had a kitten, she would let it sleep on the pillow beside her so it wouldn't bother me in the night. Life in the fast lane.

When Hilda came down, she was dressed to go out.

"Want to join us?" I asked.

"Thank you, no," she said. "I'm off to Ray-elle's Beauty Salon."

"Thinking of getting a new do?" said Jess.

Hilda patted her red hair with a degree of satisfaction. "Oh, I think my old do will suffice."

"I like it," Taylor said. "In oil paints that colour is called 'raw sienna.' It's one of my favourites."

"Mine too," said Hilda.

Gary Stephens was an hour late picking up Jess. He'd called in mid-afternoon to say he'd be at our house by 5:00, but it was close to 6:00 when he pulled into the driveway.

"Sorry I'm late," he said. "The skiing was just too good." He was wearing cross-country ski clothes, and I saw his skis on the rack of his car, but he didn't radiate the sense of physical well-being of someone who'd spent the afternoon outdoors. As he stood in the hall, his handsome face was pale, and he smelled, not of fresh air, but of liquor and cologne. I wondered who the lucky woman was this time.

"It wasn't a problem," I said. "The kids had a great afternoon. They built a snow fort. Jess could have stayed for supper if he'd wanted."

"Thanks, babe, but Sylvie has something planned." He smiled his slow, lazy, practised smile. "You know how she is," he said.

You and me against the little woman. It was an ugly tactic, but before I had a chance to respond, Jess was in the hall.

"Dad, you've gotta see the fort we built. Come on. We made forty-six snowballs."

As Jess grabbed his father's hand, Gary Stephens was transformed as he had been Hallowe'en night. There was such naked love in his eyes as he looked at his son that I felt a rush of feeling towards him. Five minutes before I'd wanted to come down on him like a fist on a grasshopper, but he was a complex man, and he evoked complex emotions.

Angus and I were just finishing the salad when Hilda came in.

I checked her hair. "No new do?" I asked.

"No," she said, as she hung up her coat. "But I did come away with some interesting new perspectives on Maureen."

"From whom?" I asked.

"From Ray-elle herself. Joanne, Maureen did not work at Ray-elle's at the time of her death. Ray-elle had, and I quote, 'canned her' the last week in October."

"But the paper said . . ."

"Ray-elle didn't believe there was much to be gained in giving the newspaper the complete story. She reasoned that since Maureen was dead and Shirley Gault was suffering enough, there was no need to dig up the past."

"I guess that makes sense," I said.

"There's more," Hilda said. "And this doesn't make sense. At least not to me. The day after Kevin Tarpley died, Maureen Gault came by the beauty shop and offered to buy Ray-elle out."

"Where would Maureen get that kind of money?"

Hilda came over and took a slice of cucumber out of the salad bowl. "I don't know, but apparently she said she could pay cash. Joanne, the asking price for that business would be significant. Ray-elle told me she had just finished renovating." A smile flickered at the corners of Hilda's mouth.

"What's so funny?" I asked.

Hilda shook her head. "That place. Joanne, everything in Ray-elle's is pink. Floor, walls, chairs, uniforms, everything."

"Maybe Ray-elle had Superstar Barbie's decorator," I said.

Taylor, who was setting the table, heard a name that interested her. "I saw a lady on TV who had nineteen operations so she could look like Barbie," she said.

"Good lord," I said, "why would she do that?"

Angus handed me the salad. "You don't want to know, Mum," he said. "How long till we eat?"

"Not long," I said. "The pasta has to cook."

"Time enough to see my snow fort," T said.

"I had to ask," said Angus, as he followed his sister out the back door.

I turned to Hilda. "How about some Chianti while you tell me what you found out."

I poured each of us a glass. Hilda took hers and raised it. "To puzzle solving," she said. "Although, to be frank, my visit to Ray-elle's has yielded more questions than answers." Hilda sipped her wine. "Joanne, let me practise what I preach and put some chronology to all this.

"When I got to the shop, Ray-elle was at the appointments desk and Cheryl, a young woman who plays a pivotal role in this story, was sweeping up. There weren't any customers. I introduced myself, and Ray-elle said she was just about to close anyway and she asked Cheryl to get me some coffee. When Ray-elle was finished, she told Cheryl she could leave, and Ray-elle and I went to a little room at the back, so she could smoke. Joanne, even her lighter was pink. It was in a kind of sheath made of pink leather, and the case she kept her cigarettes in was covered in pink leather, too."

"I used to have a cigarette case like that," I said, "except mine was white. I haven't seen a set like that in twenty-five years. I take it Ray-elle is, as the French say, 'of a certain age.'"

"She is," Hilda agreed. "And of a certain type. I liked her, Joanne. She's a school-of-hard-knocks person, physically strong and experienced. To look at her, one would think there wouldn't be much in life that would intimidate her . . ."

"But something did," I said.

"Not something, Joanne. Someone. The first thing Ray-elle said to me after we sat down was that she wasn't sorry Maureen Gault was dead because Maureen scared the shit out of her." Hilda raised an eyebrow. "You do realize I'm giving you Ray-elle's words verbatim."

"I do," I said. "Now, what did Maureen do to Ray-elle to scare her so badly?"

"It's an ugly story," Hilda said. "Cheryl, the girl who was sweeping up when I arrived at the shop, is a person with some serious limitations intellectually. She does odd jobs around the shop, sweeps up, cleans brushes and combs, that sort of thing. But Ray-elle has her wash hair, too. She says Cheryl has a gentle touch, and the customers like her." Hilda smiled. "Cheryl really did seem like a pleasant young woman. At any rate, last month, Cheryl came to Ray-elle and told her Maureen was forcing her to hand over her tips. It didn't amount to much, and when Ray-elle confronted her, Maureen said she didn't need the money."

"Why did she do it then?"

Hilda's face was grave. "Ray-elle said that Maureen seemed to get her kicks just from making the girl do her bidding."

"What did Maureen do when she was fired?" I asked.

Hilda picked up the wine bottle and filled our glasses. "She laughed in Ray-elle's face. Said she didn't need to work anyway, because she was about to come into some major money." Hilda looked hard at me. "It wasn't braggadocio, Joanne. The day after Kevin Tarpley died, Maureen paid a farewell visit to Ray-elle's. According to Ray-elle, Maureen was dressed expensively and ostentatiously. She said something cruel to Cheryl, queened it over the other women who work in the shop, then she went over to Ray-elle and offered to buy the shop. She said she could pay cash. When Ray-elle told her to get out, Maureen turned ugly. She said, 'Like I would ever want to buy a dump like this.' Then she picked up an open bottle of peroxide solution and threw it in Ray-elle's face. Ray-elle still has a nasty burn."

"Did she go to the police?"

Hilda shook her head. "She was afraid to, Joanne. She said she was afraid of what Maureen Gault would do if she crossed her."

That night I couldn't sleep. Every time I closed my eyes,

Maureen Gault was there. Finally, I gave up, went downstairs, and made myself some warm milk. As I sat at the kitchen table with my mug, Rose came into the room and sat with me; in Rose's house, people didn't come down for warm milk in the middle of the night.

From the kitchen window, I could see the ice on the creek. In the November moonlight, it looked dark and sinister. A child had drowned in that creek. When they had searched for the body, the police had brought up all kinds of ugliness: stolen bicycles and grocery carts; empty whisky bottles and used condoms; a weighted gunny sack full of small skeletons that turned out to be feline.

That afternoon, when I was certain the child's body had been taken away, I had walked along the levee. The banks of the creek were still littered with the objects the police had dredged up. Until that morning, those objects had been part of the tenebrous life of the creekbed. In the pale spring light, they had looked both mean and alien and I had hurried from them.

I rinsed my mug, put it in the dishwasher, and turned out the kitchen light. I had to get some sleep. In the morning it would be my turn to dredge.

Seven

I DIDN'T want to remember the last hours I spent with my husband on the day of his death. The morning of December 27 was cruel in every sense: the weather was viciously cold, and, the night before, Ian had come in very late and we had quarrelled. We weren't people who fought often and, as Ian got ready to leave that morning, we were silent, stunned, I think, by the pall of bitterness that hung in the air between us. I kissed my husband as he left, but I didn't tell him I loved him, and I didn't say goodbye. I was angry at him for deciding to drive through a blizzard because he felt he had to honour the outcome of a stupid coin toss, and I was angry at him because I thought he had treated me badly at the caucus office party the night before.

That party had seem jinxed from the beginning. The idea had been a good one: an afternoon of skating and tobogganing in Wascana Park for the families of members and staff who were in town for the holidays, then, in the evening, Boxing Day drinks in the east wing for the adults. But the wind had howled all afternoon, and most of us with children stayed away. After lunch, Ian had gone over to his office to get caught up on his mail, and he had called before dinner to say he wouldn't be home, and that I should come straight to the party and he'd see me there. As I was dressing, Angus came into our bedroom and threw up. I felt his head. He was feverish, but not worryingly so. I cleaned up, gave him a bath and some children's Tylenol, and called Ian at the office to tell him I wasn't coming. There was no answer. By the time Angus got out of the tub, he seemed better. Mieka was babysitting her brothers, and the party was only a few blocks away at the Legislature, so I decided to go after all.

It was a fine night. The wind had died down, and the air was clear and cold. The evergreens in front of the Legislature were strung, as they always were, with blue and white lights, but that year the park commission had suspended a giant illuminated snowflake over the face of the old building. It was sensational, and as I walked past the pictures of our former premiers and heard the music drifting down the marble corridors, I thought that one last Christmas party wasn't such a bad idea after all.

My merry mood didn't last long. The stately old Opposition Caucus Room was full of people, but Ian wasn't one of them. I got a drink and went over to Ian's secretary, Lorraine Bellegarde. She was wearing a red and yellow Métis ribbon shirt and a fringed leather skirt; it was a festive outfit, but Lorraine did not look cheerful. I didn't have to ask why. Lorraine was a perfectionist, and she'd been in charge of the festivities that day. I knew her well enough to know how acutely she'd be feeling the weight of the afternoon's failure. She told me she hadn't seen Ian. She also told me not to worry, but it was too late for that. I started moving around the room, asking if anyone had seen my husband. No one had, and the terrible possibilities began their assault on my consciousness: a holiday accident; a heart attack; a fatal slip on an icy step. By the time Ian walked through the door I was half sick with worry. He looked weary and preoccupied, but I didn't pity him.

"Where were you?" I said.

"Leave it alone, Jo," he said, and there was an edge to his voice that angered me.

"It would have been nice to know where you were," I said. "Angus is sick."

A flicker of alarm passed over his face, then he seemed to relax. "If it was serious, you wouldn't be here." Then he'd smiled, "Come on, relax. Angus is probably just suffering from too much Christmas."

"What if it had been serious?" I said.

"Well, it wasn't, so that's a moot point, isn't it? Look, Jo, I'm having a great time. Standing here listening to you being pissed off is exactly what I want to be doing right now. But, if you don't mind, I'd like to get a drink. Then, I'll come back and you can continue with whatever the hell it is you think you're doing."

I watched as he went to the bar and poured himself a drink. He downed it in a single gulp, poured another one, and started towards me. I was furious. I looked around for someone to talk to. Howard Dowhanuik was alone by the window. He was wearing the red plaid vest he had worn to every holiday function since I'd known him. Howard always made a point of drawing our attention to what he called the Dowhanuik tartan, but the vest had always done a pretty good job of calling attention to itself. In that evening of strange currents and jagged edges, it had been a reassuring sight.

I don't remember what Howard and I talked about, but I do remember that Ian joined us, and that, at some point, Lorraine came over and reminded Howard that the Caucus Office had to send someone to speak at Charlie Heinbecker's funeral the next day. Mellowed by good scotch, Howard had been avuncular as he gathered all our members together. I don't remember who came up with the idea of the coin toss to decide who would drive to Swift Current. Like most ideas that people come up with when they're drinking, it seemed inspired. Two people would toss, and the loser would meet a new opponent and toss again, until the outcome had been decided. When Ian lost, he had raised his glass to me. "At least I'm lucky in love," he'd said, and his voice had been heavy with irony.

I hadn't answered him. Lorraine Bellegarde had come over and told me there was a phone call. It was Mieka. Angus had thrown up again and was asking for me. I told Mieka I'd be right home. When I'd looked for Ian to tell him I was leaving, he was gone.

Three times during the evening I called the caucus office. Ian wasn't there. It must have been after 2:00 when I heard the front door, and a half-hour later than that when Ian finally came upstairs. I watched as he undressed in the moonlight, his long pale body as familiar to me as my own.

"Where were you?" I said.

His voice was infinitely tired. "Where you left me. At the party. Now I'm here, and I want to go to bed."

"Not until you tell me what's going on," I said. "Ian, you weren't at the party. I called. Nobody could find you."

"I stepped out for a while. Satisfied?"

"No," I said, "I'm not. Ian, we've never lied to each other. Where were you tonight?"

"Jo, if you'd stop badgering me, I wouldn't have to lie to you. This is my business, not yours. Now, for the last time, leave it alone."

"Go to hell," I said, and I turned my back to him. We slept fitfully, angry and apart. The next morning he showered and left. Seven hours later he was dead, and the marriage which had been the best thing that ever happened to me was over.

That was how the party had looked from my perspective, but there'd been other people there, and they would have other stories. I looked at my watch. It was too late to call anybody. All I could do was sit and watch the back yard fill up with snow until I was tired enough to sleep.

The next morning, as soon as I got in from taking the dogs for their run, I called Howard at his apartment in Toronto. He was happy to hear from me, but less happy when he heard what I was calling about.

"Jesus, Jo, I thought we agreed you'd stay out of this."

"No, Howard, you agreed. Look, the universe is not exactly unfolding as it should around here."

When I'd finished telling him about the way the arrows were pointing in the Maureen Gault case, Howard's voice was sombre.

"What can I do?"

"Tell me what you remember about the party the night before Ian died."

"You mean the one at the caucus office? Christ, Jo, that was six years ago."

"It's important, Howard. At least, I think it might be. The problem is I don't remember much about it at all. Angus was sick, and I went home early. I don't even know for sure who was there."

Howard's voice was thoughtful. "We were all there, weren't we? I remember Andy was. His mother was down for the holidays, and he brought her. Old Roma Boychuk, there was a political asset for you. She kept sniffing at the food. Finally she went up to Lorraine Bellegarde and said, 'How much you pay for all those little sausages and the crackers with the raw meat?' When Lorraine told her, Roma hit the roof. She spent the rest of the evening going around telling everybody how they'd been ripped off. 'Next time, get me. For that money I make you a five-course meal, and the meat will be cooked!'" He laughed again. "Lorraine was really steamed.

"Anyway, Roma and Andy were at the party, and Craig was there with Julie. He sure did better the second time around, didn't he? That Julie was something else . . . That night was the only time I ever remember seeing Craig stand up to her."

"What happened?"

"Julie came over to me with some hot piece of news, and Craig told her to put a lid on it."

"What was the news?"

"I don't know, but I don't imagine it was much. Julie

always had a mean little story or a nasty rumour. Remember how she used to say, 'There's something I feel I have to share with you . . .'? It was always dirt.

"Let's see, if Marty and I were still together, she would have been there, but I don't remember if we were still together."

"That's probably why you're not together now," I said.

"You're probably right," he agreed.

"Jane O'Keefe was there with that fat lawyer from Saskatoon. You know, the one who dyes his hair."

"Billy Clifford?" I said. "I never knew they were an item."

"They weren't. Billy would have taken a bullet for Jane, but she was just using him as a blind."

"For what?" I said.

"For an affair she was having with another guy," he said. "Jo, let's get on to something else here. With all my nasty evasions and innuendos I'm beginning to sound like Julie Evanson."

"Howard, if that other man is somebody I know, it may be important. Was he?"

There was silence. When Howard spoke, his voice was sad. "I guess it doesn't matter any more. It's been over for years. The other guy was Gary Stephens."

"Oh, Howard, no."

"It wasn't just a fling. At least not on Jane's side. She was really in love with him. In fact, she kind of fell apart that night at the party. I don't know whether they'd had a fight or what, but Gary disappeared part way through the evening, and Jane went after him."

"Howard, I just can't believe this. Was Sylvie there?"

He laughed. "Jo, as you just discovered, I can't even remember if my own wife was at the party, but I don't think Sylvie was there."

"No," I said. "When I really think about it, Sylvie wouldn't have been there. She never had much interest in Gary's political life."

"She never had much interest in Gary," Howard said. "At least she hadn't for a while."

"I just can't believe that Jane would have an affair with Gary. She and Sylvie have always seemed so close."

"They're still close," Howard said. "Gary's the one who seems to have been frozen out."

"Howard, do you think Sylvie knew?"

"If she didn't, she was the only one. We all knew."

"I didn't," I said.

Howard sighed. "Well, now you do. Look, Jo, can I call you back? I'm supposed to be taking Marty to brunch. She divorced me once for never being there; I'm trying to get back into her good graces."

"Marty's good graces are worth getting back into," I said. "But, Howard, can I just have one more minute? Please? Did Tess Malone come that night?"

Howard's voice was testy. "I don't know, Jo." Then he added more kindly. "Tess always went to everything, didn't she? Look, I'm sorry if I'm sounding pissed off, but I've told you everything I remember."

"You left out Ian," I said. "How long was he there?"

"Off and on all evening, I think. Jo, it's been six years. People weren't punching in and punching out. I don't remember how long Ian was there."

"Try, Howard, please."

He sighed. "Well, I know he was off with that old guy at the beginning."

"What old guy?"

"I don't know who he was. Ian and I came into the building together that night. When we got to the caucus office, there was an old man waiting on the doorstep. I heard him tell Ian his name. Can't remember what it was, but it was one of the good names."

"Ukrainian?" I said.

He laughed. "Right, a good Ukrainian name like Dowhanuik. Anyway, the old man was very agitated. Ian tried to calm him down. I remember he put his arm around

the old man's shoulder and walked him down to the end of
the hall."

"And?"

"And nothing. I went inside and took care of a few things
before the party. I never thought anything more about it. I
still don't. Jo, you've been around politics long enough to
know there's always some sad sack hanging around with a
gripe or a problem. It comes with the territory."

"I know," I said. "Today I'm the sad sack, and I've kept
you long enough. Have fun at brunch. Give Marty my
love."

"I will."

"Howard, one last thing."

"Yeah?"

"Watch your language."

He sighed heavily. "Oh shit, that's right. Swearing drives
Marty crazy."

I hung up. One down. Four to go.

When I walked into the kitchen, Angus was pouring
juice and Taylor was eating Eggos. On my plate was a
drawing of a woman: thin and glamorous, but recogniz-
ably me.

"T," I said. "This is terrific! On the best day of my life I
never looked this good."

"I gave you planes," T said, smiling.

"So you did," I said. "Thanks T. You improved on God."

She shook her head. "Oh, Jo. Like I could," she said, and
she went back to her Eggo.

When Hilda came down, she was dressed to travel. She
made herself a plate of scrambled eggs and toast, and ate
standing at the counter.

"Did you phone Carolyn Atcheson and ask if you could
come?" I said.

Hilda shook her head. "It's far too easy to say 'no' on the
telephone."

"If she won't see you, it's a long drive for nothing," I said.

Hilda's back was ramrod straight. "She'll see me,

Joanne. I'm not a person who permits a door to be barred against her."

"Aren't you going to church?" Angus asked innocently.

"Not today," Hilda said.

Angus looked at me hopefully. "Mum . . .?"

"Okay," I said. "We'll all backslide today. But after today . . ."

"I know, I know," Angus said, but he was already on his way to the phone to arrange a game of shinny.

I turned to Taylor. "It looks like it's you and me against the world, kiddo," I said. "How would you like to visit a pregnant lady?"

Manda Traynor sounded excited at the prospect of company. "Jo, you haven't seen our new house yet. Craig loves to show it off. And Taylor and I can play with Alex P. Kitten and Mallory."

"You have cats," I said.

"Two beautiful little Persians," Manda said.

"They have cats," I said to Taylor as I hung up.

She jumped up from the table and headed upstairs. "I'll be ready fast," she yelled over her shoulder.

Craig and Manda's new house was only about six blocks from us, so Taylor and I walked. It was a dreary November morning. The sky was overcast, and the only splashes of colour in the muted tones of the city streets came from orange Hallowe'en leaf bags leaking soddenly onto the snow.

"I'll be glad when people start putting up their Christmas decorations," I said to Taylor.

"Me too," Taylor said. "I'm going to make Jack a Santa hat and put him back out on the front porch."

"Swell," I said.

Taylor smiled up at me. "It will be swell, won't it?"

When Craig opened his front door to us, Alex P. Kitten and Mallory were waiting. Taylor was ecstatic. "Look," she said as she reached out to grab one of the ginger cats. "Their hair's the same colour as Miss McCourt's."

The cats didn't stick around long enough for me to make a comparison. They high-tailed it down the hall with Taylor in hot pursuit.

"Looks like it's going to be a long morning for Alex P. Kitten and Mallory," I said to Craig.

"They like company, and so do we," he said, and he savoured the word *we* as if it were newly coined.

"How's Manda doing?"

"She's terrific. The baby's in position now. It should be any day." He lowered his voice. "Jo, how are you doing? I've been working on the assumption that if you'd needed a lawyer, you'd have called."

"I would have," I said. "But the fact that I'm standing here doesn't mean I'm out of the woods. Craig, I need help."

"Why don't you go in and say hi to Manda? Then we can talk."

Manda was in the kitchen taking cookies out of the oven, and she was wearing a bright red apron that had CHILDBIRTH, A LABOUR OF LOVE written on the bib. Her dark hair was tied back with a red ribbon and her face was shining. When she reached out to hug me, I could smell cloves and cinnamon.

"Jo, I'm so happy you're here."

"Me too," I said.

Somewhere in the house a cat screeched. I waited, but there was no answering howl from Taylor. "I guess Taylor's learning that loving a cat isn't easy," I said.

Manda looked serious. "Jo, loving a cat is very easy. All the same, maybe I should go and give Taylor a few tips about getting acquainted. That'll give you two a chance to get caught up."

Craig turned to me. "Why don't we go down to the family room? The chairs are more comfortable."

The family room had floor-to-ceiling windows on the

wall that looked out onto the back yard. Against the window, a trestle table bloomed with plants: azalea, hydrangea, fuschia, and a huge Christmas cactus.

"This is beautiful," I said.

"Manda and I bought the house for this room," Craig said. "We thought it would be a great place for the kids."

"Kids plural?" I asked.

He grinned. "Why not?"

"You're really happy, aren't you?" I said.

He nodded. "Happy and very humble. Not many of us get a second chance, Jo. Come here, I have something to show you."

There was a small table in the corner. It was filled with pictures from a political life – not grip-and-grin photos, just pictures of friends. Craig picked one up and handed it to me. "Here's one you'll like," he said. It was a photograph of me, as pregnant as Manda Evanson was now. I was slumped into an easy chair, asleep; propped against the wall beside the chair was a stack of VOTE KILBOURN lawn signs.

"It was fun at the beginning, wasn't it?" Craig said softly.

"Oh, yeah," I said. "It was fun."

"Ian was a terrific guy."

"He was," I agreed.

I picked up another picture. This one was of Gary, Ian, and Andy sitting around the kitchen table in our old house. As befitted men who were about to change the world, they looked very serious.

"I took that picture," Craig said. "We used to sit at the table for hours arguing about policy, remember?"

"Sure," I said. "In those days, I was the one who made the coffee."

I looked at the picture again. All that idealism and commitment. Now Ian and Andy were dead, and Gary Stephens didn't care about anything above his belt.

I turned to Craig. "What happened to Gary?" I said. "What changed him?"

Craig's eyes were sad. "I don't think you can ever point to one thing when a person changes that much. But it started with Sylvie's book."

"*The Boy in the Lens's Eye*?" I asked, surprised.

"No," he said, "the first one, *Prairiegirl*. That book was the beginning of the end of his career in politics."

"Those girls were from Gary's constituency, weren't they?"

"That didn't bother Sylvie," Craig said, and I was surprised at the asperity in his voice.

"You don't think she should have taken those pictures."

"Jo, I don't give a damn about her taking pictures, but the world is full of young girls. Why Sylvie had to photograph those particular girls is beyond me. She was one who had everything. She had the money and the talent. She must have known what those pictures would do to Gary's career. And she went right ahead. They used to love Gary out there. He grew up in those hills."

"And they stopped loving him after Sylvie's book?"

"Not everybody, but a lot of people felt betrayed. Especially the old ones. They were proud of Gary. They thought they knew him, and they thought he stood for what they believed in."

"God, the Family, and the Land," I said.

"Exactly. Have you seen the pictures, Jo? I don't know anything about art, but I do know the law, and I could have argued a case that, taken out of context, those pictures were pornography. The parents of those girls agreed to let Sylvie photograph their daughters because she was Gary's wife. For them, what she did was a breach of trust."

"And they blamed Gary because he should have kept his wife in line," I said.

Craig nodded agreement. "They're good people, Jo. But the attitudes of a lifetime aren't easily changed."

"I know that," I said. "But Gary won the next election. They might have had to hold their noses when they voted, but those people gave him a majority, Craig. If Gary had toughed it out, they would have come around."

"He was toughing it out. Then there was some more trouble. The pictures had made Gary vulnerable, and he resigned his seat."

I looked again at the photograph in my hand. "Sometimes, it seems as if there's a curse on all the Seven Dwarfs."

Craig shook his head. "This wasn't a curse. This was a problem of Gary's own making." In the yard, two chickadees were fighting at the bird feeder. Craig was silent as he watched them.

"What did he do?" I asked.

"One of his clients discovered Gary had been dipping into his funds."

"I never heard anything about this."

"It was the spring after Ian died, Jo. You were going through a pretty bad time of your own. Besides, Gary's friends took care of it, or at least we tried to. We put some money together to cover the deficit, but the client was a farmer in Gary's constituency, so, of course, word got around. *Prairiegirl* had pretty well undermined whatever loyalty Gary's constituents felt they owed him. It was only a matter of time before the rumours finished him, so he resigned."

"Craig, this doesn't make sense. Why would Gary have to steal? Sylvie's got money."

Craig moved closer to the window. The chickadees were still at it. "I guess Gary thought the problem was his. It had to do with his land. Apparently, he'd borrowed pretty heavily from the Farm Credit Corporation, and he couldn't make his payments."

"Same old story," I said. "And Ian always said Gary couldn't resist the path of least resistance."

"Well, he paid for it," said Craig. "He resigned from a job that he loved, and he's been a pretty sorry excuse for a human being ever since."

"He is that," I said, and I felt weighed down by sadness.

Craig dropped an arm around my shoulder. "Come on, let's get some tea. You look like you could use a bracing cup of camomile."

"Manda's into health food?" I said.

"With a vengeance," he said. "There are nights when I'd give five years of my life for the sight of organ meat."

The camomile tea was bracing and the cookies, molasses and whole wheat flour laced with wheat germ, were solid but tasty. Manda was as fascinated by babies and cats as Taylor was, so the table talk was lively.

After Taylor and I had said our goodbyes and started off down the sidewalk, I turned to look back at Craig and Manda. She was standing in front of him, enclosed in the circle of his arms. On the front door behind them was the wreath of dried apple slices and berries Manda had made to celebrate fertility. As they waved, I was grateful that the curse of the Seven Dwarfs seemed to have passed them by.

Taylor and I had lunch at McDonald's. While she ate, she made up a list of the names she would call her kitten, if, that is, she ever was to have a kitten. I thought of her birthday three days away and wondered how much grief Sadie and Rose's aging hearts could take.

Taylor was still talking about kittens when I pulled up in our driveway. Angus was home. I could hear the rhythmic pounding of the CD upstairs in his bedroom, but Hilda wasn't back yet. I took some chicken breasts from the freezer and made a sauce of yogurt, lime juice, and ginger to put on them after they were grilled. We could have couscous and a cucumber salad with the chicken. A nutritionally faultless meal from the woman who'd let her daughter eat two Big Macs, a large fries, and a cherry pie for lunch.

It was close to 3:00 by the time Hilda got home, and she was buoyant.

"I don't need to ask how it went," I said. "Obviously, Carolyn Atcheson didn't bar the door against you."

"At first she almost did," Hilda said, "but once she invited me in and began to talk about Maureen Gault, she was unstoppable. I think it was cathartic for her."

"Good," I said. "Let's go in where it's comfortable and you can tell me about Carolyn's catharsis."

Hilda settled back into her favourite chair in the family room. "To start with," she said, "Maureen seems to have affected Carolyn's life profoundly, but I have the sense that, until today, she hasn't discussed the girl with anyone."

"Maureen Gault was just her student," I said. "Why wouldn't Carolyn talk about her?"

Hilda shrugged. "For the same reason most of us avoid talking about a situation we've bungled."

"What did she think she'd bungled with Maureen?"

Hilda's voice was grim. "Just about everything. Joanne, Carolyn says Maureen Gault was pathological, and I trust her assessment. She's a woman who uses language carefully."

"If she knew Maureen was pathological, she must have brought in a professional," I said.

"It wasn't quite that simple. According to Carolyn, Maureen seemed normal enough when she started high school. In fact, she was quite a success socially. There was always a group of girls around anxious to do her bidding, and she thrived."

"What went wrong?"

"Maureen overplayed her hand. According to Carolyn, she had to dominate every situation and manipulate every relationship. The more she could manipulate and humiliate her little group, the better Maureen seemed to feel about herself. Of course, it didn't take long for the girls to grow weary of being props for Maureen's self-esteem. They tried to break away and that's when the trouble began."

"Serious trouble?" I asked.

"Serious enough. There were threats. A girl opened her locker one morning and found her schoolbooks smeared with human faces. Another girl's house was broken into, and her clothes were shredded. Another's dog was killed."

"And the school let this go on?"

"Carolyn went to Maureen's mother with the name of a psychiatrist. Of course, Mrs. Gault was furious. She kept demanding proof."

"And there was none," I said.

Hilda shook her head. "Maureen Gault was too clever to carry out the revenge herself. She kept her distance and used a confederate."

"Kevin Tarpley," I said.

Hilda nodded. "Kevin Tarpley."

"And they were never caught," I said.

"No," said Hilda. "They were never caught."

I leaned forward in my chair. "Hilda, did Carolyn Atcheson say anything about what Maureen and Kevin did to Ian?"

Hilda looked away.

"What did she say?" I asked.

Hilda's voice was low with anger. "She said she wasn't surprised. She always knew it was just a matter of time before Maureen discovered murder."

That night, as Hilda and I were finishing our after-dinner coffee, the phone rang. It was Jane O'Keefe asking if we could get together. I arranged to meet her at her office at the Women's Health Centre the next day, after classes. After I wrote the time of our meeting on my calendar, I decided I might as well fill up my dance card, and I called Tess Malone. She agreed to meet me in the Beating Heart offices at 2:00 that same day.

When I hung up, I was satisfied. The work of Sister Mouse was going well.

Eight

THE Regina Women's Medical Centre was located between a Mr. Buns Bakery and a bicycle store in a strip mall on the north side of the city. Jane had told me they chose the space because the parking was free and the rent was cheap, but there had been no penny-pinching in the reception area. Jonquil walls blazed with Georgia O'Keeffe desert prints, a brass bowl of fat copper chrysanthemums glowed on the reception desk, and the crystal clarity of a Mozart horn concerto drifted from a CD player on the antique credenza in front of the window. The Women's Medical Centre had been decorated co-operatively by a group of pro-choice women in the city, and despite what Tess Malone told the public, the Centre had ended up owing more to *Better Homes and Gardens* than to Sodom and Gomorrah.

The receptionist had just finished announcing me, when Jane came out and motioned me to follow her down the hall. My gynecologist's office was decorated with posters from pharmaceutical companies: a pictorial history of contraceptive devices, a cross section of the uterus – instructive, but not exactly *trompe-l'oeil*. Jane's walls were filled with some serious female art: a Jane Freilicher amaryllis, so lush I wanted to touch it; an exuberant Miriam Schapiro abstract; an electric Faith Ringgold story quilt. On Jane's desk in a chased silver frame was a photograph of her with

Sylvie. They looked to be in their middle teens. Tanned and grinning, they faced the camera. Life was ahead.

Jane didn't waste any time getting to the point. "Howard called," she said.

"I thought he might," I said.

"He said he told you about Gary and me."

I nodded.

She looked at me levelly, "And . . .?"

"And I don't understand. You're so close to Sylvie and you're too . . . smart, I guess, is the word I'm looking for."

Jane raised her eyebrows and laughed. "Smart has nothing to do with it, Jo. This morning I had breakfast with a cardiologist who smokes two packs a day. Ask her about the relationship between what we know and what we do."

"I didn't mean to sound judgemental," I said. "I know this isn't any of my business. But, Jane, you know, don't you, that when I talked to Howard I wasn't just digging for dirt."

Jane smiled. "You've never struck me as the logical successor to Julie Evanson. I can read, Jo. I've seen the papers. But can't you leave the investigating to the police?"

"No," I said, "I can't. Jane, I didn't kill Maureen Gault and, in my more optimistic moments, I'm reasonably sure the police are going to find that out, too. But until they do, I'm in limbo. Every day, I just get up and go through the motions, and it's getting to be a drag."

"I know. The sword-hanging-over-your-head syndrome. We see it all the time in patients dealing with serious illness. The conventional wisdom is that the best way to deal with a hanging sword is to grab hold of it, take control."

"That's what I'm trying to do," I said.

"Fair enough," she said. "What do you need to know?"

"Could we start with the caucus office party the night before Ian died? There were all those undercurrents. Something was going on. Do you remember anything at all that might be significant?"

Jane winced. "I hardly remember anything about that

party except that it was one of the worst nights of my life.
For starters, it was the end of my relationship with Gary. I
guess we'd been heading in that direction since Jess was
born, but I loved him, Jo. I even had this fantasy about Gary
and Jess and me becoming a family. Crazy stuff, but when
you let your loins do your thinking, you're not always rational. Anyway, as soon as I saw Gary that night, I took him
down to my office, threw my arms around him, and tried to
rekindle the flame."

"And it didn't rekindle," I said.

She shook her head. "I asked him if he'd told Sylvie
about us, and he looked at me as if I was insane. No, scratch
that. He looked at me as if he didn't have the slightest idea
what I was talking about.

"I went back to the party and did the sensible thing. I've
been drunk twice in my life. Once was the night I finished
exams in my last year at medical school, and the other time
was that night. I was so drunk I don't even know how I got
home. I didn't wake up until the next afternoon. When I
remembered what had happened with Gary, I rolled over
and went back to sleep. I didn't get out of bed for a day and a
half. The morning I finally decided I'd better pull myself
back together, I turned on the radio and heard that Ian had
been killed. It seemed as if the whole world had gone to
hell." Jane raked her fingers through her hair. "That was
the worst winter."

"Yes," I agreed, "it was." I took a deep breath. "Jane, do
you remember anything else about the party? Howard told
me Ian was talking to an old Ukrainian man. Did you see
them?"

Jane's eyes widened. "I saw the old Ukrainian man, but
he wasn't with Ian. He was with Tess." She laughed. "It
would have been funny if it hadn't been so awful. After my
true love walked out on me and I was well on my way to getting pissed, I decided to step out and get some air. I wanted
to get as far as possible from Gary, so I didn't go down the
main stairs. I went over to the west wing and went down

those stairs at the end of the hall. When I got to the landing, what to my wondering eyes should appear but Tess Malone grappling with a gentleman and making one hell of a racket. In my less than competent state, I thought they were having sex, then I noticed Tess wasn't crying out in ecstasy. She was trying to get away from him. I went over to them, and that put an end to it."

"Was he trying to rape her?" I asked.

"No, not that. I don't know what he was trying to do, but I remember he said something like, 'You stick your nose in, and now I got no more daughter.' Does that mean anything?"

"Not to me," I said. "Was that before Tess was involved with Beating Heart?"

Jane snorted. "Sometimes I think Tess has been involved with Beating Heart since she was a beating heart, but this was before she was there full time. Do you think the scene with the old man could be connected with her work there?"

"Sounds like it might, doesn't it?" I said. "Tess encourages the girl to go through with her pregnancy and something goes wrong." I picked up my coat. "I don't know, but I'm going to ask the person who will."

The offices of Beating Heart occupied the second storey of an old building on Pasqua Street. It was less upscale than the Women's Medical Centre, just a single big room with a couple of small alcoves that I guessed were used for counselling. Here, the music was chartbusters from a radio on an untended desk, and the pictures on the wall were of the graphic didactic school. Tess was standing at a table covered in boxes. On the window ledge behind her, a cigarette burned in a yellow ashtray.

She smiled when she saw me, but, for once, the smile was thin, and her manner was guarded.

"I suppose you'd like to get right to your questions," she said.

"Yeah," I said. "I would."

I looked at her. Every golden curl was shellacked into place, and she was wearing a jumpsuit that looked vaguely military. The idea of her grappling with anyone seemed ludicrous. But Jane's memory on that point, at least, had seemed clear.

I took a deep breath and began. "Tess, I need to know more about that party at the caucus office the night before Ian died. Jane O'Keefe remembers seeing you in a . . . situation . . . with an old Ukrainian man."

A flush started at Tess's neckline and moved slowly up to her face. "Jane was drunk that night. Did she tell you that?"

"Yes," I said, "she did."

Tess picked up her cigarette and drew heavily on it. "Well, she was seeing things."

"I don't think so," I said. "Howard saw the man, too."

She seemed to flinch. "With me?"

"Was he with you?" I asked.

"He had some sort of constituency problem."

"To do with his daughter," I said.

This time there was no mistaking Tess's reaction. She looked as if she'd taken a blow. "I don't remember," she said.

"Think," I said. "It could be important."

"It was six years ago, Joanne. I told you I don't remember, and I think you're out of line hectoring me like this."

"Tess, I don't mean to hector, but this isn't a tea party. I'm in a lot of trouble. Just tell me the truth. I can't promise I won't repeat what you tell me, but I can promise I won't reveal anything I don't have to."

She took another drag of her cigarette. "There's nothing to tell, Joanne. It was a man with a constituency problem."

"Do you remember his name?"

"No." She picked up a cloth from the desk, opened the box nearest her and removed a plastic foetus. Then, very gently, she began to wipe the dust from its moon-shaped skull. "I think you'd better go now," she said.

I moved closer to her. "I'm going to keep asking questions, Tess. If you remember anything, let me know."

She didn't answer me. She put the foetus she'd been dusting back in the box and picked up another. This one was larger, but still snail-like, wrapped in on itself, otherworldly.

"Tess, do you remember how, in the old days, when we got into a battle about policy, you used to invite everybody over to your house to eat?" I moved close and put my hand on her arm. "You used to say there wasn't a quarrel in the world that a pan of cabbage rolls and a bottle of rye couldn't straighten out. Do you want to find a place with cabbage rolls and see if we can straighten this out?"

She didn't answer. But when she turned to replace the foetus in the box, I saw her eyes were filled with tears. It was like seeing a general cry.

My pulse was racing when I stood on the landing outside Beating Heart. Tess knew the old man's name, and I was sure that when she had a chance to think things over, she would tell me. She was a decent person, and she would want to help. I looked at my watch. Two-thirty. Taylor wouldn't be home for another hour. I had time to find out how that last evening had looked from another seat at the head table.

Gary Stephens's office was in the same building as my dentist's. It was a cheerless cinderblock building on the corner of Broad and 12th. At the top of the stairs on the second floor was a sign with Gary's name and degree in block letters and an arrow pointing toward his law office. When I opened the door, I had two surprises. The first was that Ian's old secretary, Lorraine Bellegarde, was behind the front desk. The other was that she was obviously in the final stages of packing up the office.

When she saw me, she came over and took both my

hands in hers. Lorraine was so tiny it seemed she could buy most of her clothes in the children's department, but there was nothing child-like about her organizational skills or her grasp of politics. Ian's trust in her had been absolute, and she had been a friend to us both. Lorraine and I had lost touch in the last few years, and as we stood, surrounded by packing boxes, grinning at each other, I wondered why.

"What are you doing here?" I said.

"Trying to get all this stuff out before the landlord catches me."

"Gary's moving his office?"

"Well, he's moving out of here. But this is all going into storage." She picked up a roll of masking tape and cut a length from it. "I don't know what Gary's going to do. I guess, as they say, he's exploring his options."

"I can't imagine you working for a man like him."

"Nobody's perfect, Jo. Anyway, I'm not working for him for much longer."

"It didn't work out?"

"It worked out. For a while, anyway. Gary has his faults, but I've always found him easy to get along with. And I liked the quiet around here." She placed the tape carefully along the top flaps of a packing box. "Unfortunately, it was too quiet."

"The firm was having trouble getting clients?"

She narrowed her eyes. "Look, Jo, maybe we shouldn't be talking about this. Anyway, you're the one who's got the mega-problem these days. Have the cops managed to find out who killed Maureen Gault?"

"No, that's why I'm here. I need to talk to Gary. Will he be back today?"

She shrugged. "I don't know. Gary's not exactly the poster boy for effective office practices."

"If he comes back, ask him to call me, would you? I don't want to go to his house. Sylvie thinks I'm Public Enemy Number One."

"I wouldn't let that keep you away."

"It won't," I said.

"Jo, can I tell Gary what you want to see him about?"

"Sure. Tell him I want to talk to him about the day before Ian died."

Her body tensed with interest. "They've found something, haven't they? Ian's death wasn't just lousy luck. There was a reason he was killed."

"They haven't found anything," I said, "but I think I have." As I told her about the evidence pointing to Maureen Gault, I could see the anger in Lorraine's eyes.

"You think she planned to kill him?"

"That's exactly what I think."

"But why would she want him dead?"

"I don't know, but I'm going to find out. Lorraine, could there be anything in Ian's appointment book that would shed some light on this?"

"Such as . . . ?"

"Such as the people he saw the last week. Maybe there was somebody out of the ordinary. Howard and Jane remember an old Ukrainian man who was around the night of the party. Does that ring a bell?"

She shook her head. "It's been such a long time, Jo." She smoothed the masking tape on the box in front of her. "I can tell you right now there won't be a clue in the last week's appointments. Ian wasn't there. Remember, you two took off the week before Christmas to go cross-country skiing with the kids."

"We went down to Kenosee. I'd forgotten." I said.

Lorraine picked up on the disappointment in my voice. "Don't give up on the office angle completely, Jo," she said. "Even if Ian wasn't there, I would have kept a record of his messages." She looked around the room. "I'm just about through here. I'll go over to the Legislature. I packed all Ian's stuff and sent it to the archives. It shouldn't be any problem to dig up Ian's appointment book. If anything looks interesting, I'll call you."

"Thanks, Lorraine," I said.

She came over and slid her arm around my waist. "Come on, I want to show you something." She took me over to the big plate-glass window that looked down on a parking lot. The area was a favourite for prostitutes and for the johns who sought them out.

Lorraine pointed down. "That's where Gary parks his car," she said. "All last summer one of the street girls used his car as her office: sitting on the fender, fixing her makeup in the outside mirror, even lying over the hood and working on her tan when there wasn't any action. I must have volunteered twenty times to go down and tell her to beat it, but Gary wouldn't hear of it. He said everybody needs one place where they won't get hassled."

"And the point of the story is . . .?"

Lorraine shook her head and smiled. "I don't know. Maybe just that Gary hasn't turned into as much of a rat as you think."

I hugged her. "Let's keep in touch, Lorraine."

One more errand and I could go home. By the time I left the Humane Society I was forty dollars poorer and a kitten richer. It was windy and cold when I drove into the Nationtv parking lot. I stuck the kitten inside my coat, and as I walked into the building I could feel the sharpness of its claws through my sweater. The door to Jill's office was open. She was on the phone, and she motioned for me to come in. When I took the kitten out of my coat, she said a fast goodbye to whoever she was talking to and leapt to her feet.

"I don't believe my eyes," she said. "You with a cat."

"I don't believe my eyes either," I said. "But here she is, and I'm appealing to you as a cat person to take care of her until after Taylor's party tomorrow."

"I accept," she said. "You can always count on cat people." She took the kitten from me and began stroking under its chin. I could hear the kitten's motor-hum of satisfaction. "So Taylor was the one who finally broke you down. How many times did the other kids ask for a cat?"

"Don't remind me," I said. "But it was all Taylor wanted."

Jill held the kitten against her cheek and rubbed. "How do you think Sadie and Rose are going to feel about an interloper?"

"They'll probably put out a contract on me," I said.

She looked at her watch. "The sun's over the yardarm somewhere. Do you have time for a drink?"

"I do," I said, "but you don't." I pointed to the cat. "You have responsibilities. Jill, could you bring her over tomorrow around 3:30? I thought the adults could get together for cake and a glass of wine when the kids had wound down a bit."

"I'll be there, at 3:30. Cat people are punctual to a fault, but of course now that you're a cat person yourself, you'll be learning that."

I stopped at the mall on the way home and bought the rest of Taylor's presents. After I'd hidden them in the basement for wrapping later, I came upstairs and started dinner. I felt edgy but good. The answers seemed to be coming closer, I could feel it. I was rubbing rosemary into the lamb chops when the phone rang. It was Lorraine Bellegarde.

"I've got something," she said. "There was a stack of phone messages stuck in the appointments book. I guess after we heard about Ian, someone put them in there and forgot about them. Come to think of it, that someone was probably me. Anyway, there were the usual messages from constituents and government departments."

"How about from the Seven Dwarfs?"

"They all rang in. Do you want me to check who called when?"

"Could you?"

I wrote down the information and thanked her.

"And now for the *pièce de resistance*," she said. "There were fifteen separate messages from Henry."

"Who's Henry?"

"I'm not sure, but I think he may be your old Ukrainian

man. He called and called that last week. I remember him
now. A sad old guy. He was always blowing his nose. Anyway, the bad news is he wouldn't leave his last name. The
good news is he left his number."

"Bingo," I said. I repeated the number and wrote it down.
"Thanks, Lorraine. Ian used to say he could always count
on you to come through."

"Anytime, Jo," she said softly. "Anytime."

My heart was pounding as I dialled Henry's number.
There were two rings. Then the operator's voice: "Your call
cannot be completed as dialled. Please check the listing
again, or call your operator for assistance." I hung up and
looked again at the number. It could be long distance. I
dialled "1" and tried the number again. This time I got
through.

A young man answered. In the background, country
music blared.

"Yeah," he said, not unfriendly.

"Could I speak to Henry?" I asked.

"There's no Henry here, lady."

I felt my heart sink. "He's an older man. Ukrainian."

He sounded kind but exasperated. "Lady, there's three of
us share this house. None of us are Henry, none of us are
older, and none of us are Ukrainian."

"Wait," I said. "How long have you had this number?"

"Three years." He started to hang up.

"Where are you?" I said. "Where do you live?"

"Lady . . ." His voice was edgy.

"Just tell me the name of the city, please. It's important."

He laughed. "It's no city, lady. This is Chaplin, Saskatchewan, population 400."

I felt a rush. Chaplin. I should have known.

I had one more phone call to make. I dialled Beating
Heart and got the machine. "Someone would be happy to
help you during regular office hours which were . . ." I hung
up and opened the phone book at the M's. Tess Malone's

home number wasn't listed. I dialled Beating Heart again and left Tess a message. "I need to talk to you about Henry," I said, and I left my name.

The phone rang again just as I was sliding the chops under the broiler. It was Jill.

"Did Taylor ask specifically for a female cat or was that just a whimsy of yours?"

"If I picked out a male, don't tell me," I said.

"Okay," she said, and the line was silent.

"I've changed my mind," I said. "Tell me."

"You chose a male," she said.

"How do you know?"

"I just lifted his tail and looked: three dots, not one. Next time, take me with you."

"There won't be a next time," I said, gloomily.

She laughed. "See you tomorrow."

After supper, Hilda took Taylor down to the library to return her books. I asked Angus to wrap presents while I made the birthday cake.

"What did we get her?" he asked.

"A case of cat food. A cat dish. A Garfield T-shirt and a book of cat cartoons from *The New Yorker*."

"Did we also get her a cat?" he said.

"A little ginger male. The man at the Humane Society says he's part Persian. What do you think about getting another pet?"

"I think it's amazing. Everybody knows how you are with cats. It's cool that you got one for T." He snapped his fingers. "Really cool. Okay, where's the wrapping paper?"

An hour later, when Taylor and Hilda came back, the presents were wrapped and the cakes were made. Taylor looked into the flowerpots critically.

"How did you make the dirt?"

"The way the recipe says to make it. A bag of Oreos pulverized in the food processor."

"And the mud?

"Chocolate pudding and Dream Whip."

"And the jelly worms are in there?"

"All $5.27 worth."

She nodded. "Should I bring Jack in tonight or wait till tomorrow?"

"You're bringing Jack in?"

"For the party. For the centre of the table."

"T, he's getting pretty saggy. There are other things you could have as the centrepiece."

"Like what?"

"Angus had a clown head made out of a cabbage one year and an octopus another time. They were both pretty cute. And when Mieka was about your age, she had a doll with a cake skirt. Peter had a firehat three years in a row. You can pretty much use anything."

"Good," she said. "We'll use Jack." She leaned over and kissed me goodnight. The issue was settled.

Hilda was out with friends for the evening. After I tucked in Taylor, I made myself a pot of Earl Grey, sat down at the dining-room table, and thought of all the birthday parties that had been celebrated around it. I'd been a young mother when Mieka and Peter had had their parties. Children who had sat at this table singing "Happy Birthday" to my children were now old enough to have children themselves. And I was forty-nine. Not young.

Ian must have wasted a hundred rolls of film taking pictures of the kids' birthdays. He always managed to snap the shot at just the wrong time. We had a drawer full of photos of blurred children, of children with satanic red eyeballs, and of me, looking not maternal but menacing, as I poised the knife above the birthday cake. Memories. But there were other memories. Better ones. Memories of the times after the parties when Ian and I would clean up, pour a drink, cook a steak, and be grateful for another year of healthy kids.

When I went upstairs to get ready for bed, Rose was in Angus's room sitting on the cape he had worn Hallowe'en

night. I thought of the ginger cat, and went in and sat down
on the floor next to her. I put my arms around her neck.
"Changes for you tomorrow, old lady," I said. Full of trust,
she nuzzled me. "Just remember," I said, "adversity makes
us grow." She stood up expectantly. "We're not going anywhere tonight," I said. I picked up the cape. "Except down
to the basement to put this back. Look, it's covered in dog
hair." I brushed off the cape and headed downstairs.

The trunk I'd taken the cape from Hallowe'en night was
still open. I decided to check through the clothes inside to
see if there was anything Peter or Angus could wear. I found
a couple of sweaters and a pair of dress slacks that looked
possible. I was sorting through a stack of sport shirts when I
found the wallet. It was in a small bag, like a commercial
Baggie, but of heavier plastic. The boys, never inspired in
their choice of gifts, had given it to Ian that last Christmas.
A young constable had brought the wallet, Ian's keys, and
his wedding ring back to me after the trial. The wedding
ring was upstairs in my jewellery box, and I'd given the keys
to Peter when he started driving. I didn't remember putting
the wallet in the trunk, but there was a lot I didn't remember about those months after Ian died.

I undid the twist-tie on the bag and took out the wallet.
In the upstairs hall, the grandfather clock chimed. I opened
the wallet. The leather was still stiff, and the plastic photo
case was pristine. Christmas afternoon Ian had made quite
a show of cleaning out his old wallet and transferring everything worth transferring to the new one. The boys had been
very pleased. I looked through the photo case. There wasn't
much there: Ian's identification, some credit cards, the
kids' school pictures, Ian's party membership, and one
picture of all of us that I'd forgotten about. We'd been in
Ottawa, taking turns snapping pictures of one another in
front of the Parliament Buildings, when a young man asked
if we'd like a family picture. It had turned out well. I looked
at us, suntanned and smiling in our best summer clothes,
and I could feel my throat tighten. I reached inside the

plastic to pull the photo out. There was another picture behind it, and I slid it out too. I hadn't seen this one before. It was a Santa Claus picture from a shopping mall.

A woman, very young, very pretty, was sitting on Santa's knee, holding a baby up to the camera. On the back, in careful backhand, she had written: "He looks just like you. I love you. J."

I'd been so anxious to make the pieces fit. Maybe, at last, they'd all fallen into place. Ian's anger when I'd pressed him about what he was doing that last day. The old man who'd confronted him the night of the party. "Now I got no more daughter." And this child. Crazily, I remembered my fortune in the barm brack Hallowe'en night. The tiny baby doll.

I looked at the child the girl was holding. "He looks just like you." I tried to see the resemblance, but I couldn't. The baby didn't look like Ian; he just looked like a baby.

I put the picture into the pocket of my blue jeans. Then I slid the wallet back into its plastic bag, and carried it upstairs. I didn't stop to put on boots. I plodded across the deep snow of the back yard, to our back gate, opened it, and walked down the lane to the garbage bin. I didn't hesitate before I threw my husband's wallet into the garbage.

Nine

THE first thing I saw when I awoke the next morning was the picture on my nightstand. In the full light of morning, the woman seemed even younger and more lovely than she had the night before. I thought about the day ahead and felt the heaviness wash over me. Somehow I had to get through Taylor's party. When I'd managed that, there was just the rest of my life to muddle through.

The phone was ringing when I stepped out of the shower. I grabbed a towel, tripped over Sadie and yelled at her so viciously that she ran out of the room. My coping mechanism seemed to have short-circuited.

My caller was Inspector Alex Kequahtooway.

"I know it's early to phone, especially on a holiday," he said, "but I have news."

"Go ahead," I said, and my voice sounded dead.

"It's good news," he added quickly. "You're in the clear, Mrs. Kilbourn. The reservations clerk you talked to the night of the murder has had a chance to give her story some sober second thought. Now that she's had time to reconsider, she realizes that when you left your name and address for the lost and found, it must have been after 11:05, not at 11:00 as she previously told us."

"It's still just her word, isn't it?" I said. "She could change her mind again."

"I don't think so," he said. "This time she has the hotel's telephone records to keep her memory fresh. The records say that on the night of the murder, someone at the reservations desk made a long-distance call to Wolf Point, Montana, at 10:47. The call was not completed until 11:05. Now, the only connection between the Hotel Saskatchewan and Wolf Point, Montana, seems to be the reservations clerk's boyfriend. He's working at a western-wear store in Wolf Point."

"That still leaves ten minutes," I said dully. "I found the body at 11:15, and that's when the police came."

I could hear the edge in Inspector Kequahtooway's voice. "That's where we had a break, Mrs. Kilbourn. It turns out that somebody found the body before you did."

"Who?" I asked.

"Another guest at the hotel. He's been out of the country for a couple of weeks. When he read about the case in the paper, he got in touch right away. A good citizen. He says when he went to get his rental car to drive to the airport, he saw a woman lying by that old Buick in the parking lot. He says he remembers the time because he was in a hurry. It was 11:00."

"Why didn't he call for help?"

Alex Kequahtooway's voice was impassive. "He had a plane to catch. It was dark. From where he was parked he couldn't see the woman's face. He thought she was, and I quote, 'just another drunken Indian.'"

"I'm sorry," I said.

"For what?"

"That the world is such a shitty place," I said.

"It does have its moments, doesn't it?" He paused. "Mrs. Kilbourn, are you ill? You don't sound like yourself."

"I'm not myself, Inspector," I said. "But thanks for calling." I hung up.

I was in the clear. I could stop asking questions. I could stop trying to make the pieces fit. Life could go back to normal. I looked at the picture of the young woman. She was wearing blue jeans and a white sweater. Against the cheap red suit of the mall Santa, her blond wavy hair seemed charged with life. Her face was serene. Her eyes, slightly upturned at the outer edge, looked steadily into the camera. The curve of her breasts behind the baby suggested fullness, and the flesh on her arms was taut with abundance. The baby she held in those arms was like her, solemn, plump, and beautiful.

"Not everybody trusts paintings, but people believe photographs." That's what Ansel Adams said. I caught sight of myself in the mirror. What truth would a photograph of me convey? My hair, still wet from the shower, was slick against my skull, and my face was pale and haggard. I was forty-nine years old. It wasn't going to get any better. I pulled the towel tight around me. I wanted to vanquish that beautiful young woman with her lovely baby. I wanted to rip her picture into a dozen pieces and flush it down the toilet.

But even as I picked up the picture, I knew she couldn't be vanquished. I had to know who she was. I had to know what she had meant to Ian. I had to know whether the child she held in her arms was his, and I had to know how she was connected to his death.

I reached for my jeans and a sweatshirt, changed my mind, and chose a soft wool skirt that always made me feel attractive, and a cashmere sweater the colour of a pomegranate. After I'd dressed, I sat down in front of my mirror and brushed my hair. Then, I picked up the foundation cream and began to smooth it over my face.

A thousand years ago, Hilda had said, "Follow the strands back to the place where they join. Of course, you'll have to scrutinize your husband's life, too." Back then, *scrutinize* had seemed to suggest such a pitiless intrusion that I'd rejected the idea outright, but now I knew Hilda was right. I had to know the truth. I brushed the blush across the soft pads of my cheeks. "Chipmunk cheeks," Taylor had said. The girl in the picture had great cheekbones, high and sloping. Who was she?

"This is between you and me, Ian," I said aloud. And as soon as I heard the words, I knew they were true. No one but I should be part of this next phase of the investigation. I had to convince Hilda and Jill that, because the chase was over, life was back to normal. I dabbed the eyeshadow brush in sable brown and touched the corners of my eyelids.

If Ian hadn't been the man I thought he was, no one else was going to know. We'd been married twenty years, and whatever that marriage meant to him, I wasn't going to expose him. I picked up the mascara, leaned towards the mirror, and began darkening the ends of my eyelashes. There was something reassuring about seeing my eyes looking as they always had. I filled in my lips with colour, slid on my best gold bracelet, and put in my new gold hoop earrings.

My reflection in the mirror looked assured and in control. I hid the woman's picture under a pile of nighties in my bottom drawer and started downstairs. Before I walked into the kitchen, I took a deep breath. I wasn't an actress, and this performance had to do the job. I had to convince everybody I cared about that the nightmare was over, and happy days were here again.

Hilda and the kids were already at the breakfast table.

When she saw me, Hilda nodded approvingly. "Don't you look attractive."

"It's Taylor's birthday," I said.

Taylor jumped up. "And you said that, as soon as we were all here, I could open my presents."

"If that was the deal, then I think you'd better get started," I said, pouring myself coffee.

She didn't need to be told twice. Five minutes later, the table was covered with wrapping paper, and Taylor was beaming.

I sat down beside her. "What's your best present?" I asked.

She picked up a box of art pencils Hilda had given her. "These cost eighty-five dollars. Fil, my teacher, has some just like them, and he told me."

I knew Hilda's funds were limited. "You really shouldn't have," I said.

"An artist can always use a patron," she said tartly.

Taylor smiled at Hilda. "Thanks," she said. "Thanks a lot. And thanks for all the cat stuff, Angus. Too bad I don't have a cat."

Angus winked at me broadly, but Taylor didn't notice. She'd found something else that interested her and had run to the window. "Look, the sun came out!" she said.

I went over and stood beside her. The sun was high, the sky was blue, and the trees in the back yard sparkled theatrically with hoarfrost. I put my arm around her shoulder. "Hey, a real party day," I said.

She looked up at me. "Lucky, eh?"

"Very lucky," I said.

When I turned from the window, Hilda was watching me carefully. "You seem wound a little tightly this morning," she said.

"I'm just excited," I said. "I didn't want to take the edge off Taylor's gift opening, but I had some good news this morning." As I told Hilda about my conversation with Alex Kequahtooway, I could see the relief in her face.

"This means your life can go back to normal," she said.

"So can yours," I said. "Hilda, I can't thank you enough for being here with us when we needed you. We couldn't have made it without you."

Her eyes narrowed. "That has a distinctly valedictory tone. Am I being given my walking papers?"

I went to her. "Never. I just thought you'd be missing your life in Saskatoon."

"Well," she said, "Advent does begin in less than three

weeks. The Cathedral choir will have all that splendid Christmas music to get ready."

"And you're their only true alto," I said.

She frowned. "You're sure you're all right?"

"Never better."

"If you say so," she said. "Now, if you're going to preserve that sense of well-being, you'd better eat something. Have something substantial, Joanne. We have an arduous day ahead."

After breakfast, I made some calls: to Peter, to Howard, to Keith, and finally to Jill. As the relief and congratulations swirled around me, I tried to sound like a woman whose world had just been restored to her. It wasn't easy.

Taylor's party was a success. No one got hurt; no one cried; no one got left out. The worm cakes were a hit, and the party hat I'd put on the jack o'lantern covered the dent in his skull and made him look almost festive. Taylor was as happy as I'd ever seen her, but I couldn't wait for the afternoon to end. I wanted to be alone to look at the picture and make plans.

At 3:00, the parents began to come for the kids. Sylvie and Jane came together to get Jess. The O'Keefe sisters were wearing camel-hair coats, and as they stood in the doorway with their faces flushed from the cold, laughing about something Jess had said that morning, I thought blood really must be thicker than water.

When they came inside, Jane took her boots and coat off. "I have something for the birthday girl," she said. She pulled a small, prettily wrapped package out of her bag.

"Why don't you and Sylvie stay and watch Taylor blow out her candles?" I said. "The kids had Sylvie's worm cake, but there's something a little more orthodox for the adults."

Surprisingly, Sylvie didn't hesitate. "Sounds good," she said, and she began to take off her things.

When Gary came five minutes later, it seemed churlish

not to ask him to stay, too. So I did. For a woman who wanted to be alone, I was moving in the wrong direction.

At 3:30 on the dot, Jill arrived. We were still standing in the doorway when Craig and Manda Evanson pulled up in the driveway. Craig's arm was tight around Manda's shoulders as they came up the walk. Manda was holding a red wicker basket. She held it out to me. Inside was a checked blanket embroidered with the words: SHHHHH. KITTEN SLEEPING.

Craig looked at the pink balloons on the door. "We don't want to interrupt anything," he said.

"I told Craig I had to see Taylor's face when she met her cat," Manda said. She patted her belly. "At this stage, he has to indulge me, but don't worry, Jo, we'll be gone before you know it."

"Don't be silly," I said. "Come in and have some cake."

Manda grinned. "Are you sure?"

"Absolutely."

"In that case," she said, "make mine a double. I'm in a state of severe cake deficit."

The first minutes after the kitten entered our house were about as bad as I'd always imagined they would be. Sadie bared her teeth, and Angus banished her to the back yard. Rose took one look at the interloper and ran down to hide in the basement. Angus went after her to soothe her nerves.

Taylor, of course, was transported. Manda and Jill clucked over her, showing her how to hold the cat and what to feed it. At the end of five minutes, Taylor was an experienced handler; the kitten was purring, and she handed it to me. I stroked the cat's head. The purring stopped, and the cat curled around and swiped viciously at my face. Jill glared at me disapprovingly. "Jo, when you pat a kitten on its head, you awaken its sexual feelings. Cats have very violent sex. You were lucky you didn't get your face clawed off."

I gave the kitten back to Taylor. Owning a cat was going to be even worse than I thought.

Hilda waited till there was relative peace, then she went into the kitchen and came back with two bottles of Asti Spumante.

"I thought this would be a nice accompaniment for the cake," she said.

Gary opened the Asti, Craig poured, and I turned out the lights and lit the candles on the cake. As Craig proposed the toast, Taylor held the glass with her thimbleful of wine gravely.

"To Taylor's sixth birthday," Craig said. "May there be many happy returns."

We drank and then he turned to me. "And to Jo. May there be brighter days ahead."

I looked at the faces in the circle. The candlelight made them look younger, but also less familiar and, somehow, more menacing. Now was as good a time as any to make my announcement. "Good news," I said. "The brighter days are already here. If Taylor ever blows out her candles, I'll tell you what's happened. Come on, T, make a wish."

Taylor didn't move. She was staring at the cake, paralyzed.

I dropped down beside her. "T, what is it?" I asked.

She leaned towards my ear. "I don't know what to wish for," she whispered. "I've always wished for a cat."

"Wish that your cat will learn to get along with the dogs," I said.

She nodded, closed her eyes, wished, and blew.

As soon as we had our cake and wine, I told them about Alex Kequahtooway's phone call. Gary was standing beside me and he kissed my cheek. "Great news, babe," he said.

When he moved away, I saw Jill, shaking her head and trying to suppress a smile. Gary Stephens was not one of her favourites. Craig was ebullient. "I knew it was just a matter of time," he said, and he squeezed Manda's shoulders so hard, she cried out. The O'Keefe sisters stood together, smiling but silent.

Craig picked up a bottle of Asti and refilled our glasses, and the conversation moved happily towards the inconsequential. Not surprisingly, we talked about names: a good name for Taylor's kitten; wise choices for Craig and Manda's baby.

My mind drifted. Ian and I had spent hours deciding on names for our children. Our most intense talks always seemed to come when I was in the bathtub. Ian would wander in, say something salacious about pregnant women, flip down the toilet lid, and read from a book of names he'd bought. Then we would laugh at the horrors and try out possibilities till the bath water got cold.

We had been very happy. I closed my eyes, shutting out the memories. When I opened them, Manda was leaning towards me.

"Who is Walter Winchell?" she asked.

"What?" I said, startled. "I'm sorry, Manda, I was a million miles away. What did you say?"

"I asked you who Walter Winchell was. We were talking about whether it's good to name a baby after her parents, and Hilda said Walter Winchell named both his children after him: his son was Walter and his daughter was Walda. Everybody laughed, but I don't know who Walter Winchell is."

"You don't have to," I said. "Just don't name your baby after him."

Manda yawned and stretched lazily. "Gotcha," she said. She put her head back against her husband's chest. "I've had enough fun, Craig. Time to go."

Manda and Craig moved towards the front hall. It wasn't long before the others followed. I was almost home-free, and I felt a rush. In minutes, I would be on the phone talking to Tess Malone. Confronted with Henry's name, Tess would tell the truth, and I would be one step closer to the young woman in the picture.

As I was down on the hall floor, helping Jess find his boots, it hit me. Tess's number was unlisted. A phrase Howard Dowhanuik had used the morning after Maureen Gault's murder flashed through my mind. I'd been surprised that Sylvie and Jane had gone to Tess's for a drink after the dinner, and Howard had said, "Tess and Sylvie are tight as ticks."

I looked up at Sylvie. "Have you got Tess Malone's home number?" I asked.

"What do you want it for?" she said.

Jane smoothed over the rudeness with a smile. "More questions about Tess's old Ukrainian?"

"His name is Henry," I said.

Jane knotted her scarf with her capable surgeon's hands. "I thought you'd be out of the cops-and-robbers business now that you're in the clear."

"I am," I said. "I just wanted to ask Tess if she was free for lunch one day next week."

Without a word, Sylvie picked up a pad by the phone and wrote down the number.

"Time to leave," Jane said. "Come on, Sylvie, let's go."

Already dressed for the outdoors, Jess stood with his father. Gary Stephens's hand was resting on his son's shoulder.

"Say goodbye, Jess," Jane said, and she pushed Gary's hand from his son's shoulder and propelled the little boy towards the door.

"Bye," Jess said. And he vanished into the night, closing the door behind him.

As he stood staring at the space where his son had been, Gary Stephens's face was bleak. "Goodbye," he whispered, and his voice was so soft I could barely hear it.

After everyone had driven off, Hilda went to the kitchen to clean up, and the kids took the kitten down to the basement to start the reconciliation process with Rose. Jill and I were left alone in the front hall.

"I take it the inspector's news means I'm off duty."

"It does," I said. "You can go back to painting your nails and sticking pins in pictures of Nationtv vice-presidents."

"Speaking of Nationtv," Jill said, "Keith Harris called from Washington this morning. He sends you his love."

"Swell," I said.

"He'd like to talk about human-rights violations among some of our trading partners on Saturday's show. It's okay with Sam Spiegel if it's okay with you."

"It's okay with me," I said. "That's right up my alley."

"I'll bet that's why Keith suggested it," Jill said, then she touched my hand. "I'm glad everything worked out, Jo. I was really scared."

Her gaze was so open and her affection so palpable that I almost told her the truth. Then I remembered how Jill had revered Ian, and I steeled myself. "I'm glad everything worked out, too," I said.

It was after 9:00 when I finally managed to get into my bedroom, close the door, and dial Tess's number. Late in the afternoon, Alex Kequahtooway had told the press about the evidence clearing me. I guess he'd decided it was time for the old squirrel dog to shake things up a bit. The telephone had started ringing during dinner, and it hadn't stopped. I'd never been very good at faking, and all evening I had cringed at the falseness of my voice as I tried to sound euphoric.

There were two phone calls that didn't require acting. The first was from Peter. He had been a rock, but now the worst was over. As he relaxed into the concerns of a third-year university student – the inequities of exam timetables, gossip about friends, hints about what he wanted for Christmas – he sounded relieved to be back to normal.

Mieka and her husband, Greg, called from Galveston to wish Taylor happy birthday, and their joy in being young and in love and discovering the world together was so tonic, I almost didn't tell them about the deaths of Kevin Tarpley and Maureen Gault. But we'd always told the kids that families couldn't function without trust, so after I'd listened to Mieka's descriptions of the beauty of the old houses along

the Gulf of Mexico and Greg's account of how great a
bucket of crayfish tastes when you wash it down with a
schooner of Lone Star, I gave them the essentials. They
were shocked, but as I answered their questions, I could feel
them relax. The crisis was, after all, in the past, and as we
rung off, I could hear the happiness returning to their
voices.

Finally, the phone grew silent, the kids were in their
rooms, and I was alone. I was so tense that my hands
were shaking as I dialled Tess's number. There was no
answer. I couldn't believe it. I had been so certain the
answers were within reach. Ten minutes later, I tried
again. After that, I tried every ten minutes until, finally,
exhausted, I fell into bed.

For the next two days I tried to find Tess. She wasn't at
home, and she wasn't at Beating Heart. No one knew where
she was. The man who answered the phone at Beating
Heart told me not to worry. Tess would show up. She
wasn't the kind of woman to leave town without telling
anybody. I told him that's why I was worried. Have a little
faith, he said, and I promised him I would try.

Friday, I took Hilda to the Faculty Club for lunch before
she drove back to Saskatoon. We ate liver and onions and
made plans for Christmas. I loved her, but as I watched her
manoeuvre her old Chrysler Imperial out of the university
parking lot, I was relieved. Hilda was a hard person to
deceive, and I was certain she knew I was concealing something critical from her.

I had three students to see that afternoon. When the last
one left, I pulled the picture of the young woman and her
baby out of my bag and propped it against my coffee cup. I
tried Tess's home number. There was no answer. I looked at
the picture and I knew I was tired of waiting. It was time for
action.

The receptionist at Beating Heart had a great smile, eye-
glasses with bright green frames, and a sign on her desk that

said, I'M MICHELLE, PLEASE BOTHER ME. But she turned her face away when I held the picture up and asked her if she knew the woman who was sitting on Santa's knee.

"We don't discuss clients," she said.

"Was this woman a client?"

Michelle pushed her chair back as if she was afraid I would force her to look at the picture. "I don't know," she said woodenly.

I moved closer to her. "This is important," I said. And then I added, "It's a matter of life and death."

It was an unfortunate choice of words. Michelle leapt up from her desk and returned with an older woman who bore a startling resemblance to the actress Colleen Dewhurst and who looked as implacable as Colleen Dewhurst had looked when she played Aunt Marilla in *Anne of Green Gables.*

"Look," I said, "I think I got off on the wrong foot here. I'm a friend of Tess Malone's. I've been trying to reach her, but I can't. I need to find this young woman."

When the two women exchanged a quick, worried glance, the penny dropped. They thought I was the enemy.

"I'm not trying to get her to change her mind about going through with her pregnancy," I said. "If you'll look at the picture, you'll see she already had her baby. It was at least six years ago. But I have to find her. It really is a matter of life and death."

For the first time, the older woman smiled. She held out her hand. "I wish you'd said at the outset you were a friend of Tess's. I think Michelle and I jumped to the wrong conclusion about you." She spoke with a slight accent, pleasant and lilting.

"My name is Joanne Kilbourn," I said.

"Irish?" she asked.

"My husband's family were," I said.

"Every last member of my family is Irish," she said. "My name is Maeve O'Byrne. Now let's look at your picture. What did you say the girl's name is?"

"I didn't say. I don't know."

Maeve O'Byrne pulled out a pair of reading glasses. As she looked at the photo, I held my breath. It didn't help. She shook her head and handed the photo back. "I don't recall her," she said.

"Don't you have files?"

When she answered, there was a hint of asperity in the lilt. "Yes, we have files, Mrs. Kilbourn. And like most organizations, we classify them by name. Since you don't know the girl's name, we have nothing to go on. At any rate, you say this was over five years ago. If there was a file, it would have been destroyed. We cull inactive files after five years."

"So I'm out of luck."

"I'm sorry."

The phone rang and Michelle answered it. "Just a minute. I'll see," she said. She put her hand over the mouthpiece and looked up at Maeve. "That's the paper," she said. "They're asking if we want to keep our ad in the personals. Tess used to check every day to make sure it was there and there weren't any typos."

Maeve sighed wearily. "Sure, tell them to keep it in. What does it say, anyway?"

Michelle asked the person on the other end of the phone, and she repeated the words for Maeve: "'If you're pregnant and alone, we're here. Beating Heart can help.' Then there's our number."

"That sounds acceptable," Maeve said. She turned back to me. "I wish Tess were here. She's good at taking care of matters like that."

"I wish she were here, too," I said. I wrote my home and office numbers on a card. "Please, if you hear from Tess, let me know."

"I will," Maeve said.

She was as good as her word. The next Wednesday when I came in from my senior class, the phone in my office was ringing. It was Macve O'Byrne. "Good news," she said. "Tess called."

"Where is she?" I asked.

"She didn't say."

"When will she be back?"

"She didn't say that either." I could hear the impatience in Maeve O'Byrne's voice. "The point is," she said, "Tess is all right, and I'm glad she called because I was about to phone the police."

"Maybe that's why she called," I said.

"What?"

"Nothing. Thanks, Maeve. I mean that. I know how busy you are."

"If I hear anything more, I'll be in touch," she said.

"I'd appreciate that," I said, and I hung up, more discouraged than ever. Every lead seemed to be turning into a dead end.

I spent the rest of the week teaching classes, trying to bring about a *détente* in the war between our pets, and reading up on incidences in which nations had censured trading partners for human-rights violations. Human rights had turned out to be a popular subject. The switchboards had been jammed on the call-in segment of our show, and we were revisiting the topic on Saturday night.

By the time I drove Taylor to her art class on Saturday I felt as if I was handling life again. I'd marked half a section of essays on the neo-conservatism of the eighties. I'd talked to a colleague who'd just come back from Mexico with documents that made me wonder again about the ethics of two electoral democracies entering into a trade agreement with a quasi-dictatorship. Most importantly, it seemed my peacemaking efforts with the animals were paying off. The dogs no longer snarled when the kitten came into the room, and he no longer arched his small back and hissed every time he saw them. Taylor still hadn't given her cat a name, but it seemed he was here to stay.

When I walked into the gallery gift shop and found two inspired Christmas presents within five minutes, I knew I was on a streak. There was a lineup at the cash register, so I left the bronze cat I'd chosen for Taylor and the box of stained-glass tree ornaments I'd picked out for Greg and Mieka on the counter and went back to browsing.

There were several copies of *The Boy in the Lens's Eye*, but there was only one copy of *Prairiegirl*. I picked it up and began leafing through it. I was not an expert on photography, but even I knew the pictures were brilliant. Seductive, by turns naive and knowing, the prepubescent girls posed for the camera. The photographs were stunning, but they were also disquieting.

The oldest of the children in the photographs was no more than thirteen. Exulting in the changes in their young bodies, they had shown themselves to the camera. They were innocent, but what about the person behind the camera? I thought of Sylvie's cool, unwavering gaze and her blazing talent, and I knew that, for better or worse, I would never see the world as she did.

The picture of the girl lying on the dock was almost the last one in the book, and it stopped my heart. The girl had been swimming; her thin cotton panties were soaked and her hair curled wetly against her shoulders. The wood of the dock beneath her was dark and rough textured; set against it, the soft perfection of her body seemed incandescent. Technically, that contrast must have been what gave the picture its power, but I didn't care about technique. All I cared about was the girl. The ecstasy she felt that day on the dock was frozen in time, but the girl herself had grown up. She had become a mother, and she had her picture taken again. This time she was sitting on a mall Santa's knee and holding her baby. I pulled the photograph I'd found in Ian's pocket from my purse and held it against the photograph in *Prairiegirl*. Unmistakably, the face was the same.

I was shaking so badly I could barely turn the page, but I had to know if she was there again.

She was. In the last photo in the book, two young girls stood against a split-rail fence. Their arms were around each other's waists and their faces were turned toward one another. The picture was called "Friends." One of the friends was the girl from Ian's picture; the other was Maureen Gault.

Ten

Whenn I put the copy of *Prairiegirl* on the counter of the gallery shop, I felt dazed. The woman behind the cash register gave me poinsettia-patterned gift boxes for the bronze cat and the Christmas ornaments. After she'd rung through the book, she looked up brightly. "Shall I gift-wrap this?"

"It's mine," I said.

"The best presents are always those we give ourselves, aren't they?" she said, and she turned to the next customer.

As I waited in the lobby for Taylor, I read the introduction Sylvie had written for *Prairiegirl*. It was full of art talk about purpose and explanations of how she had used an eight-by-ten-inch view camera for the photographs. There was nothing there for me. I turned the page. In the acknowledgements, Sylvie thanked "the girls of Chaplin, Saskatchewan, whose luminous beauty was a gift to the camera." She did not thank the parents who had trusted her to preserve their daughters' innocence in their photographs.

My mind felt clearer than it had since the moment I found the photograph in Ian's jacket. The girl in the Santa photograph was from Chaplin. I sat in the lobby of the gallery assessing possibilities. My first thought was to call Sylvie. I rejected that. If Ian had been involved with this young woman, his infidelity was my private grief. Sylvie was out.

The girls were all from Chaplin. There was no doubt in my mind now that Chaplin was the key. The desolate moonscape behind the sodium sulphate plant flashed through my mind. Chaplin was a company town and a small one. Carolyn Atcheson, the teacher Hilda had visited, had known Maureen Gault. Surely, she would know at least something about her best friend. The next day was Sunday, a good day to take a long drive to visit a stranger.

By the time Taylor came from her class, full of talk about Fil and his teachings, the adrenalin was pumping. That night on "Canada This Week" I argued passionately for the need to demand stringent human-rights protections from our trading partners. When the program ended, Jill came over and paid me her highest compliment. "That worked," she said, and she offered to buy me a cup of Nationtv cafeteria coffee. Afterwards, I drove home and looked through *Prairiegirl* again. The next morning, after church, I set out for Chaplin.

It was an ugly day. The sky was heavy with snow, and the countryside looked as if it had been sculpted out of iron: iron-grey clouds and iron-grey land joined by a steel-grey sky. The only colour between Regina and Parkbeg came from the Christmas lights on Chubby's Cafe near Belle Plaine.

I was grateful when I left the flatness of the farmlands and hit the gentle hills of ranch country. The hills seemed to offer protection against the heaviness of the looming sky. I'd always loved this short-grass land. Ian and some of the other members of the Legislature had come here to hunt each fall. They were seldom gone for longer than three days, but three days had been enough to transform them from their everyday selves into strangers whose faces were dark with beards and who smelled of wet wool and stale liquor and something unidentifiable and primal. Boys' Night Out.

It had been six, maybe seven years since I'd been here. I hadn't driven this far west on the Trans-Canada since Ian died, and as I neared the spot on the highway where he'd been killed, I was tense.

Incredibly, I drove right by it. As the desolate mountain of sodium sulphate behind the Chaplin plant loomed up out of nowhere, I realized that somehow I'd missed the cut-off to the Vermilion Hills where my husband died. I hadn't even recognized it. As I turned off the highway into the town of Chaplin, I thought of a reservation Ian and I had driven through in Montana where each fatal accident along the road was marked by a wooden cross that had been decorated by the grieving families. At the time, we'd thought the plastic flowers and baby booties and beadwork necklaces which decorated the crosses were mawkish. Now I wasn't so sure. It would have been good if there had been something to mark the place where my husband died.

I pulled into the Petro-Can, bought a cup of coffee, and asked the mechanic for directions to Carolyn Atcheson's house. It was two blocks away. On my way into town I'd noticed the school. It was very modern: terra cotta with cobalt-blue eaves and trim. The mechanic pointed towards it.

"She lives on First Street, so she can keep an eye on that school of hers. She's got a right; it wouldn't have been built without her. She taught the whole school board."

Carolyn Atcheson's house was small, neat, and care-fully kept. Her walk was shovelled, her rosebushes were wrapped in sacking for the winter, and the brown paint on her gingerbread trim and front door was fresh. The name C. ATCHESON was burned into a wooden sign nailed above her mailbox. When I saw the light inside the living room, I was relieved. It had been quixotic to drive from Regina to Chaplin without calling ahead. I knocked on the front door, and a dog somewhere in the house began to bark, but no one came out to see why. There was a large front window. I made my way between the rosebushes and stood on tiptoe to peer in. The dog, an ancient terrier, flattened his face against the window barking at me. Everything inside was shining, but no one was there.

A snowflake fell, and then another. A gust of wind came out of nowhere, rattling Carolyn Atcheson's wooden shutters. I thought of driving home through a snowstorm and shuddered. It had all been for nothing; I hadn't learned a thing. I turned to walk back to the car. "Shit," I said. "Shit. Shit. Shit. Shit. Shit."

Head bent against the wind, I didn't notice the man come out from the house next door. But he noticed me.

"That's no language for a lady," he said.

"Sorry," I said, and I kept walking.

"Wait," he said. "Are you looking for Miss Atcheson? If she isn't home, she's at the school. She leads a pretty simple life."

"Thanks," I said, and I turned and walked the half-block that took me to Chaplin School and into the not-so-simple life of Carolyn Atcheson.

She must have seen me coming, because she had the door open before I knocked. She looked like teachers I could remember from my childhood: big, over six feet, and ample, not fat, but what another generation would have called a fine figure of a woman. Her hair was salt-and-pepper grey and cropped short. She did not look pleased to see me, but she was of the old school. No matter how she felt, she would not be rude.

"Come down to my office, Mrs. Kilbourn. You'll be more comfortable there."

"You know who I am."

"I watch television," she said.

As I followed her down the empty hall, the years melted away. The principal was taking me to her office. She was not happy, and I had to think quickly.

Carolyn Atcheson's office did nothing to put me at ease. It was a no-nonsense place. Barren of photographs, plants, or personal mementoes, her oak desk gleamed. On the wall behind her was a brass plaque. KNOWLEDGE IS POWER, it said sternly.

Carolyn motioned me to the chair on the student's side

of the desk; then she sat down. She didn't waste time. "I'm surprised to see you, Mrs. Kilbourn. From what I've read and heard, I thought the police had cleared you."

"They have," I said. "But I still have questions."

"About Maureen Gault," she said.

"About Maureen Gault, and about someone else, too," I said. I pulled the copy of *Prairiegirl* from my bag, found the page I was looking for, and slid the book across the desk to her.

"I need to know about this girl," I said. "What can you tell me about her?"

It had been a shot in the dark, but it found its mark. Carolyn Atcheson's face went white, and she grabbed the edge of her desk as if she needed something to hold on to. Outside in the hall, the bells announcing a class change rang and the sound echoed hollowly through the empty school. Carolyn Atcheson didn't move.

"I need to know about her," I repeated.

"She was a student here," Carolyn Atcheson said.

"And a friend of Maureen Gault's," I said. I reached across and turned to the photo on the last page of *Prairiegirl*. "Look," I said.

She turned away. "I've seen the picture," she said.

"Have you seen this one?" I asked, and I slid the Santa Claus picture across to her.

Carolyn's face seemed to grow even paler. Her dark eyes burned across the space between us. "What are you after?" she asked.

I looked at the plaque on the wall behind her. "Knowledge," I said. "I'm after knowledge. Tell me everything you know about the girl in those pictures and Maureen Gault."

She stared at me.

"Maybe your files would help," I said.

"I don't need files," she said thickly.

"Miss Atcheson, this is very important. A woman's life is at stake." As soon as I said the words, I knew they were true. The life that was at stake was my own.

What I said seemed to jolt her. She closed her eyes and rubbed her temples. Then she leaned towards me. "I assume Hilda McCourt told you something of my history with Maureen Gault."

"Yes," I said, "she did."

"In all the years I've taught, Maureen was the only truly evil student who ever crossed my path." For a moment Carolyn Atcheson seemed stunned by the enormity of what she had said, then she straightened her shoulders and continued. "My mother used to tell us that nothing is wasted. Maureen inspired me to do a great deal of reading in psychology. If I ever meet another student like her, I'll know what to do. But I didn't know what I was dealing with in that girl, and that's why I failed everyone so badly. Maureen Gault should have been stopped years ago."

"Yes," I agreed, "she should have been."

Carolyn half turned her chair so she was facing the window. As she leaned forward to watch the snow, her voice became almost dreamy. "From what I've learned, Maureen could be classified as a primary psychopath. She truly believed she was superior to everyone around her. The guiding principle of her life was to force others to recognize and acknowledge her superiority."

"Hilda told me that Maureen was very popular when she started high school."

Carolyn Atcheson seemed to find it easier to talk without facing me. "Her leadership skills were remarkable for a girl her age. I've read since that this is not atypical of her illness. At any rate, as long as everyone accepted her as leader and did her bidding, Maureen functioned. It was when the other girls got sick of being manipulated and dominated that the trouble started."

"That's when the attacks on the other students began," I said.

Carolyn's voice was sad. "Yes, and that's when she began her relationship with poor Kevin."

"He was the only one who stuck by her," I said.

"No, not the only one," Carolyn said. "That girl in the picture was Maureen's best friend. She never gave up on Maureen either."

"Who was she?" I asked.

"Her name . . ." Carolyn stopped speaking for a moment. Then, shoulders sunk in defeat, she murmured, "Her name was Jenny Rybchuk."

My heart was already pounding, but I had to know more. "What was Jenny Rybchuk like?"

Carolyn turned from the window, and I saw that there were tears in her eyes. "Innocent. Sweet. No matter what Maureen did, Jenny always forgave her, tried to understand. They'd known each other since they were babies. The families lived next door to one another. Henry was so erratic . . ."

"Henry," I repeated, remembering the man who had sought Ian out at the Legislature the night before he died.

"Henry Rybchuk," Carolyn said. "Jenny's father. When Jenny was growing up, her friends were afraid to go into the Rybchuk house because Henry was so unpredictable. When he was sober, he was decent enough, but when he was drinking, he could be violent." She hesitated. "There were rumours that his feelings for Jenny went beyond what a father should feel for his daughter. It must have been a terrifying life for a child, and lonely. Of course, Maureen went there. That one was never afraid of anything. She spent so much time with the Rybchuks that I think Jenny came to look upon her as a kind of sister."

"How did Maureen look upon Jenny?"

Carolyn laughed bitterly. "I'm sure she thanked her lucky stars that fate had sent her a friend as compliant and as needy as Jenny. I suppose when they were children, Maureen didn't mistreat Jenny any more than any strong-willed child mistreats a more passive friend. In my experience, children are as fond of power as anyone – and as easily corrupted by it. But eventually I think Maureen's role in their relationship became more sinister than

deciding which game the two of them would play . . ."
Carolyn fell silent.

"Maureen used Jenny," I said.

"Oh, yes," Carolyn agreed. "Maureen used Jenny. That
girl knew how to use goodness."

"How did she react to Jenny's pregnancy?"

For a beat, Carolyn was silent. Finally, she said, "Jenny
didn't tell her until after the baby was born."

"If she didn't tell her best friend, whom did she tell?" I
asked.

Carolyn looked away. "I don't know."

I didn't believe her. "Did Jenny tell the baby's father she
was pregnant?"

Carolyn's voice was edgy. "I told you I don't know whom
else she told."

"But she told you," I said gently. "Carolyn, Jenny told
you she was pregnant, didn't she?"

"I was the one she came to," Carolyn said, her voice
breaking. "It was such an act of trust . . ."

"She must have felt very close to you."

"She didn't have anyone else. Her mother was dead.
Henry was impossible."

"Why didn't she go to Maureen?"

Carolyn shook her head. "I honestly don't know. All I do
know is that she came to me. It was the day before Good
Friday. The students had been dismissed for the Easter
holidays. I was just getting ready to leave myself when
Jenny knocked at my door."

Unexpectedly, Carolyn smiled. "Isn't it funny, the
things you remember? Jenny came in and sat down in the
chair you're sitting in now. I can still see her. She usually
had her hair brushed back in a French braid, but that day it
was loose. She was wearing a turquoise windbreaker and,
on her lapel, she had a little Easter pin. It was a rabbit carrying a basket of eggs."

"And she told you she was pregnant?"

"Yes, she came straight to the point. She told me she was pregnant and that she wanted an abortion. I didn't believe her."

"You didn't believe she was pregnant?"

Carolyn shook her head impatiently. "Oh, I believed that all right. Student pregnancies are all too common in this school. What I didn't believe was that she wanted an abortion. I wouldn't have been the one Jenny'd come to if that was truly what she wanted."

"You're opposed to abortion?"

Carolyn looked at me levelly. "I'm a Roman Catholic, Mrs. Kilbourn. So was Jenny. I think her mind told her that one course of action was logical, but her heart told her differently. We talked for a long time that afternoon, but nothing I said convinced her. She was poised between two very painful alternatives, and she was eighteen years old. She needed guidance, and I wasn't adequately prepared to give her that guidance."

"So you took her to Beating Heart," I said.

Carolyn looked surprised.

"And the woman you saw there was Tess Malone."

Carolyn's eyes widened. "Yes, that was her name."

"What happened next?" I asked.

"Nothing," she said dully. "Jenny had the baby. She gave it away. She went back to school."

"Where is she now?"

"I don't know."

"As close as she became to you, she never got in touch?"

"No," Carolyn said, "she didn't."

"One last thing," I said. "Who was the baby's father?"

For a moment she was silent. Then she murmured. "That doesn't matter any more. Mrs. Kilbourn, don't persist in this. Any answer you find is just going to cause pain. You've been cleared of any suspicion of wrongdoing. Leave Jenny Rybchuk's child in peace. Please."

When I told Carolyn Atcheson I was leaving, she fluttered her hand in a vague signal of dismissal, but she didn't bother getting up. At the office doorway, I turned to say goodbye. Through the window behind her, I could see the snow falling, rhythmic, inexorable. Carolyn Atcheson didn't notice it. Sitting at her desk, back ramrod straight, hands clasped in front of her, Carolyn was the prototype for the class's most obedient student.

When I got back to my car I checked the clock on the dashboard. Three o'clock. Two hours till dark. I had time to pay one more visit. There were too many gaps in Carolyn's story. Erratic as Henry Rybchuk might be, I needed to talk to him.

When I got to the Petro-Can station, the mechanic who'd directed me to Carolyn's house was out front checking the oil in a Camaro. I pulled up next to him and rolled down my window. I noticed the name embroidered on his shirt pocket was Maurice. "I need your guiding skills again, Maurice," I said. "How can I find Henry Rybchuk?"

He smiled, revealing some missing teeth. "Maurice is long gone. My name is Bob, but there was a lot of wear left in Maurice's old shirts. Besides, I kind of like 'Maurice.' It's distinctive. Now, about Henry Rybchuk. You'll need more skills than mine to find him," he said. "Old Henry's been dead for over five years."

The driver of the Camaro went inside, and Bob and I talked a little longer. He said Henry had committed suicide. Shot himself to death in the basement of his house. He remembered Jenny, but he hadn't seen her in years either. "I'll tell you one thing," he said. "She didn't come back for the old man's funeral. After the announcement of the old man's death appeared in the obituaries in the Swift Current paper, Wrightman's Funeral Home – that's in Swift Current, too – got an envelope of cash and some instructions about the burial. It was anonymous. Most of us figured the envelope came from Jenny. Nobody tried very hard to chase her down. We figured if Jenny had managed to get away from that old bastard, she was better off."

I mentioned Maureen Gault's name, and Bob dismissed

her with a one-word epithet. When the driver of the Camaro came back out and started honking his horn, I got the addresses of the Gault and Rybchuk houses, thanked Bob for his help, and doubled back through town.

Factory Road was the last street on the west side of Chaplin. It looked out on a desolate landscape of salt stock-piles and tanks for the water run-off from the sodium sulphate factory. Numbers 17 and 19 were at the end of the street, set apart from the other houses. They were small bungalows with the boxy, stripped-down look of wartime housing, but the house in which Maureen Gault had grown up had fallen on hard times. Motorcycles, in various stages of disintegration, filled the carport; the front window was covered by a tattered American flag; and a doll lay abandoned on the front steps.

I pulled up in front of the Rybchuk house. Like Carolyn Atcheson's, this house was hard-scrubbed and cared for. A young woman was out shovelling the snow, and she came over as soon as she saw me. She was wearing a leather jacket with the logo of the sodium sulphate mine on the breast pocket, and her nose was running from the cold. When I rolled down the car window, she wiped her nose on the back of her mitten and grinned.

"Gross, huh?"

"We all do it," I said.

"Right," she said. "Now what can I do for you? I'll bet you're looking for a way out of Chaplin."

"No," I said, "I'm looking for the Rybchuk house."

The young woman's face grew solemn with the importance of being forced to break bad news. "They don't live here anymore. Old Mr. Rybchuk died. I'm sorry to be the one to tell you."

"That's all right," I said.

She leaned closer to me. "You know, you're the first person who's come and asked for them since we bought the house, and that'll be six years in May."

"I think old Mr. Rybchuk was pretty reclusive," I said.

She rolled her eyes. "I'll say. Imagine nobody coming to ask about you in all that time. Listen, do you happen to know his daughter? Nobody cleaned out the house before we bought it, so there was a lot of junk. We sold most of the stuff in a garage sale, and burned the rest in the burn barrel out back, but I couldn't burn her pictures. Maybe it was an identification thing. She's like my age, and I kept thinking I wouldn't want anybody to burn my pictures and stuff." She looked at me winsomely. "Since you're here and all, could I possibly impose on you to get them to her?"

"I'd be happy to."

"Great," she said. She threw her shovel into a snowbank and ran indoors. She came back with a box which she handed through the window to me. It was bigger than a shoebox, but not much. A box for winter boots, maybe. Someone had covered it in wallpaper, white with a pattern of ballerinas in pastel tutus. There was a yellowish stain on the wallpaper, and the box smelled musty.

"Sorry about the stink," she said. "It was in the basement, and you know how they are."

I thought about Henry Rybchuk committing suicide in the basement, and I shuddered.

The girl's brow furrowed. "You will get it to her, won't you?"

"I'll do my best," I said.

It took an act of will not to open the box before I got home, but I managed. When I walked through the front door, Taylor came running, eyed the box hopefully, then held her nose.

"What's in that?" she asked.

"Just some old pictures that were in somebody's house."

"Okay," she said, then she lowered her voice. "Angus is making dinner. It's a surprise, so act surprised."

"I will," I whispered back. "What are we having?"

She pulled me down, put her mouth beside my ear, and stage-whispered, "Cinnamon buns!"

"Great," I said.

"Remember the surprise."

I gave her the thumbs-up sign, turned towards the kitchen, and said loudly. "I'd better go get dinner started."

Angus came peeling out. He was wearing a shirt that said NOBODY WITH A GREAT CAR NEEDS TO JUSTIFY HIM-SELF, and he had a ring through his left nostril. It hadn't been there when I'd left him at lunchtime.

"Angus!" I said.

"I told the guys you were the coolest mother. I said my mother lived through the sixties, this won't be a problem for her."

"You were wrong," I said.

"I knew it," he said gloomily. Then he brightened. "I made cinnamon buns."

"You thought I could be bought for a cinnamon bun?"

He grinned. "I thought it was worth a shot."

That night we sat at the kitchen table, ate cinnamon buns, and watched the snow. The kids drank milk, and I drank Earl Grey tea. When I got Taylor into bed, and Angus was in his room listening to Crash Test Dummies and doing his algebra, I poured myself a glass of Jack Daniel's, picked up the box with the ballerinas on it, and went to my room.

I was glad I had the bourbon. Jenny Rybchuk's whole life was in that box. Her report cards, stacked neatly, were tied together by a thin blue ribbon. I looked at them all, and I read the teachers' comments on Jenny's development as avidly as a parent. ("Jenny is a sensible girl, whose co-operative attitude makes her a valued member of the class. She should work harder on Math." "Promoted to Grade 7 with honours. Good work, Jenny!!!") There were pictures, too. Baby pictures. School pictures. Thirteen of them. I arranged them in order on my bedspread. Kindergarten to Grade 12. The pictures were the kind a photographer who travels from school to school takes. Watch Jenny grow. Standard poses against standard backgrounds, yet something about them nagged at me. They were familiar somehow, as if I'd seen them before. Like a word on the tip of my tongue the connection was there, but I couldn't make it. I put the pictures back and closed the box.

But there was one photograph that I couldn't seem to put away. It was in black and white. Jenny looked to be about five or six, and she was wearing a flower-girl's dress. There was a blur of guests in the background, but she was alone and unsmiling. Her dress looked as if it was made of taffeta, she had a crown of flowers in her hair, and she was looking directly into the lens. There was something unsettling about those unblinking eyes. She seemed to be looking ahead into the future, collapsing the distance between past and present, seeking me out.

That night I couldn't sleep. Sometime in the early hours of morning, I turned the lights on and picked up the flower-girl picture from my nightstand. "What happened to you, Jenny?" I said. "Where are you now?" I knew I had to find her, but if I was going to find Jenny, I had to find Tess Malone.

At 5:30, I gave up on sleep and went downstairs. It was too early for the paper to be delivered, so I went out back and got an old issue out of the Blue Box. The paper's classified offices opened at 9:00. I wrote down the number. Then I turned to the classified ads and ran my finger down the column until I found what I was looking for. "If you're pregnant and alone, we're here. Beating Heart can help."

I picked up a pencil and started to write. Three minutes later, I had what I wanted: "If you're ready to talk about Henry and Jenny, I'm ready to listen. JK."

The receptionist at Beating Heart had said that Tess checked the classifieds every day to make sure its ad was there. If I was lucky, she'd keep on reading. My ad would be the one right after Beating Heart's.

Eleven

My ad in the personals column appeared for the first time on Tuesday. There was no response, and life went on. The jack o'lantern was still on the deck, and Taylor still hadn't named her cat. Angus's nose had become infected over the weekend and, by Wednesday, he had to admit defeat and take the ring out. "Temporarily," he said, but I recognized a window of opportunity when I saw one. As soon as the ring was out, I called Jill and asked her to come over and take some family pictures for our Christmas cards.

Thursday afternoon, there was a half-day holiday at Taylor's school, so she came to the university with me. She brought her sketchbook and the drawing pencils Hilda had given her for her birthday. On the way to my office, we stopped off at the cafeteria for a can of pop, a bag of chips, and box of Junior Mints; then we went to the departmental office where Rosalie Norman agreed, reluctantly, that if there was an emergency, Taylor could call her. All the bases had been covered. Still, when I picked up my notes to go to class, I was anxious.

"Are you sure you're going to be all right?" I asked.

Taylor was adjusting my desk lamp so the light fell on her sketchpad. "I'm fine," she said without looking up. "There are a couple of things I really want to work on." As I watched her choose a pencil from her case, I marvelled for the hundredth time at the metamorphosis that Taylor underwent when she was making art.

An hour later, when I came back from class, she was still at work.

"How did it go?" I asked.

She held up her sketchpad. "Take a look," she said.

She had drawn Jess Stephens, surrounded by a series of quick line drawings of her kitten. The cat sketches were fluid and funny, but the drawing of Jess was remarkable. Taylor's art teacher, Fil, had told me she still had a lot to learn about technique, but she'd captured Jess: the dreamy little boy with the great cheekbones and the eyes that tilted upwards and made him look always as if he were laughing.

I had seen Jess Stephens a hundred times, but it wasn't until I looked at Taylor's drawing that I knew why the pictures of Jenny Rybchuk had nagged at me. I tried to remember the months before Jess was born. Sylvie had gone to a fertility clinic in Vancouver. Later, because the doctors knew the pregnancy would be a difficult one, she had spent the last months of her pregnancy at the clinic and had the baby there. That had been the story. Sylvie and her baby had come back in the fall. Jess was six now. Taylor had gone to the party for his sixth birthday in September. The baby in Jenny Rybchuk's arms in the Santa picture seemed to be two or three months old. It all fit.

When I got home, there was a message from the classified department of the paper. Did I want my ad in for another three days? I called back and said I did, but I was going to change the wording. I wanted the new ad to read: "If you're ready to talk about Jenny and Jess, I'm ready to listen, JK."

Tess Malone called Saturday night. I'd just gotten back from the station after doing our show, and I was in that state that Angus calls wired but tired.

Tess just sounded wired. "I saw your ad, and you've got to take it out of the paper. You have no idea what you can bring down on yourself if you pursue this."

"Is Jess Stephens Jenny Rybchuk's son?"

"Jo, why are you meddling in this?"

"I'm not meddling," I said. "Tess, it's important that I know the truth."

"Dammit, Jo. Leave it alone."

"I can't," I said. "I need to understand what happened. Tess, you've known me for years. Give me a little credit. I'm not stirring this up just to make trouble."

She sighed. "I know you aren't." For a moment, she was silent. I hoped the silence was a good sign and it was. When she finally spoke, her voice was resigned.

"I hope you're not going to be sorry you forced this, Jo. I don't know how you found out, but you're right. Jess is Jenny Rybchuk's son."

"And you knew her," I said. "You met her when Carolyn Atcheson brought her into Beating Heart."

"Yes."

I felt a rush of excitement. "What was she like?"

"Young. Scared. Decent. Trying hard to do the right thing. I'd only been a volunteer at Beating Heart for three or four months when Jenny came in. I would have remembered her even if . . ." Her voice trailed off.

"Even if what, Tess?"

"Even if . . . if she hadn't been one of the first girls I counselled. Sometimes it's so easy to get a girl to see that having the baby is the right option. But when Jenny started to talk to me, all I could think of was how amazing it was that she was even considering going through with the pregnancy."

"Carolyn said Jenny was poised between two very painful alternatives."

"That about sums it up. Jenny was a very loyal girl, but when she talked about her home situation and what her father would do to her if he knew she was pregnant, I understood why she was considering abortion. When she came to Beating Heart, she was already three months' pregnant. High-school graduation was another three months away. All her life she'd worked towards getting that diploma. It was her ticket out of hell, Jo. I know that sounds melodramatic, but that's the way it was. Once she had her Grade 12, Jenny wouldn't be dependent on her father anymore."

"From what Carolyn said about Henry Rybchuk, that must have been a powerful argument."

"It was," Tess agreed, "but it wasn't the most powerful. Jenny's biggest concern wasn't herself. It was her baby. She was worried sick about what might happen to her baby if she gave it out for adoption. I guess she knew first-hand what an abusive parent could do to a child, and the idea that her own child would be raised by people about whom she would know nothing terrified her."

"So you convinced her to have the baby and give it to Sylvie and Gary."

"You make it sound as if I was just using Jenny to do a favour for friends. It wasn't like that. Abortion is wrong, Jo, and, in her heart, Jenny Rybchuk knew that. She knew a foetus wasn't just a collection of cells that you scrub away like dead skin. She knew she'd never forgive herself for committing murder. Sylvie and Gary offered the perfect solution. It wasn't common knowledge at the time, but before Jess came into their lives, Gary and Sylvie's marriage was in serious trouble. They'd just turned forty. There was no baby, and it didn't look as if there was ever going to be one. They were desperate.

"All I had to do was pick up the phone. I could save the marriage of two people I cared for, keep a fine young girl from making a mistake that would ruin her life, and make certain a baby came into this world. It all seemed so right."

"And so you made the call."

"Yes," she said. "I made the call, and that night Sylvie and Gary came down to Beating Heart to talk to Jenny. They were all so excited and so committed to making sure the baby had a wonderful life." She was silent for a long while, then she said, "It should have been perfect." She sounded as if she was speaking to herself, not to me.

"What went wrong?" I asked.

"Nothing," she said flatly. "Everything worked out the way it was supposed to. Jenny got her high-school graduation diploma. Carolyn Atcheson went to old Henry Rybchuk and told him she'd found his daughter a job babysitting for a family on Vancouver Island, starting in June, and that she was arranging to have Jenny write her final exams in B.C."

"And Henry Rybchuk went along with that?" I asked.

"According to Carolyn, he was relieved. He'd been laid off at the plant, and money was tight. He gave Jenny his blessing. She went to Vancouver, and, a few days later, Sylvie joined her. They stayed together until Jess was born. Sylvie didn't want to miss any part of the experience."

"They must have become very close."

Tess's voice was dead. "I guess they did." She sighed. "Jo, I don't want to talk about this any more. I've told you everything you need to know. Goodnight."

"Don't hang up. Please, don't hang up yet. I need to know one more thing." I could feel my muscles tense. "Tess, who was the baby's father?"

"What?" she said.

"I said, do you know who Jess's father is?"

"The name's in our records," she said.

"Who was it?"

"I can't tell you that."

"Was it Ian?"

The shock in her voice seemed genuine. "Whatever made you think that?" she said.

"Then it wasn't him?"

"Of course not." For the first time that night, she sounded like the old Tess, gruff and confident, and I remembered how often that gruff confidence had got all of us through a tight spot. Now it sounded as if she was the one in a tight spot.

"Tess, are you all right?" I asked.

"It doesn't matter," she said. "Just take the ad out of the paper, Jo. Please." Then she hung up.

I went to my purse and pulled out the picture that had been in Ian's wallet. Now that I knew the truth, the photo had lost its power. It was just a picture of a shopping mall Santa, a pretty young woman, and a baby whose father was a man I didn't know. The big question had been answered, but there were others. Why had Ian been carrying the picture? What had Henry Rybchuk talked about with Ian and then with Tess the night before Ian was murdered? Why had Henry Rybchuk committed suicide? And, most naggingly, where was Jenny Rybchuk?

I opened the box of Jenny's mementoes, and put the Santa Claus picture on the top. As I replaced the lid, I thought about the girl who had pasted ballerina-covered wallpaper on to an old box to make it pretty. Jenny's Grade 6 teacher had said she was a sensible girl, and a sensible girl would know when it was time to put away the past. By now she probably had another baby and a new life.

That night I slept deeply and dreamlessly. The next morning I woke up to fresh snow and a sense of hope. It was Advent Sunday. As I made the coffee, I remembered our old minister saying that the first Sunday in Advent always reminded him of a song from *West Side Story*. When I stepped into the shower, I knew exactly how he felt. "Something's coming," I sang and, as I soaped up, I thought it was about time for something good to come whistling down my river.

Angus was the altar boy at church, and as he lit the candle, I felt my heart beat faster. To celebrate the start of the Christmas season, we went to the Copper Kettle for brunch. At the buffet, Taylor and Angus competed hotly to see who could heap the most food on their plate. As I watched them tottering back to our table, plates piled high with roast beef and ribs and perogies, I was so embarrassed I wanted to sink through the floor, but they told each other jokes all through lunch and laughed so hard that the owner of the restaurant gave them each a free dessert. "You two are good for business," he said. When we came out of the restaurant, Taylor decided to dance all the way down Scarth Street because she was so happy. As I watched her twirling around in her snowsuit and her boots, I knew my something good had already come. You could always count on Leonard Bernstein.

Monday after class, a student called asking for an appointment and, as I checked my calendar, I saw there were only twenty-four shopping days till Christmas. I made a quick list of people I was buying presents for and headed for the mall.

Inside the Cornwall Centre, it wasn't hard to feel the holiday spirit. Beside the fountain in the centre courtyard, a three-storey tree soared towards a skylight; in front of the toy store, Santa was ho-ho-ho-ing on his big red chair inside the North Pole; and every loudspeaker in the mall was blaring "Silent Night."

I was coming down the escalator in Eaton's when I saw her. She was in the accessories department, comparing two scarves. She seemed so absorbed that, for a split second, I thought I might get away unscathed. But just before the escalator got to the main floor, Julie Evanson looked up and saw me. There was no escaping her.

She was wearing her platinum hair in a new and becoming feathered cut, and her cherry-red wool coat fitted her trim figure like the proverbial glove. The look was strictly Liz Claiborne, but I knew Julie had made the coat herself. As she had told me many times over the years, she made all her own clothes. She also told me that, with a figure like mine, which must be difficult to fit, I'd find I'd look much smarter if I made my own clothes, too. That was Julie.

"Christmas shopping, Julie?" I said.

She smiled her dimpled smile. "All my shopping's done, Joanne. And wrapped."

"Mine, too," I said, crossing my fingers the way my kids did when they told a lie.

"I guess shopping kept you busy when everyone thought you'd murdered that girl."

"Not everyone thought that, Julie. The police didn't. That's why I'm standing here now."

She looked thoughtfully at the scarf in her hand. "That poor girl," she said. "Choked to death. It was good luck that you got off, wasn't it?"

"It wasn't luck," I said. "It was justice. I didn't have anything to do with Maureen Gault's death."

She shrugged. "So you say. But try as I might, I can't forget the little chat I had with Maureen the day you and I met in the Faculty Club."

"What are you talking about?"

"I just told you. I had a fascinating tête-à-tête with Maureen Gault the day before she was killed. She was coming out of the elevator in the Arts Building. You know, the building where you have your office," she added helpfully.

"I know where my office is, Julie. What did Maureen tell you?"

Julie frowned. "I'll have to make sure I remember exactly what was said. After all, Maureen isn't here to defend herself, is she? On second thought, maybe it would be better if I didn't say anything at all."

I started to leave. "Suit yourself," I said. "I'm too old for this crap."

She reached out and touched my sleeve. "I don't remember you as being profane, Joanne. But I guess I can't blame you for being anxious about what Maureen might have said to me before she died."

"Julie, please."

"All right. It was a brief encounter. I was on my way to your office to see if you'd buy some tickets to the fashion show. I was just passing the bookstore in the Arts Building when Maureen Gault got off the elevator. I recognized her, and went up and introduced myself." Julie dimpled. "I said I was a friend of yours. You're not the only one who can stretch the truth, Joanne.

"Anyway, Maureen said, 'When you see her, tell her I'm looking for her.' Of course, I asked why, and Maureen said,

'I want to ask her if she's feeling different about any of the Seven Dwarfs these days.'"

I remembered the crude X's someone had drawn over the faces of Andy Boychuk and my husband the day Julie ran into Maureen. There didn't seem to be much doubt anymore about who had wielded the felt pen. "Did she say anything more?" I asked.

"I forced her to say more," Julie said proudly. "I asked Maureen point-blank what she knew about the Seven Dwarfs. At first she seemed angry at the question, then she laughed and pointed to one of the displays in the bookstore window. They hadn't taken out the Hallowe'en decorations yet, and there was a skeleton propped up against a stack of biology books. Maureen jabbed at the window in front of it and said, 'There's your answer, blondie. I know where the Seven Dwarfs hid their skeleton.'"

Julie must have seen the fear in my eyes. "Just a figure of speech I'm sure, but in retrospect, it does seem chilling, doesn't it?" She looked at her watch. "Four o'clock, already. How the minutes fly when we're with friends."

She thrust the scarf she was holding into my hand. "Here, Joanne, you take this. All those colours. It's more the kind of thing you'd wear." She turned on her heel, and steered her way effortlessly through the other shoppers in accessories. I felt as if someone had run me over with a truck, but then Julie had always been the queen of the hit-and-run artists. The scarf she'd thrust at me was still in my hands. Julie was right. That brilliant swirl of colour was the kind of thing I liked. When it came to insights that could wound, Julie had a knack for being right. She also, much as I hated to admit it, had a knack for finding out the truth. As poisonous as she was, I had never known Julie to lie.

I put down the scarf. Christmas shopping was over for the day. I had to find out if Julie had stumbled onto some ugly truth about the Seven Dwarfs.

When I walked past the North Pole on my way out, I

could hear the soft, anxious voices of the young mothers waiting with little girls in fussy velvet dresses and little boys in Christmas sweaters and new corduroy pants. "Don't forget to smile," the mothers said. "Don't forget to tell Santa what you want him to bring you. There's nothing to be afraid of . . ."

Jenny Rybchuk had stood in a line like that with her son. Where was she now? When her father said, "Now, I got no more daughter," what had he meant? As I drove up Albert Street, I could feel the anxiety beginning to gnaw.

I didn't wait to take my coat off before I dialled Howard Dowhanuik's number in Toronto.

He was furious. "A skeleton! Don't you know better than to listen to Julie? Christ, Jo, after all these years . . ."

"Howard, as awful as Julie is, I've never known her to lie."

"Maybe she's turned a corner since we knew her."

"I don't think it's that simple. Howard, Maureen Gault was murdered the day after Julie saw her. What if the skeleton Maureen was talking about wasn't figurative? What if she really did chance upon something about the Seven Dwarfs? Do you have any idea what she might have been talking about?"

"No, I don't, and to be frank I'm pissed off that you think I would. Jo, I may lack finesse and I may be a little crude, but I'm an officer of the court. We take an oath. Do you think I could know about a stiff being stashed somewhere and say, 'Oh well, one of us was responsible for that murder, so I'll overlook it'?"

"I'm sorry," I said.

"You should be," he said. Then his voice was kinder. "That goddamn Julie makes us all crazy. Just forget it, Jo."

"I'll try," I said.

But I couldn't. I dialled Craig Evanson's number. When Manda answered, I hung up. After enduring the hell of a bad marriage for twenty years, Craig had found a great wife and a great life. He didn't need to revisit his past. Besides, there was a chance Howard was right. It was possible that Julie was just making me crazy.

I went upstairs to change my clothes before dinner. I pulled on my blue jeans and a long-sleeved T-shirt Mieka had bought years ago at a concert. The Go-Go's. Another blast from the past. When I reached down to pick up my sneakers, I saw the corner of the ballerina-covered box under the bed, and I felt the panic rising.

"Where are you, Jenny," I murmured. I picked up the telephone and dialled the number of my new friends in the classified department. This time I wasn't fancy with the ad: "URGENT : I must speak to Jenny Rybchuk or anyone knowing her whereabouts. Joanne Kilbourn." I left both my office and my home numbers. I didn't want to take a chance on missing her.

The ad appeared in the late edition of Tuesday's paper. Wednesday morning as I pulled onto the parkway on my way to the university, I noticed the silver Audi behind me. When I turned into the university, the Audi stayed with me, but it sailed by when I drove into the parking lot in front of College West, and I forgot about it. Two hours later, as I started home, it was there again. The Audi's windows were tinted. Whoever was driving it had an advantage over me in our game of hide and seek. I looked for it when I stopped for groceries at the IGA, but it had disappeared. When I drove home, the Audi was behind me all the way, but it was nowhere in sight when I parked in front of our house. The first thing I saw at home was Taylor balanced on the railing on the front porch with a string of Christmas lights in her hand and a look of grim determination on her face. At that point, the Audi slipped to the back of my mind where it stayed the rest of the evening.

Peter called after supper to say he was coming home Saturday to study for his mid-term exams. Taylor, who had been standing beside me, holding her kitten and listening to my half of the conversation with Peter, looked at me expectantly when I hung up. "Now is it time to get out the Christmas stuff?" she asked.

"It's time," I said. "Come on, we'll go downstairs and dig out the decorations. But you're going to have to keep that cat out of harm's way till we're done." I looked at the animal in Taylor's arms. It wasn't a ball of ginger fluff any more; it was starting to get a rangy adolescent look. "T," I said, "when are you going to decide on a name? You're supposed to do these things when the animal is young enough to learn."

She rubbed the spot under her cat's neck thoughtfully. "I keep changing my mind. Angus says I should call him 'Dallas' after the Dallas Cowboys. What do you think?"

"Dallas? It sounds okay to me."

Taylor shook her head. "I hate it." She moved the cat into his favourite carrying position, with his body against her chest and his head looking back over her shoulder. "Come on, kitten, let's go put you in our room." As she walked out the door, I caught the cat looking at me in a defiant teenager way, and I knew he would make me pay for banishing him.

Taylor and I spent the rest of the evening decorating. We were just winding fake holly around the staircase rail when the phone rang. It was Inspector Alex Kequahtooway.

"I thought I'd call and see how you're doing, Mrs. Kilbourn."

"I'm fine," I said. "How are you?"

"Fine," he said. "Mrs. Kilbourn, I was wondering what you were doing Friday night."

I felt my heart sink. "Friday night? I don't remember. Inspector, what's happened?"

He laughed. "Nothing's happened, Mrs. Kilbourn. It's not last Friday I'm interested in. It's this Friday. I was wondering if you wanted to go to the symphony with me. They've got some hot-shot guest violinist and he's doing a Beethoven sonata. That day in my office, you said you liked Beethoven."

"I do," I said.

"Well?" he asked.

"I'd love to," I said.

"Shall I pick you up at about seven?"

"Seven would be great," I said.

The next day as I drove to school thinking about what I'd wear on Friday night, I noticed the Audi again. I'm a cautious driver, but I tried a few tricky manoeuvres to see if I was imagining that the Audi was following me. It was right with me all the way to the university turnoff. When I got to my office, I called Alex Kequahtooway. He wasn't at headquarters, but I left a message, and when he called back a half-hour later, I told him about the Audi. He said he'd look into it. When I drove home after class, the Audi was gone, and I thought it might be handy dating a cop.

Friday night, Inspector Alex Kequahtooway was on my doorstep at the dot of 7:00. I'd had my hair cut at a new place that cost three times as much as my old place, and I was wearing a black silk dress so chic that even Julie Evanson would have approved.

Alex Kequahtooway did too. "You look great," he said, as he held out my coat for me.

"You look pretty spiffy yourself," I said.

He smiled. "I guess if the compliments are over, we can go."

The kids came down to say goodbye, and we walked out to the curb where the taxi Alex had arrived in was waiting. It was a gorgeous night, warm for December, and starry. We had the idea at the same time. "Let's walk," we said in unison. Alex sent the cabbie on her way with a Christmas tip generous enough to make her smile. I ran back to the house, put on my heavy boots, and we started for the park. As we walked through the snowy streets, we didn't talk much, but it wasn't an awkward silence. When we rounded the corner by the Legislature, Alex climbed through the snow onto a little spit of land overlooking the lake. He held his hand out to me to follow. There was a full moon, and the ice on the lake seemed to glow.

"When I was a kid, we used to walk on the lake by the reserve all winter. Christmas Eve we'd walk across to church, then we'd come back, and all my aunties would make pies. That's what I remember about Christmas. Lying in bed, smelling pies baking, and hearing my aunties laugh." He turned to me. "What do you remember?"

"Nothing that good," I said. "Come on, let's walk across the lake."

"Are you sure? It's longer."

"I don't mind," I said. "I want to start this year's store of Christmas memories off with a bang."

We jumped off the shore and walked across the ice in the moonlight. Neither of us mentioned the case that had brought us together, and neither of us mentioned the Audi. We talked about good things: Christmases and hockey and ice-fishing, and I think we were both surprised when the lights from the Centre of the Arts loomed ahead of us.

We were late. The lobby was almost empty, and we slid into our seats, laughing and out of breath, just as the orchestra struck the opening chord of the Shostakovich Fifth. My heart was pounding from the walk, and the Shostakovich kept it pounding. At intermission, I said to Alex, "I've had enough excitement, let's just stay here."

He laughed. "That's exactly what I feel like doing. I'm wearing dress shoes, and my feet haven't hurt like this since I was a beat cop."

The audience drifted off, and I picked up the program. "Which sonata are they doing?"

He shrugged.

I looked at my program. "The Kreutzer," I said. "Wouldn't you know it."

"You don't like it?" he said.

"I love it. It's just that the Kreutzer Sonata was as close as my husband and I came to having a piece of music that

was 'our song.' Tonight's the first time since Kevin Tarpley
was killed that I haven't spent the whole evening thinking
about Ian. You and I were having such a good time . . ."

"We still are," he said. "If you want to remember,
remember. Let the memories come." He leaned towards
me. "You had a good marriage, didn't you?"

"Yes," I said, "I did. My friend, Jill, is a journalist, and
she says, in her business, there's nothing like death to air-
brush the past. I try to remember that when I think of Ian.
He wasn't perfect. Neither was I. But there wasn't a day in
our life together when Ian and I didn't know that being
married was the best thing that had ever happened to either
of us."

"Twenty years of a good marriage is about twenty years
longer than most people get," Alex said.

"I know," I said, "but it still wasn't long enough for me."

He reached out, took my hand, and we settled back in
our seats, holding hands till the audience came back, the
lights dimmed, the musicians came onstage, and the guest
violinist stepped forward and played, unaccompanied, the
heart-stopping opening of the Sonata No. 9 in A Major. The
piano replied, then, after a few bars of tentative approaches,
piano and violin began their tempestuous pursuit of one
another in the presto, and I closed my eyes and remembered
the first time I'd heard the Kreutzer Sonata. Ian and I were
at the University of Toronto. It was January. We'd been dating for a couple of weeks, and I was sitting in a classroom on
the second floor of Victoria College waiting for my English
class to begin. Suddenly, Ian was there. He wasn't wearing
his jacket, and he looked half-frozen. Without a word, he
grabbed my hand and led me down Vic's worn marble stairs
and outside, through the snow, to a little record store
around the corner on Bloor. There was a listening booth at
the back. We went in. Ian's coat and books were on the floor
where he'd left them, and the LP of the Kreutzer Sonata was
on the turntable. Ian turned on the record player, I heard the
violin's luminous entry, and my life changed for ever. We

took the record back to Ian's room, and that afternoon we made love for the first time. Afterwards, as we lay in the tangle of sheets, listening to the violin and piano play their separate and confident variations on the single beautiful theme of the second movement, I knew that, whatever else happened in my life, I would have known what it was like to be happy. Four months later, Ian and I were married.

Onstage in the Centre of the Arts, the piano and violin were moving from the tarantelle to the sensuous passage before the finale. Alex Kequahtooway looked closely at me, reached into his pocket, and gave me his handkerchief. I leaned forward to listen to the final dazzling burst of virtuosity, and the movement was over. The musicians bowed to the audience, the applause swelled, and I mopped my eyes and blew my nose. When I was through, I turned to Alex. "Not many men carry a real handkerchief anymore."

He smiled. "My mother always made me carry two hankies. 'One for show. One for blow.' "

"I may need both of them," I said.

"It's a powerful piece of music," he said.

"There's a Tolstoy story where a character says the Kreutzer Sonata should never be played in a room where women are wearing low-necked dresses."

Alex Kequahtooway raised an eyebrow. "Tolstoy may have had a point there."

We walked home through the park. The temperature had risen, and the snow on the trees looked heavy and wet. Suspended from the wrought-iron lampposts along the path were globes of light that reflected red and green and white on the slick pavements.

"Do you think we'll have a green Christmas?" I said.

He shuddered. "I hope not. I can remember only one green Christmas, but it was awful. No snow for tobogganing, and the ice was too thin for skating."

A car speeded by, splashing water on us.

"Never a cop around when you need one," Alex said mildly.

I laughed. "I wouldn't say that. You were there when I needed someone to take care of that Audi. Incidentally, it seems to have decided to play hide and seek with somebody else. I didn't see it at all today."

"Good."

"I probably over-reacted," I said. "But there's been so much weirdness in my life lately."

I could see his body tense. "Such as?"

"Such as an old friend – no, not a friend, an acquaintance – telling me something disturbing."

Alex turned to me. "What did you hear?"

The decision to tell him didn't take long. I was sick of secrets. "I guess I should tell you who the acquaintance was first. It's a woman named Julie Evanson."

"Craig Evanson's first wife," he said.

I looked at him questioningly.

He shrugged. "Mouse work," he said.

"Right," I said. "You must know more about the Seven Dwarfs than we know about each other."

"Probably," he said.

"Then you know that Julie Evanson will never be anyone's candidate for humanitarian of the year," I said.

He smiled. "That seems to be the consensus."

"Nonetheless," I said, "Julie's no liar."

As I told Alex about Julie's encounter with Maureen Gault, we didn't break our stride, but when I repeated Maureen's line about knowing where the Seven Dwarfs had hidden their skeleton, Alex stopped abruptly. In the street light, I saw that his expression was all cop. "Did she elaborate?"

"No, that's not her style. Julie's the surgical-strike-and-withdraw type. She's happy just to leave you standing there bleeding. But that's not the point. The point is I think Julie really believes she knows something. Look, Alex, tell me if I'm getting into an area you can't talk about, but when you were investigating all of us, did you find anything really questionable?"

In the light his face was unreadable. "Was there something to find?"

"I don't know," I said.

"This case isn't over, Joanne. There are things I can't talk about with you." He took both my hands in his and turned me towards the light so he could see my face. "Do you understand?" he asked. "There are things you're better off not knowing."

I felt a chill. When I shivered, Alex Kequahtooway put his arm around my shoulder. We walked home that way, not talking but close. When we turned the corner onto my street, I pointed at my house. "Look," I said, "we're the only house without Christmas lights. I guess I'd better get out my ladder tomorrow."

"Do you need somebody to hold it steady?"

"Are you volunteering?"

"I guess I am."

"You're on," I said. "Is 9:00 tomorrow morning too early? My son's coming home from university around lunchtime. He puts up the lights every year; it would be great if they were blazing when he pulled in."

"Nine's fine," he said.

We were standing in front of my door. "Do you want to come in for a drink?"

"No, thanks," he said. "Nine o'clock comes early."

"I had a good time tonight," I said.

Alex Kequahtooway reached out and touched my cheek. "So did I." Then his face grew serious. "Be careful, Joanne. Don't take any chances."

I unlocked the front door. "Don't worry," I said, "I'm a very prudent person."

Twelve

SATURDAY morning I woke up to the radio weatherman telling us we were in for a record-warm December 5. "Get out the sunscreen, folks," he said. I looked out my bedroom window. Maybe not sunscreen weather, but there were patches of dark ground beneath the melting snow, and I could hear water dripping off the eaves. When Alex came, his windbreaker was open, and Angus refused to wear a coat at all.

"Somehow, when I envisioned this, I thought we'd all be rosy-cheeked in our toques and ski-jackets," I said.

Angus shook his head. "Dream on, Mum."

Alex and I put the lights on the house while Angus and Taylor did the trees. When we were through, Taylor brought her pumpkin out and placed it on top of the painted cream can I was going to fill with pine boughs and red velvet bows. She smiled at Alex. "Can you light him up, too?"

Alex looked at me questioningly. I nodded. "It can be done," he said, and he threaded the lights expertly through the pumpkin.

"Good job," Taylor said approvingly.

"You'd be amazed at the things they teach us at the police college," he said.

Angus ran in the house and turned on the lights, and the four of us stood on the soggy lawn assessing our handiwork.

In the rotting snow, the lights looked like decorations for a used-car lot, and there was no denying that Jack was more battle-scarred than ever.

"I think my Hallmark Christmas just went down the dumper," I said.

"Let it go," Alex said. "We'll come up with something better."

I smiled at him. I liked the sound of that *we*.

We had an early lunch because Alex was on duty at noon. Peter drove up just as he was leaving. As I saw Peter pull up out front, I tried to think how his old green Volvo would look to someone who hadn't known it as long as we all had. Rust had eaten serious holes in the car's body, and the trunk was tied shut with a piece of rope, but the homemade canoe rack on top was still in A-1 shape. I turned to Alex. "As a cop, are you are obligated to do something about a car like Veronica?"

He pointed towards the Volvo. "That's Veronica?"

"Peter's pride and joy," I said.

Peter came, and after the hugs and the introductions, Alex pointed to the canoe rack.

"You enjoy the water?"

Pete grinned. "Sure, but I don't have a boat. That thing just came with the car. It seems kinda pointless to take it off."

Alex nodded in agreement. "Who knows? One day you might get a kayak or something."

Pete's grin grew even wider. "Exactly," he said, and he shot me a look of triumph. I had never been a fan of that canoe rack.

Angus and Taylor came out and hauled Pete into the house to show off the cat and see if he'd brought them anything. Alex watched their retreating backs thoughtfully. "Nice kids," he said.

"Thanks," I said. "I was afraid that between Peter's car and Taylor's superannuated pumpkin you'd be ready to write us off by now."

He shook his head. "Actually the car is pretty much like most of the cars I had when I was a kid, and Taylor's pumpkin looks like my captain." His words were casual, but when he turned to me, his dark eyes were grave. "Are you planning to stay pretty close to home today?"

"I've got our TV panel at 6:30. Till then, I hadn't planned much beyond visiting with Pete and getting ready for the show."

"Good," he said.

"Is something wrong?" I asked.

"I don't know," he said, "but it never hurts to be careful."

Our topic that night was changes in the delivery of the health-care system, and I spent the afternoon catching up on Peter's news and rereading my notes. It was a subject I was up on, but the questions viewers called in were quirky sometimes, and I wanted to be prepared. As Alex said, "it never hurts to be careful."

We ate early, and I was at Nationtv by 6:00. I had trouble finding a parking place. When I got to the entrance I remembered why. There was huge fir tree in the middle of the galleria, and the area around it was filled with people. I spotted Jill at the far end of the room, talking to a cluster of technical people who were watching a choir arrange themselves on a makeshift stage. When Jill saw me, she gave one final instruction to the camera people and came over.

She was wearing a dark green silk skirt and a matching blouse covered in Christmas roses. In her ears were gold drop earrings which, on closer inspection, turned out to be reindeers.

"You look like the spirit of Christmas," I said.

"Thank you," she said. "I'd like to find the fuckhead vice-president who came up with this community tree-lighting idea. Do you know the network's doing this all across Canada? Coast to coast, people are jumping in their cars so they can come down to their local Nationtv station, hang their trinket on our tree, and get a glass of warm apple juice and a dead doughnut. And people like me are trying to figure out where we're gonna find the money to pay all our technical people time-and-a-half. Do you know what I was doing when you came? Setting up to re-shoot a segment because a little girl in the front row of the choir peed herself in the middle of 'Frosty the Snowman.' She didn't even stop singing. The cameramen noticed it dripping off the edge of the stage."

I started to laugh.

"It's not funny, Jo," she said. Then she started to laugh, too. "Well, maybe it is funny, but a real friend wouldn't have laughed. Come on, let's go downstairs. We can run through the show when you're in makeup."

After I was made up, Jill and I walked onto the set. I sat in my place, and Leslie Martin came over and clipped my microphone on my jacket. She was wearing dark green tights, a red and white striped jerkin, and a red stocking cap with a jingle bell on the end.

"Do you get time-and-a-half for being an elf?" I asked.

"You bet your boots! And guess whose boyfriend is getting a Nordic Track for Christmas." Leslie flashed me a grin that was far too lascivious for one of Santa's helpers. "I can hardly wait to rub up against those sculptured pectorals."

Through my earpiece I could hear Jill's voice. "I was just talking to Keith," she said. "I think he and the lady lobbyist must have had a falling out. He says he's coming home for Christmas, and he wonders if you'd take it amiss if he asked you for dinner."

"I wouldn't take it amiss," I said, "but I may have other plans. I've met somebody else . . ."

"Do tell," she said.

I started. Then the monitor picked up Sam Spiegel in Ottawa, the director began counting down, and we were on the air.

It was a good show. Keith outlined the more provocative proposals for revamping the American health-care delivery

system, and Sam and I talked about some of the initiatives
the provinces were taking at home. There were the usual
ideological flare-ups about who had the right to expect
what from whom, but we were spirited rather than vicious,
and when the phone-in segment started, the callers
seemed, for once, to be more interested in light than heat.
The questions were fair and perceptive, and I relaxed and
enjoyed myself. Sixty seconds before the end of the show,
I was half-listening to Sam talk about wellness models,
when the moderator in Toronto said, "Time for one more
quick question. Go ahead, Jenny from Vermilion Hills,
Saskatchewan, you're on the air."

I heard the woman's voice. "Help me," it said. And that
was all it said. I looked over to Jill in the control booth; she
was rolling her eyes back in a "what next" way. In Toronto,
the moderator was signing off. We all said goodnight, and
the light on the camera went dark.

I unclipped my microphone and went into the control
booth. "Who was that last caller?" I asked.

"Crank or prankster, take your pick." Jill said.

"Can you check with Toronto and see if they got that
woman's last name?" I asked.

Jill shrugged and punched a button. "Toronto, did you
get a surname on that last caller? Okay. Yeah, we do know
how to grow them out here. Thanks." She looked up at me.
"No surname," she said. "Just Jenny, from Vermilion Hills,
Saskatchewan. Never heard of it," she added.

"I have," I said. "Can you find out who cut off the call?"

Jill asked, then turned back to me. "They cut her off in
Toronto."

"Thanks," I said.

I didn't stop to take off my makeup. I grabbed my coat
from the hook in the green room and ran upstairs and across
the crowded lobby. On the stage, another children's choir
was singing, and a group of little kids was sitting on the
floor around the tree stringing popcorn and cranberries.

Jenny's phone call seemed to be a cry from a different world. I was so preoccupied, I didn't notice the man at the reception desk until it was too late. I ran straight into him. When he turned, I saw that the man was Paschal Temple.

As soon as he recognized me, his face lit up with pleasure. "I was just watching you over there on the television. With all this crowd, I couldn't hear too well, but you looked very pretty. Well, this is good luck. I was just leaving something for you."

"Did you come down here just to see me?" I asked.

"No, I'm killing two birds with one stone. We brought Lolita's choir down to be on TV." He gestured to a children's choir just coming off the stage. "They're so excited. Me too. Watching how they make a TV show was fun. Anyway, I'm sure you're busy, so just let me give you my little package. It's poor Kevin's Bible. The warden gave it to me because he knew it had come from me originally." He opened the Bible and took out a folded piece of paper. "I would never have thought to give the Bible to you, but when I looked inside, I found this, and I remembered you were interested in it."

He handed me the Bible. I took it and unfolded the paper. It was a photocopy of the Biblical Character Building Chart that Paschal had shown me the night I'd gone to Bread of Life Tabernacle. Kevin had printed his name in capital letters on the top of the page and he'd printed pairs of letters beside some of the biblical passages that dealt with character-destroying qualities. The letters printed next to the notation for Wilful Blindness were my initials, JK; the biblical reference was to Psalm 146, the verse Kevin had sent me. I checked the other letters. Kevin's own initials appeared beside the entries for Cowardice and Impurity. The initials MT were printed beside Pride and Falsehood. Maureen had received a letter too. There was a final set of initials, but this one didn't have a character-destroying quality listed next to it. There was just a biblical reference.

Paschal Temple was watching me closely.

"Do you know what Exodus 20:13 is?" I asked.

His eyes were grave. "It's the sixth Commandment: Thou shalt not commit murder."

"Thank you," I said. "Look, I'm sorry. I have to leave. It's an emergency."

"Can I be of any help?"

I shook my head. Then I changed my mind. "You could add me to your prayer list," I said, and I started for the door.

There were still cars coming into the parking lot behind Nationtv. A van waited as I pulled out of my spot, and it squeezed in as soon as I was clear. When I nosed out onto the street, I saw the silver Audi in my rear-view mirror. It was coming out of the parking lot behind me, and I had a pretty good idea now who was driving it. Suddenly, I was icily calm. I drove carefully along the streets that I knew would be fully lighted. When I got home, I used the electronic eye and drove straight into the carport. I used the door between the carport and the kitchen to get inside. When I was safely in the house, I leaned against the kitchen door and closed my eyes. So far, so good. Upstairs in the family room, I could hear the sound of the television and of Taylor and the boys laughing. I dialled the number of the Regina police.

"Inspector Kequahtooway, please."

There was silence. Then a click, and a woman's voice.

"Inspector Kequahtooway is not on duty. Can someone else help you?"

"No," I said. "Do you have his home number?"

"We can't give out home numbers, ma'am."

"Right," I said, and I hung up and dialled Craig Evanson's number.

He answered, sounding breathless and excited. "We're on our way to the hospital, Jo. The baby's coming. Manda's contractions are five minutes apart."

"Craig, I won't keep you. I just need to get some directions. When you guys went hunting in the Vermilion Hills, you stayed in a cabin. I need to know how to get there."

As Craig gave me the directions, I sketched a quick map. My icy calm was starting to melt. I was scared, and I didn't want to leave anything to chance. I stuck the map in my purse, went up to my room, and changed out of my TV clothes into blue jeans, a sweater, and boots. I might have to move quickly, and I wanted to be ready. I walked down the hall to the family room. Taylor and the boys were watching *Blazing Saddles*. It was the beans-around-the-campfire scene, and Taylor was roaring.

"Pete, I need your car keys," I said.

"They're in my jacket pocket," he said. "Can I use your car?"

"No," I said. "Not tonight. Stick close to home, would you?"

Peter looked up from the screen. "You look kind of intense. Are you okay?"

"I'm fine," I said, and I hoped I sounded more certain than I felt.

I walked back upstairs and down the hall to the front door. Through the window, I could see the silver Audi parked down the street about half a block. It had started to rain, and the pavement looked slick. Peter's jacket was hanging on the coat-rack. I found the keys, then I looked again at the jacket. It was an Eddie Bauer, rainproof, with a hood I could pull over my head. I put the jacket on. When I pulled up the hood, it covered the sides of my face. Peter's book-bag was on the floor, and I picked it up and slung it over my shoulder. The empty book-bag gave me an idea. I went back up to my room, pulled the box of Jenny's mementoes out from under the bed and slipped it into the book-bag. Downstairs, I checked my reflection in the hall mirror. In the dark and with my head down, I could pass for Pete. At least that's what I was hoping.

There was no point in delaying. I opened the front door and ran towards Pete's car. I didn't look in the direction of the Audi until I got to the corner of Albert Street. When I checked my rear-view mirror, the Audi was right where I left it, and I sighed with relief.

Regina's streets were busy, but there weren't many cars on the Trans-Canada. It was 8:30 on a Saturday night, three weeks before Christmas. People had places to be; no one would be driving in this strange winter rain storm unless they had to.

The rain. If the temperature dropped five degrees, the highway would be lethal. But, as my grandmother used to say, there's no point jumping off a bridge till you come to it. I tested Veronica's brakes a couple of times. They held. For better or for worse, I was on my way, and I had to think about what I was going to do when I got there.

I tried to formulate a plan. The objective was clear enough: I had to get Jenny out. It was the obstacles that were shadowy. I didn't know what I'd be walking into. Jenny had been able to phone. That meant she was alone. But if she was alone, why hadn't she run away? I couldn't get the pieces to fit.

As I drove onto the overpass by Belle Plaine, the car started to make a gasping sound. I looked at the gas gauge, and uttered an expletive my grandmother would not have approved of. The needle was hovering a hair's breadth away from empty. I patted the dashboard. "Come on, Veronica," I said, "Pete says you're one hot car. You can do this. You can make it." She continued to climb, but she was coughing badly. I tried to visualize the highway ahead. Chubby's Café and Gas Station was along here somewhere, but where? The rain continued to fall. The car continued to cough. Then, from the top of the overpass, I could see a fuzz of light on the right-hand side of the road. "Please let that be Chubby's," I said as Veronica coasted down the overpass onto the highway.

I was in luck. The café was less than a kilometre down the road, and Veronica made it right to the tanks before she coughed her last. Chubby himself filled her up. When he'd finished, I gave him my credit card and showed him my map.

"I have to get down there tonight," I said. "Do you know of a shortcut I could take?"

He took the map between his thumb and forefinger and walked inside where there was light. I thought I had never seen a human being move so slowly. When he came back, he handed me my credit card and the map.

"No shortcut, not in this weather," he said. "Just stay on the highway till you see the sodium sulphate plant." He gave me my credit card. "Jeez, just a minute, I forgot something," he said, then he turned and lumbered heavily towards the bright lights of the café. When he came out, he reached through the window. "Merry Christmas," he said, and he handed me a candy cane.

"Same to you," I said. I finished the candy cane just as I came to the turnoff for the Vermilion Hills. As soon as I hit the grid road, I knew I was in trouble. The car started to fishtail on the wet gravel, and by the time I straightened it, I could feel the sweat running down my back.

There was no consolation when I looked up into the hills. In the spring, the Vermilion Hills are as beautiful as their name. In the summer, they're alive with wildflowers. But in the winter, stripped of the softness of grass and flower, they are primordial and terrifying. That night, as I followed the hairpin curves of the dark road that took me into their heart, I was engulfed by a fear that seemed as atavistic as it was intense. Then, out of nowhere, a deer leapt across the road ahead of me, and I felt the fear lift. I wasn't alone.

I held the map up to the light on the dashboard. I was almost there. A kilometre farther, I saw the yard-light of the cabin glowing dimly in the dark and the mist. I pulled

onto the shoulder of the road, and began to walk. I wasn't
sure who was in the cabin, but there didn't seem to be much
point in announcing myself.

The rain was cool on my face, and the air was fresh.
I took some deep breaths. "I'm coming, Jenny," I said, and
I felt strong and clear-headed. I stood for a moment, getting my bearings. The cabin was set back about a hundred
metres from the road. It was isolated. The last lights I'd
seen had been fifteen kilometres back. This was short-
grass country, and there weren't many trees around, but
there was a windbreak of what looked like caraganas on
the north side of the cabin. It would be a place to run if I
needed one.

I could feel the adrenalin rush as I started for the cabin.
The curtains were pulled tight, but as I moved closer I could
hear music inside; it sounded like a radio or a TV. I told
myself it was Lolita Temple's choir and that, if they were
singing, nothing bad could happen to me.

I went to the front door and knocked. For a moment, the
only sound was the music, then I heard someone coming
towards me. When the door opened, I was facing Tess
Malone.

"I knew you'd come for Jenny," she said.

"Where is she?" I asked.

"Dead," Tess said, and she turned away from me.

"But the phone call . . ."

Tess looked ghastly. Her hair, always so carefully
sprayed in place, had come loose. In fact, it seemed as if
everything about her had come loose. Behind the thick
lenses of her glasses, Tess's blue eyes always seemed perceptive, but this night she wasn't wearing her glasses, and
her eyes looked unfocussed. Even her body looked slack
and shapeless.

"What happened to Jenny?" I said.

"She changed her mind," Tess said.

On the television, a child began to sing "The Little
Drummer Boy." I glanced towards the set, hoping to see the

familiar images of the Nationtv Christmas party, but the picture on the screen of the old black and white TV was so fuzzy, all I could make out was the shape of the singing child. It was a slender reed to cling to.

Tess went over and turned the sound down, then she started back towards the couch. She moved slowly. There was an open fireplace, with a roaring fire, and the room was stiflingly hot, but she pulled an afghan around herself.

"Tess, you've got to tell me what's going on here."

She lowered herself onto the couch. Beside it, there was a metal TV table. On it were the leftovers from a frozen dinner, an overflowing ashtray, and two packs of du Mauriers. Tess reached for a cigarette and lit it. I took the ashtray to the fireplace and dumped it, and came back to her.

"There's a bottle of rye over there," Tess said.

"Forget the rye," I said. "We have to get out of here."

She dragged deeply on her cigarette. "I'm in more danger out there than I am here. Get the rye, Jo. I'm tired of secrets. I want to talk."

"Tess, we have to go to the police. I don't think you understand everything that's happened."

When I told her about Julie's dark reference to a skeleton and the initials opposite the sixth Commandment on Kevin's list, Tess sagged, and when she spoke, her voice was small. "It isn't the way you think it is," she murmured.

"Then it's true."

"Yes, but . . . Jo, please let me tell you what happened."

"Tess, are we safe here?"

She laughed. It wasn't a nice laugh. "As safe as anyone is anywhere." She gestured towards the whisky. "Please, Jo."

I picked up the rye. There were no clean glasses. I took a dipper of water from the corner, rinsed two of the cleaner glasses, and poured rye into them.

I took a sip of my whisky. The warmth helped. "Okay," I said, "start talking."

Tess pulled her afghan tight around her. "How does Julie find out these things?"

I shook my head. "It doesn't matter. All that matters is that Julie's information was right. What happened to Jenny Rybchuk, Tess?"

"She died. It was six years ago, Jo, and it wasn't a murder – at least not the part we were involved in. It was an accident. A terrible, terrible accident."

"What are you talking about, 'the part we were involved in'?"

Tess went on as if she hadn't heard me. "It should never have happened," she said. "Everything was going so well. Jess was a perfect baby. Gary and Sylvie were there when he was born, did you know that?"

I shook my head.

"They were the most beautiful family. Jane and I went out to the airport when they brought the baby home. They were so happy. We thought Jenny was happy, too. It seemed as if everything had just fallen into place. Jenny had been writing to her father all summer. He hated having her away from him, but the plant had laid him off because of his drinking. He was having serious money problems, and he was relieved Jenny was paying her own way. Jess was born the first week in September, so Jenny was able to visit her father in Chaplin before she started university in Saskatoon. Everything went off like clockwork . . ." Her voice trailed off, and her eyes were remote.

"Except . . . ," I prompted.

Tess's voice was filled with pain. "Except Jenny couldn't forget her son. She started phoning Sylvie and Gary. At first, they didn't mind; in fact, I think they were pleased that she cared so deeply about his welfare. They told her about how much weight Jess was gaining and what he was doing, but no matter how much they told her, it was never enough. She hungered for her child, Joanne. It was that simple. Nothing could satisfy her but having him back. When the calls got truly desperate, Sylvie asked me to go to Saskatoon and talk to Jenny."

"And you went?" I asked.

"Of course I went, Jo. I was responsible." She spit out the last word with loathing.

"You tried to do the right thing," I said weakly.

"That doesn't exempt me from responsibility," she said, and, for the first time that evening, there was something of the old Tess in her voice. "Intention doesn't count, Jo. Just results. And the results of what I had done to Jenny Rybchuk were devastating. She wasn't the same girl I'd seen in Regina. She was thin and ill and driven. She said she had made a terrible mistake, and I had to help her get Jess back."

Tess lit a fresh cigarette off the stub of her first one. She dragged deeply and coughed till the tears came.

"Jo, I was so cruel to her. I told her she'd made an agreement, that life was about choices, and that Sylvie and Gary could give Jess a far better life than she could dream of. I said it was time for her to face facts, and walk away from the past.

"Until I die, I'll never forget the look of betrayal in that girl's eyes. Do you know what she said to me?" Tess's voice broke. "She said, 'You're the one who told me a baby isn't just a collection of cells a woman can walk away from.' After that, there was nothing more I could say except good-bye. I turned my back on her, Jo. It was a terrible abnegation of responsibility, and a fatal one."

I could hardly bring myself to say the words. "Tess, Jenny didn't commit suicide, did she?"

Tess's laugh was bitter. "No, she didn't commit suicide. God forgive me, maybe it would have been better if she had."

"What happened?"

"She went to the baby's father, and asked him to help her." Tess looked toward the fire. Finally, she said, "The father was Kevin Tarpley."

"Kevin Tarpley," I repeated stupidly. "I don't understand."

"There's nothing to understand. It was just one of those

sad, stupid things. Maureen and her mother were visiting relatives for Christmas. Kevin was supposed to keep an eye on their house. You know, make sure the furnace was on and the pipes didn't burst. Apparently, one night during the holidays, Henry Rybchuk got drunk and started in on Jenny. She ran next door, and Kevin just happened to be there."

"But when Jenny found out she was pregnant, she didn't tell Kevin."

"No. She didn't tell him until I turned her away. That was at the end of November. A week later, Gary called. Someone had taken Jess from his carriage on the porch of their house. Sylvie was in Toronto making arrangements for a show. Gary said they put Jess in the same spot every afternoon because it was protected, and he thrived on all the fresh air and sunshine. That day he'd only been out for a few minutes. Gary was pretty sure Jenny must have been watching the house. She'd left a note, saying she knew that legally she still had time to change her mind, and she had. She wrote that she was sorry and she would be in touch.

"We didn't hear a word about Jess till the next day at noon. I wanted to call the police, but Gary was sure Jenny would come to her senses. We knew the baby was safe. There was that at least, but the wait was still terrible. Sylvie and Gary had wanted a child for so long. Gary and I sat in the living room and talked about Jess and all the plans they'd had for him . . . It was like a death . . . There was that sense of loss, and the feeling that nothing would ever be the same again.

"And then at noon, the phone rang . . ."

"Jenny kept her word," I said.

Tess picked up the bottle of rye and half filled her glass. "No," she said, "it wasn't Jenny. It was Maureen Gault."

Thirteen

I THOUGHT we'd been delivered from hell," Tess said. "Maureen Gault introduced herself as Jenny's best friend, and she said Jenny was ready to talk. You can imagine how desperate Gary was to get Jess back before Sylvie came home. From the time Sylvie and Gary realized it was unlikely they'd ever have a child, their marriage had pretty much been a disaster."

"Gary's promiscuity didn't help," I said, and I found it hard even to say his name.

"Sylvie wasn't blameless, Jo. She was so angry at Gary for failing her. People do strange things when they're hurting. But she was crazy about Jess, and Gary was counting on him to give them a new start."

"That's a pretty heavy burden for a baby."

Tess nodded her head in agreement. "It is, but Jess seemed to make everything right just by existing. Gary asked me to go with him when he met Jenny. I think he was afraid of dealing with her by himself. You know how Gary's always been about confrontation. I dreaded going, but I'd failed Jenny so badly in our last meeting that I felt I owed her some support. And, Jo, you have to believe me. When we drove out here, I was certain everything was going to work out."

"You came here?" I asked.

"Maureen said Jenny needed a private place to say good-bye to her son. Gary suggested his cabin. Hunting season had just opened, and Gary had been out to the cabin the week before. And since they'd be coming from Chaplin . . ."

"Why would they be coming from Chaplin?"

Tess sighed. "Because, according to Maureen, Jenny wanted to show Henry Rybchuk his grandson before she gave him up forever."

"But he didn't know Jenny had a baby."

Tess's voice was sharp with exasperation. "I know the story is full of holes, but don't forget, all this happened before we knew Maureen Gault. When she said Jenny had told her father about the baby, we had no reason to doubt her. The truth is we wanted to believe her. Anyway, the plan was that, after they'd seen old Mr. Rybchuk, Maureen and Jenny would drive back from Chaplin and meet us at the cabin."

I stood up to take off my jacket. The room was oppressively hot, and I could feel my shirt sticking to my back. "Tess, could I open a window? I'm dying in here."

She shivered, but she nodded. "I've had this flu."

I looked at her. Her skin had an unhealthy sheen, and her lips looked dry and cracked.

"I think I should drive you into Chaplin to the doctor," I said.

Her eyes grew wide with fear. "No doctors. No police, I told you."

"All right," I said, "but I'm going to stay here with you tonight. Just let me call and tell my family I'm okay."

I went to the phone and dialled our number. As the phone was ringing, I looked around the cabin. I'd asked Ian once what it was like. He'd laughed and said, "I think you have to have a certain testosterone level to appreciate its charms." The cabin was shabby, in fact, but comfortable looking. One end of the large main room was obviously used as the living area. In front of the old sectional couch where Tess huddled, shivering beneath an incongruously cheerful afghan, there was a coffee table scarred by cigarette burns and rings from a score of drink glasses. The couch was on one side of a big stone fireplace, and a couple of over-stuffed easy chairs were on the other. The far end of the room was an eating area with a small refrigerator, a stove, and a painted wooden table and chairs. On the same side as the kitchen, there was a door to what must have been a bedroom. The main room was panelled in some dark wood. There were pictures of hunting dogs on one wall, and a number of hunting rifles mounted in racks on the wall by the door. I recognized one of them, a small 30-30 bush gun. Peter had militated unsuccessfully for a rifle like that the Christmas he was fifteen. I was remembering all the ads from hunting magazines that had littered our house that year, when Pete answered the phone. He sounded drowsy.

"It's me," I said. "Peter, did I wake you up?"

"It's okay, Mum. I was watching *Barbarella*. I must have nodded off after Jane Fonda melted the cables on Duran Duran's sex machine." He yawned. "What's going on? Inspector Kequahtooway was here looking for you. He seemed pretty worked up when I said you'd gone out."

"If he comes back, tell him I had to go out to the Vermilion Hills."

"The Vermilion Hills. What's out there?"

"An old friend in trouble," I said. "Look, I'll explain when I get home. Get the kids off to church tomorrow morning, would you?"

"Does that mean I have to go with them?"

"Of course," I said. "How else would they get there? Goodnight, Pete, and thanks. I'm glad you're home."

I found a towel, poured some water from the dipper onto it, sat beside Tess, and wiped her face. "Do you have aspirin or anything here? You're burning up, Tess."

She shook her head. "I'm all right. Just let me finish. I can't hold on to this any more."

I opened the window on the other side of the room a crack, and took a breath. "Okay, Tess," I said. "I'm listening."

She pulled the afghan closer. "Maureen Gault had lied to everyone. Jenny had no intention of giving up that baby. She'd brought Jess to the cabin so Sylvie and Gary could say goodbye to him. She really was a very sweet girl."

"Was," I repeated numbly. It was hard to think of Jenny Rybchuk in the past tense. My chest tightened. I didn't want to hear the end of the story.

Oblivious, Tess went on. "That was the first time I met Maureen Gault. She was terrifying. She'd created all this confusion and misery, and she didn't care. Jo, it was as if the pain charged her up, filled her with energy. She couldn't sit still. She kept moving around the room with this little smile on her face. Gary and Jenny were over where you are, by the window, and I was sitting on a chair close to the fireplace. It was December; the cabin was chilly, and I'd moved the chair so the baby would be warm."

Tess covered her mouth with her hand as if she wanted physically to block the words she was about to say.

"It happened so fast. When he realized Jenny planned to keep Jess, Gary said something ugly to her. She looked so hurt. I remember thinking she looked like a child who'd been punished for no reason. Then she came towards me to get the baby. Gary pushed her. Jo, I know he didn't mean to hurt her. He was just trying to get to Jess, but Jenny lost her balance. There was a sheepskin rug on the hearth. She slipped on it and fell against the fireplace."

Tess pointed towards a long piece of fieldstone at the edge of the mantel. "That caught her in the temple. Gary went to help her up. I was furious with him. I said something like 'Now look you what you've done,' but, Jo, I thought she'd just fallen. Then Gary turned her over, and I saw her eyes." Tess's own eyes were dark with horror.

"The sheepskin underneath her head was soaked with blood. I couldn't move. Gary looked as if he was paralyzed, too. I guess we were both in shock. But Maureen Gault wasn't. She walked over to the fireplace and picked up a poker that was leaning against the hearth. Then she said, 'You shouldn't have fucked my guy, Jenny,' and she raised the poker and smashed it down on Jenny's head."

I closed my eyes. I knew what Jenny's head must have looked like after Maureen Gault was through with her.

Tess was crying now. "When she was done, Maureen went over and put her arm around Gary. She said, 'From now on, when you look at that sweet baby of yours, remember that if Little Mo hadn't taken charge, little Jess would be long gone.'

"All I could think of was getting the baby out of that room. I took him into the bedroom and closed the door. I stayed there all night. Gary came in once, for a sheet. They needed it to wrap Jenny's body. I remember I heard the door to the outside open, and a car drove out. When I was sure they were gone, I went into the living room and got Jess's baby bag. There was a bottle of formula in it, and I fed him. I was back in the bedroom when I heard them drive in. After a while, I smelled wool burning. I guess that was the sheepskin. Finally, it was over. Gary came in and we drove home."

Tess looked at me in wonder. "Jo, you won't believe this, but Maureen Gault stood on the porch and waved to us when we left."

I walked over to the counter, picked up the rye bottle, and poured some into my glass. When I turned to ask Tess if she wanted some whisky, I saw that she'd closed her eyes. She was either sleeping or pretending to sleep. It didn't matter. I'd heard enough.

I turned off the overhead light. The room was stifling. I pulled my chair back and opened the window an inch more. I could see Pete's book-bag by the door where I'd dropped it. The flap had fallen open, and I could see the corner of the box of mementoes I'd brought for Jenny. I breathed in the fresh night air and tried to think of nothing. After a few minutes, I heard the sound of Tess's breathing, deep and rhythmic.

I couldn't sleep. I stared at the fire for what seemed like hours, thinking about my husband and about the dancing ballerinas on the box that contained all that was left of Jenny Rybchuk's life. And I thought about Maureen Gault with her arm raised and her derisive smile. Finally, exhausted, I must have drifted off.

It was the cold air that awakened me. I'd been dreaming about the cabin, and the rifles on the wall, and a ballerina who came in and said Anton Chekhov believed that if there was a gun on the wall in Act I, it had to be fired by the end of Act III.

At first, when I opened my eyes and saw Gary Stephens standing in front of me, I thought I was still dreaming. He was wearing a wide-brimmed rancher's hat and a yellow slicker, and he looked like the kind of mythic figure who would appear in a dream. Then I saw the rifle in his hands, and I knew this was real. I looked at the place on the wall where the rifles were hanging. The rack where the small bush gun had been was empty. It took me a minute to put it all together, but when I did, I knew Act III had begun.

Gary was looking at me intently. "Sylvie said the cops were over tonight asking questions. I thought I'd better get out here and make sure Tess was all right."

"She's all right," I said. "Put down the gun, Gary. I don't think you're in much danger from two unarmed women."

He lay the gun on the window sill beside him. It was still in easy reach, but at least it wasn't pointed at me. Gary moved closer. "What did Tess tell you?"

"Everything," I said.

"You've got to hear my side of it, babe."

Suddenly I was furious. "I think I've already figured out your side of it . . . *babe*. I know what you've done. I just don't understand how you could do it."

His voice was both seductive and pleading. "Then listen

to how it was for me. Please, Jo. Please." He paused. "For old times' sake."

"All right, Gary," I said. "I'll listen. For old times' sake."

He arranged his face into an expression of boyish sincerity. "I appreciate the chance, Jo. I really do." He took a deep breath. "None of it would have happened if Sylvie and I had been able to have kids. I know how you love your family, so you must understand it was a pretty hard thing for me to accept."

The narcissism grated. "So you coped," I said, "by having sex with every woman in sight, including your own sister-in-law, and by stealing a young woman's baby?"

He flinched. "All right, all right," he said. "I was a bastard, but Sylvie was no prize. She wouldn't stop talking about my problem – it was my problem, you know. Anyway, Sylvie wouldn't stop discussing it. It was the same thing every night. Finally, I just stopped coming home. Then, heartbroken but brave, my wife threw herself into her photography. She went down to Chaplin and shot *Prairiegirl*. That pretty well fucked up my political career. Then when she got tired of being the martyr, she decided our marriage was over, and she wanted a divorce."

"My God, if you hated Sylvie that much, why did you want to stay with her?" I asked.

"Because as lousy it was, it was the only life I had. Jo, what else was I supposed to do? When I was in politics, I'd pretty much let my law practice slide. After my wife's book came out, I didn't have much future in politics. Sylvie had all that money. It didn't make much sense to walk away from it." He shrugged. "I don't know. Maybe I just didn't think it through. But it seemed possible that, if Sylvie had a baby, we could go on the way we had for years, leading separate lives."

"But not lives paid for by separate cheques," I said.

"No," he said. "There were no separate cheques."

"So Jess was just an investment in your future."

He looked down at his hands. "Maybe, at first," he said

softly. "But Jo, you've got to believe me. From the minute I saw Jess, everything changed. I held him when he was just seconds old. I think that was first moment in my life when I knew what people meant when they talked about loving someone. It was the best feeling I've ever known. But it didn't last." His beautiful blue eyes clouded with pain. "After Jenny passed away, it was hard for me even to be in the same room with Jess. I know how things look, Jo, but I'm not a monster. Every time I looked at my son, I could see Jenny's face. I'd try to block out the memories by getting drunk or by screwing some broad I hardly knew, but no matter what I did, I couldn't forget that night. I've suffered, too, Jo. I love Jess so much, but I can't hold him in my arms without remembering . . ."

As he always was when he talked about his son, Gary Stephens was transformed, and, for a moment, I felt myself responding to him. Then I remembered.

"Ian loved his children, too," I said.

He looked at me defiantly. "It wasn't my fault, Jo. Ian was the one who wouldn't leave it alone. That night at the party he told me he'd talked to Rybchuk, and he believed Rybchuk was telling the truth, that something had happened to Jenny. Ian said it didn't make sense that Jenny would say she was going to start a new life with her son, then disappear. I tried to tell him Jenny had probably just changed her mind, but he wouldn't listen. The old man had given him a picture of Jenny with Jess, and Ian was going to take it to the police." For a beat, Gary was silent. Then, in a voice full of wonder, he said, "Ian was always such a fucking boy scout."

"And the only way to stop the boy scout was to pay Maureen Gault to kill him," I said.

Gary recoiled as if I'd hit him. "For chrissakes, Jo. He was my friend. I would never have asked anyone to murder him. All I did was tell Maureen Gault that Ian was going to be a problem. What happened later wasn't my fault."

"The Becket defence," I said.

Gary's handsome face was blank. "I don't know what you're talking about."

"Didn't you ever study the Becket defence in law school, Gary? It was on the ethics course." I stood up and began moving towards him. "Since you seem to have forgotten anything you ever knew about ethics, I'll help you out.

"It's an old case, and it explores the question of culpability. A king is having trouble with a priest who was once his friend but who's begun meddling in things the king doesn't want meddled with. The king calls in four of his most loyal knights and says, 'Will no one rid me of that meddlesome priest?' You'll notice he's careful not to instruct them to do anything wrong, but the knights aren't stupid. They know what the king wants, so they kill the priest. The king, of course, is innocent. It's the knights who did the dirty work. They're the guilty ones. Or are they?" I stepped closer to him. "What do you think, babe? Who's culpable here?"

Gary reached over and picked up his gun. "I'm not guilty of Ian's murder, Jo. The others were just a waste of skin. They deserved to die. But Ian was my, my friend."

On the couch, Tess was stirring.

I raised my voice to awaken her. "Gary, when you told Maureen Gault, 'Ian is going to be a problem,' you knew what you were doing. How much did you have to pay her to get her to kill him?"

He laughed. "You can't know much about Maureen Gault to ask a question like that. Killing was a pleasure for her. When I called her the night of the caucus party and told her Ian was going to the cops, she had a plan worked out before I hung up. All I had to do was drive her to Swift Current. She said she'd find Ian at the funeral, get a ride back to Regina with him, and talk him out of going to the police."

I could feel the rage rising. "Gary, you knew she wouldn't just talk to him. You were in this very room when Maureen Gault smashed her best friend's head in with a poker. You knew what she was capable of."

He looked at me miserably. "I didn't mean for her to kill him. Can't you believe me?"

"No," I said, and my voice was thin with fury.

He took a step towards me. "I loved Ian," he said. "You know that. I loved him."

"No," I said.

His face seemed to crumple. Finally, he whispered, "Can you forgive me, Jo? You can, can't you?"

In the firelight, I could see the tears in his eyes, but I didn't pity him, and, for what seemed like a long time, I didn't answer him. When the words did come, they seemed to tear themselves from a part of me that was beyond reason.

"No!" I shouted. "No! No! No!"

As the final *no!* hung in the air, a strange sort of calm filled the room. Gary's eyes stayed fixed on mine, then a smile started to form at the corners of his mouth. As slowly as a man moving in a dream, he swung the muzzle of the gun under his chin. For one crazed moment I wondered if the gun was loaded. Then Gary pulled the trigger, and the world exploded.

The next minutes are a jumble. Tess crawled towards the place where Gary had fallen, and I think I went to the phone to call for help. I'm not sure. What I remember are the smells: the hot metal smell of the gun and the smoky smell of the fire and the sweet, fetid smell of blood. And I remember looking down at the body to see if anything at all was left of Gary Stephens's perfect face.

Then the front door opened, and Alex Kequahtooway was there. So were a lot of other cops. The nightmare was over.

It was close to dawn when Alex and I left the cabin. Minutes after the police arrived, a squad car had taken Tess back to the city. Alex had asked if I wanted to go with her, but I hadn't. I'd waited six years, and I wanted to see this through to the end. The forensic specialists were there within an hour, and I sat by the window and watched as they measured and took photographs and put evidence into bags. When they were finished, they left, too. A few minutes later, an ambulance arrived to take Gary Stephens's body back to Regina. I stood at the door as the attendants lifted Gary's body onto the stretcher and carried him outside. As the ambulance pulled onto the grid road and started towards the highway, I turned to Alex. "Is it over now?" I asked.

He nodded and picked up my jacket. I put it on, grabbed Peter's book-bag, and stepped onto the front porch. It was the morning of December 6, but it felt like a spring day. The air, cleansed by the winter rain, was warm on my face, and I could smell the earth.

I looked up towards the road. "Where's Veronica?" I said.

"I had one of the guys drive her back," he said. "I thought maybe you'd rather be a passenger this time out."

"Fair enough," I said.

"If you think you can eat, Chubby's Café makes great bacon and eggs."

"I can eat," I said.

"My car's over there," he said, pointing towards the stand of caraganas that had been planted as a windbreak. "Pretty snazzy for a cop, I know, but I've driven reserve cars all my life, and this was a present to me from me on my fortieth birthday."

"I've always wanted to ride in a silver Audi," I said.

He grinned. "Now's your chance."

When we got to the highway, I touched Alex's arm. "Can we stop for a minute? There's something I want to leave at the place where my husband died."

Alex pulled onto the shoulder. I opened the box of Jenny's mementoes, took out the photograph of her with Jess, and got out of the car. The gravel along the side of the highway was still wet from the rain. I knelt down and picked up a stone. It was smooth and cool to the touch. On Hallowe'en night, Hilda McCourt had told me about a poet who said sudden death spatters all we know of dénouement across the expedient and wicked stones. I walked further down the shoulder of the highway, picking up stones as I went. When my jacket pockets were full, I walked back to the place where Ian died and began arranging the stones in a circle. When the circle was complete, I put Jenny's picture in the middle and anchored its corners with stones. I tried to think of a prayer, but my mind was empty. Finally, I said, "I did the best I could," and I stood up. Bits of gravel stuck to the knees of my jeans, but I couldn't summon the energy to brush them off. Lightheaded from exhaustion and hunger, I started back to the Audi.

Alex leaned across to open the car door. "Unfinished business?" he asked.

I shook my head. "Not any more," I said. I snapped on my seatbelt, and Inspector Alex Kequahtooway and I drove east towards the rising sun and Chubby's Café.

Fourteen

By the time Alex and I got back to Regina, the kids were up, dressed, and eating breakfast. The sun was pouring through the kitchen window, and Angus was describing an amazing shot his friend, Camilo, had made at basketball practice the day before. Peter was arguing that nobody but Shaquille O'Neal could make a shot like that. Taylor, who knew nothing about basketball but who was second to none in her admiration for Camilo Rostoker, was saying that Camilo could do anything. They seemed so free of care, that I hesitated before I came into the room. I knew I was bringing ugliness with me.

As soon as they saw me, the kids fell silent. I didn't blame them. At Chubby's, I'd seen my reflection in the mirror behind the counter. My skin was ashen, and my eyes were red-rimmed and swollen. At the café I had looked like a woman teetering on the edge of shock. I doubted that my appearance had improved much since then.

I started to explain what had happened back at the cabin, but I didn't get far before the horror overwhelmed me. Alex touched my shoulder. "It's too soon," he said. "Go upstairs and get some sleep. I'll tell them."

Safe in my room, I peeled off my clothes and bundled them into the laundry hamper. When I stepped into the shower, I turned the water to hot, closed my eyes, and tried to forget. Ten minutes later, the bathroom was thick with steam, the water coming out of the faucet was cold, and I hadn't forgotten a thing. As I towelled off and headed for bed, I was sick with the fear that the memory of Gary Stephens's suicide would be an albatross I would always carry with me. When I opened the door to my bedroom, I saw that the drapes had been pulled, the phone on my bed-side table had been unplugged, and the bedspread had been turned down. Alex was sitting on the windowseat.

"Are you going to be okay?" he asked.

I nodded.

"Good," he said. "There are some things I should take care of down at headquarters, but I'll let the kids know where I'm going to be, and I'll be back around supper. Try to get some sleep."

I tried. All that day, I lay in the dark, listening to the life of my house go on around me, hushed and alien. Late in the afternoon, I opened my eyes and saw Alex standing in the doorway, his silhouette dark against the bright light of the hall.

"Do you want to talk?" he said.

"Not yet. You don't mind, do you?"

"I don't mind. I have to go back downtown, but there's take-out from Bamboo Village in the kitchen. Taylor made some pretty serious inroads on the almond prawns, but there's plenty of everything else."

"Thanks," I said.

"My pleasure," he said and closed the door.

After he left, I fell asleep. When I woke up, it was mid-night and I was hungry. I remembered the Chinese take-out and headed downstairs. Sadie and Rose were right on my heels. There had been too many upheavals in their old dog lives, and they were wary.

The cardboard containers from Bamboo Village were neatly stacked on the refrigerator shelf. I'd moved them to the counter and taken the lid off the carton that held the three almond prawns Taylor had left for me when I heard a knock at the front door.

It was Jane O'Keefe.

As soon as I opened the door, she stepped into the hall. She was still wearing her white hospital coat and her picture ID.

I touched her sleeve. "Are you making a house call?" I said.

Jane looked down at the white coat, bewildered. "I thought I'd taken this off and left it in my locker." Her shoulders slumped. "I'm sorry, Jo. I don't even know what I'm doing here. I was just driving around . . . I don't want to be alone tonight."

"Neither do I," I said. "Look, I was just going to have some Chinese food. There's plenty."

I opened two bottles of Great Western, and Jane and I filled our plates and sat down at the kitchen table. We ate in silence. When she was through, Jane said, "I don't think I've eaten since yesterday. There's been so much to deal with . . ."

"How's Jess?" I asked.

"Scared," she said. "Confused. Sad."

"And Sylvie?"

"She said her goodbyes to Gary a long time ago." Jane's voice went dead. "I wish I had. I was at the hospital this morning when they brought Gary and Tess in."

"Is Tess going to be all right?"

Jane shrugged. "Physically? She should be. It's pneumonia, but I think we got to her in time . . ."

"Did you see her?"

Jane shook her head. "No. But I saw Gary. I had a patient in emergency when they brought him in. It was just bad luck." She laughed. "Of course, when it came to Gary, if I hadn't had bad luck, I wouldn't have had any luck at all."

"I'm sorry," I said.

Jane picked up her fork and began tracing a pattern of

interlocking circles on her empty plate. She seemed mesmerized. Finally, she said, "At least he didn't suffer."

Images of Gary in the last seconds of his life flashed through my mind: the pleading in his eyes as he asked if I understood, if I forgave; the curious resignation with which he positioned the rifle in the soft flesh beneath his chin.

"No," I said, "he didn't suffer."

Jane's fork hadn't stopped moving. Round and round, round and round it went. "Did he say anything at the end?" she asked softly.

"Let it go, Jane."

"I can't spend the rest of my life not knowing what happened." Her voice was thick with misery. "I loved him, Jo. I need to know why he killed himself."

She deserved the truth. "Gary killed himself because I wouldn't forgive him for killing Ian," I said.

Jane's head jerked up, and her eyes were bright with anger. "That's bullshit," she said. "Is that what he told you? That it was your fault?" She raked her fork across the plate. "That bastard. Trying to blame you. Trying to leave you with the guilt. Don't let him do it, Jo. Gary didn't die because you wouldn't forgive him. He died because . . ." She looked around wildly as if searching for an answer. Finally, she said, "He died because he'd backed himself into a corner, and there was no woman there to show him the way out." She threw the fork down and stood up with such violence that she knocked the table against me. "It wasn't your fault. And it wasn't mine. It was his fault." She was crying now. "If just once that son of a bitch hadn't taken the path of least resistance, he could have had a terrific life."

After Jane left, I couldn't get her epitaph for the man she had once loved out of my head. I don't know how long I sat at my kitchen table thinking about Gary Stephens. There were questions about him that would never be answered, but one fact was incontrovertible. Gary's weakness, his inability to withstand the lure of the easy way out, had altered the course of all our lives. It was hard not to think of what might have been, and for many hours in that endless night, I didn't even try.

During the next week, I did a pretty good imitation of a woman who was getting her life back to normal. I finished off my end-of-term marking on Wednesday. To celebrate, I went to the art gallery and bought a poster of a Harold Town self-portrait to put in Hilda's Christmas stocking. Thursday, Taylor and I made shortbread. Friday, I invited Alex to come over to meet Greg and Mieka and eat shrimp gumbo. I moved through all of this with the brisk assurance of someone who was putting the past behind her and getting on with her life. Then, on Saturday morning, Tess Malone phoned to say she wanted to see me, and I crumbled.

I drove down to Regina General just after lunch. The day was overcast and mild, and there were pools of standing water all over the parking lot. A young woman in a pink quilted housecoat was standing outside the entrance to the old wing. Her body had the soft shapelessness of a new mother. She was smoking.

When I passed her to go into the building, she grinned. "Unbelievable weather, eh?"

"Unbelievable," I agreed.

"Lucky, too," she added as she took a deep drag of her cigarette, "otherwise it'd either be give up these, or stand out here and freeze my buns off."

I climbed the back stairs up to Tess's room on the fourth floor. The stairwell smelled of hospital cooking and disinfectant. Things were better when I got up to the ward. Someone had made an effort to make the area festive. There was an artificial tree in the lounge, garlands of red and gold foil over the patients' doorways, and a huge pot of poinsettias at the nurses' station. It was cheerful, but as I walked down the corridor to Tess's room, I was far from merry.

Tess met me at the door to her room. She was wearing the blue cotton robe the hospital provides for its patients, and her feet were encased in blue paper slippers. She looked ten pounds thinner and twenty years older than she had looked the night of Howard's dinner. There was a package of cigarettes in her hand.

When she saw me, she smiled guiltily. "I was just going out for a smoke," she said.

"Tess, you're just getting over pneumonia."

"Don't lecture me, Jo. Please."

I embraced her. "Okay," I said. "I won't lecture. I'll even come with you. We can talk outside. But you have to wear your coat."

We took the elevator down, and I followed her to the steps where I'd seen the girl in the pink robe. As soon as she was out of the hospital, Tess lit up and inhaled deeply. Then she turned to me. "I can't stop thinking about them," she said.

"Them?" I asked.

She drew on her cigarette again. "All the ones who died."

"I can't stop thinking about them, either," I said.

"Maybe it'll be better after Gary's funeral."

"Maybe," I said. "When is it?"

"After the police are through with the body, I guess," she said, and her eyes filled with tears.

"Tess, perhaps you're not ready to talk about this yet."

"I thought there'd be things you'd want to know," she said.

"I guess by now I know most of it," I said. "The one thing I don't know is how Ian got involved in the first place."

Tess smiled sadly. "Ian got involved because Henry Rybchuk believed he was an honest man. That's what he told me the night of the caucus office party. He said 'the rest of you I wouldn't give a rat's turd for, but Kilbourn's different. He won't give a shit how many of you are involved in this. He'll help me find my daughter.'"

"And he was right," I said. Tess flinched, and I hurried on. "But that night at the party wasn't the first time you talked to Henry Rybchuk."

"No, it wasn't the first time," she said. "Henry Rybchuk came to Beating Heart the week before Christmas. He was already in a terrible state. Maureen had concocted some story about Jenny having to take the baby to Saskatoon for medical tests. That had put him off for a while, but when the days went by, and he still hadn't heard from Jenny, he called the place where she lived in Saskatoon. They told him she hadn't been there since early December. That's when he came to me."

"How did he know about you?"

"Jenny told him. When she told him about the baby, she told him everything. I guess she wanted him to know she'd acted responsibly about her pregnancy and Jess's birth."

"So Henry Rybchuk knew about Sylvie and Gary."

"He knew about them, all right. He'd gone to their house before he'd come to Beating Heart. He'd been trying to find somebody at home there for two days, but they were away. That empty house must have driven him over the edge. He was convinced Sylvie and Gary had taken Jenny and her baby away so he couldn't get to them."

"What did you do?"

"I lied. I told him I had no idea where Jenny was. I said I'd met Jenny once, when she'd come to Beating Heart in April, but I hadn't seen her since. He kept after me for a while, but I kept stonewalling. Finally, he seemed to realize he couldn't force an answer out of me, and he left."

"And you didn't see him again till that night at the party."

Tess shook her head. "No, I didn't. But Gary did. Henry Rybchuk came to their house Christmas night. Luckily, Sylvie was upstairs with the baby. Rybchuk was drunk. He had a picture of Jenny and her baby sitting on Santa's knee. Gary said he waved it in Gary's face and said, 'for the love of God, give me back my girl and her baby.' Gary was beside himself. He couldn't call the police, and it was only a matter of time before Sylvie came back downstairs. Then a woman walked by the house and asked Gary if she should call the police. Of course, that terrified Gary, but apparently it terrified Henry Rybchuk even more. He took off."

Tess lit a fresh cigarette from the stub of her first. "The next day he was waiting when Ian came to his office."

"And the endgame began," I said.

Tess covered my hand with hers. "I've tried to make amends. After Jenny and Ian died, I knew I had to give my life to Beating Heart. Since then, I've saved a hundred lives, Jo."

I walked Tess back to the elevator. When it came, she shook off my offer to go back upstairs with her, and she stepped inside. Just as the elevator doors began to close, she said, "It wasn't enough, was it?"

I was lucky. The doors closed before I had to come up with an answer.

On Monday, when I walked into the kitchen and turned on the radio, the announcer said that Gary Stephens's funeral was taking place that morning. I thought of what Tess had said, and I hoped she was right. Maybe once Gary was laid to rest, we'd all find some peace.

I was having my first cup of coffee and savouring the quiet when Taylor came down to breakfast, carrying her cat. As she did every morning, she handed him to me while she got his food out of the cupboard and refilled his water dish. As he did every morning, the cat stiffened at my touch and stuck his claws through the material of my robe. Our time together was, it seemed, agony for both of us. Taylor was just about to shake the dry food into his bowl, when the phone rang. "Don't let him down till I get the food in the bowl," she said, and she scampered off to see who was calling.

I tried to shift the cat's position. "Bad luck for both of us, bub," I said, "but she won't be long." With my free hand, I pulled the morning paper closer. Gary Stephens's picture was on the bottom of the front page with the details of his funeral and a précis of the news that had been our breakfast fare all week.

When Taylor hung up, I turned the paper over so she

wouldn't see the picture. She poured the food into the cat bowl.

"Who was that on the phone?" I asked.

She took the cat from me, and I could see his body go limp with joy. "Jess isn't going to school," Taylor said. "He's going to his dad's funeral." As she poured her juice and got her cereal, she was uncharacteristically quiet.

Finally, she asked, "Who goes to a funeral?"

"A person's family," I said. "His friends. The people who loved him."

"There were a lot of people at my mother's funeral," she said.

"A lot of people loved your mother," I said. "And a lot of people respected her work."

She rested her spoon against her cereal bowl thoughtfully. "Do you think there'll be a lot of people at Jess's dad's funeral?"

"No," I said, "I don't think there'll be many people there at all."

Taylor finished eating, then she got up from the table and put her bowl with the milk she always saved for her cat on the floor. "I was scared at my mother's funeral," she said.

"Of what?" I asked.

"Of what was going to happen next," she said. The cat licked up the milk. Taylor took her bowl to the sink and ran the hot water on it. "Jo, I think we should go to that funeral today."

"I don't think so, T," I said.

For a long time she didn't say anything. When she turned her face was strained and white. "If you died, I'd want Jess there," she said.

Three hours later, Taylor and I were walking up the centre aisle of Lakeview United Church. I'd been right about the crowd. I saw some familiar faces: Lorraine Bellegarde, Craig Evanson, a few people I knew from the Legislature, some members of the media, but most of the blond ash pews were empty. The band of mourners was small, too. Sylvie and Jane and, between them, Jess, looking small and sad in his new suit.

When I saw Jess, I thought of what Alex had told me about the police investigation. Everything they turned up had substantiated their theory that, for the last weeks of his life, Gary was a man possessed by his need to keep his son. The letter Kevin Tarpley had sent to Gary was in a box of unfiled correspondence Lorraine Bellegarde had packed when Gary had moved out of his office. Alex said the letter had been only three sentences long. Kevin had printed out Exodus 20:13 – the sixth Commandment: "Thou shalt not commit murder." He had promised Gary that, if he asked Jesus to forgive him, he would gain eternal salvation. And then Kevin had written a final and fatal sentence in which he told Gary he could no longer let his son be raised by a man who had sinned as Gary had sinned. There was a receipt from the private airline that had flown Gary to Prince Albert on Hallowe'en and brought him back to Nationtv in time to do the promotion for Howard's dinner. There was a bank statement showing that Gary had withdrawn all the cash in his business account the day after Hallowe'en. The amount wasn't large. Certainly, it was nowhere near the amount of money Maureen Gault had been flashing when she'd made the offer to buy Ray-elle's beauty salon.

It had taken the police a while to find the source of Maureen's bonanza. When they questioned the people Gary knew, a sad picture of Gary's activities in the days before Maureen's death emerged. He had gone to everyone he knew asking for money. He'd been so desperate he hadn't even bothered to fabricate a story. He just said he was in trouble. Most of the people Gary had gone to had already bailed him out when he'd skimmed his legal accounts after Ian died, and they turned him down flat.

Only one person was willing to help, and her identity was no surprise to me. Lorraine Bellegarde owned a small house on Wallace Street. She had been proud of the fact that it was paid for "right down to the last nail," but she had mortgaged it for Gary.

Alex had been the one to interview her, and her behaviour had baffled him. "She seems like such a sensible woman," he'd said. "Do you think he just laid on the charm or what?" I told him that Lorraine had been around Gary long enough to be immune to his charm. Then I remembered the story of how Gary hadn't let Lorraine get rid of the prostitutes who'd been using his car as pick-up point. "I guess she decided he deserved a hassle-free zone," I'd said.

Alex had shaken his head in disgust. "What kind of guy would let a woman mortgage her house for him? He must have really been a piece of work."

"He was that, all right," I said. And we didn't talk of the matter again.

In the church, Jess laid his head against his mother's arm. The service was generic: the Lord's prayer, the twenty-third Psalm, a few mournful hymns. The young minister spoke obliquely about the mysteries of the human heart and seemed relieved when he was finished.

So was I. Gary had been cremated, and, despite everything, the cloth-covered urn on the altar was painful to contemplate. When the minister said the closing prayer and invited us all to join the family in a reception room at the back of the church, Taylor looked at me expectantly. I shook my head. I'd had enough. When we came into the vestibule, Sylvie and Jane were talking to a man from the funeral home. I headed for the door, hoping Taylor and I could slip out of the church unnoticed. But Sylvie spotted me and came over.

She seemed preternaturally calm, and I wondered if Jane had given her something. Then I remembered what Sylvie had endured in the last few days, and I knew there was nothing in the pharmacopoeia that could have even made a dint in her pain. Sylvie was a strong woman, and she was drawing on her strength.

She didn't waste time on preambles. "I need to talk to you, Jo," she said. She gestured toward an area down the corridor. "Come back and have a cup of coffee." Taylor and Jess ran on ahead, and I followed her down the hall.

If I'd needed anything to depress me further on that depressing day, the reception set out for Gary Stephens's funeral would have done it. There were plates of sandwiches and dainties, two big coffee urns, and cups and saucers for at least a hundred and fifty people. We were the only ones in the room.

Sylvie led me to the corner where four chairs had been grouped for conversation. When she sat down, she clasped her hands in front of her, like a schoolgirl. I noticed she wasn't wearing a wedding ring. For a moment, she seemed at a loss. Finally, she said, "I didn't know about Jenny's death, and I didn't know about Ian. I didn't know any of this, Jo. You have to believe me."

"I believe you," I said.

Sylvie pointed to Jess and Taylor sitting at another table. "I was afraid you wouldn't let Taylor play with Jess." When she said her son's name, her voice shook. "I don't want anything more to go wrong for him."

She looked away. "Do you remember how beautiful he was, Jo?"

I was confused. "How beautiful Jess was?"

"Not Jess," she said. "Gary."

"I remember," I said.

"I don't feel anything," she said. "He's dead and I don't feel anything. There was a time when I thought I couldn't live an hour without him."

For the first time that day, Sylvie's eyes filled with tears. "How is that possible, Jo? How can a person just stop loving?"

I didn't know what to say. At the same time, I knew

Sylvie didn't need my words. At least not then. Mercifully, Taylor and Jess heard Sylvie and came over. I gave Jess a hug, then I stood and put my arm around Taylor. "Jess is welcome at our place anytime," I said. "So are you."

Sylvie nodded. "Thanks," she said. "And thanks for coming."

We started to leave, but Taylor grabbed my arm. "Jess says we're supposed to sign the book." Beside the door there was a small table with a guest book and a photograph of Gary. It was an outdoor shot. He was wearing an open-necked shirt, and he was squinting against the sun. Beside the portrait there was a vase with a single prairie lily. I signed my name in the book; under it, Taylor carefully printed hers. Ours were the only names on the page.

Craig Evanson was waiting outside the door. "I thought you and Sylvie might want some privacy," he said.

"Thanks," I said.

"How's the baby?" Taylor asked.

"Perfect," Craig said. "Would you like to see her?"

"You mean today?" Taylor said.

"Why not?" Craig said.

"Jo doesn't believe in kids skipping school for no reason."

"Seeing a new baby is a reason," Craig said.

Taylor looked glum. "It won't be a reason for Jo," she said.

"At the moment, I can't think of a better one," I said. I held my hand out to her. "Come on. Let's go."

When Manda Traynor-Evanson answered the door, she had the baby in her arms and the ginger cats, Mallory and Alex P. Kitten at her heels. Taylor didn't know who to grab first. Manda solved the problem. She asked us to take off our coats, then she turned to Taylor.

"Would you like to stay for lunch?"

"I would," Taylor said.

"So would I," I said.

"Great," said Manda. "But, Taylor, you'll have to give me a hand with the little one. Why don't you scoot into the family room and sit in the big brown chair. That's the official baby-holding chair."

When Taylor was settled, I stood behind her. Together, we looked down at the baby.

"She's beautiful, isn't she?" I said.

Taylor touched the baby's hand gently. "I didn't know babies were born with fingernails and eyelashes," she whispered. "I thought they grew those later, the way they grow teeth."

"No," I said, "they're pretty well perfect right from the start."

"She's perfect," Taylor said. Then she furrowed her brow. "Jo, what is this baby's name?"

"I don't know," I said. "There's been so much going on. I guess we just never asked."

"Ask," Taylor said.

"You ask," I said. "It won't sound so dumb coming from a kid."

Manda was standing in the doorway. "What won't sound so dumb?"

"That we don't know your baby's name," Taylor said.

Manda grinned. "Her name is Grace. After we'd bored everybody to death asking for advice and bought every book, we named her after Craig's mother."

I looked at the baby. Her hair was dark and silky, and her mouth was as delicate as a rosette on a Victorian Valentine. "Grace suits her," I said.

Lunch was fun. When Craig came home, he set up a table in the family room, so we could watch the birds at the birdfeeder while we ate. Manda had warmed up a casserole of tofu lasagna, so I was glad Taylor was distracted. When we'd had our fill of tofu, Craig and I cleared the dishes, and Taylor played with the cats while Manda fed Grace. Then we all drank camomile tea from thick blue mugs and talked about babies.

"If Grace had been a boy, what were you going to call him?" Taylor asked.

"Craig, Jr.," Manda said, shifting the baby on her hip. "We'll save it for the next one if that's okay with you."

"That's okay with me," Taylor said. "It's not a good name for a cat."

"Did I miss something here?" Craig asked.

"Taylor still hasn't named her kitten," I said.

Manda shrugged. "I've got a stack of baby name books over there, Taylor. If you like, you can take them with you when you go. We've already got a name for Kid Number Two, and when Number Three comes along, I'll get the books back."

Craig turned to Taylor. "You're welcome to the books," he said, "but I think I know a name that might work. It's the name of the man who's the patron saint of artists: 'Benet.'"

"Benet," Taylor repeated the name thoughtfully. "What do you think, Jo?"

"I like it," I said.

"So do I," Taylor said. "Because if my cat's name is Benet, I can call him Benny for short, and I really like the name Benny."

The wind was coming up as Taylor and I walked home. When we got to our corner, I saw that the boys had turned the outside Christmas lights on. The day had turned grey and cold, and the lights in front of our house were a welcoming sight. Even Jack O'Lantern looked good. During the long mild spell, his centre of gravity had shifted. From a distance, the lights inside him made him look like an exotic Central American pot.

Taylor ran ahead. She couldn't wait to tell Benny that, at long last, he had a name. Halfway up our walk, she wheeled around and waved her arms at me. "It's snowing," she yelled. "We're going to have snow for Christmas."

I looked up at the sky. Storm clouds were rolling in from the north, and with them the promise of a world that would soon be white and pure again.

BURYING ARIEL

DON'T MISS THE LATEST JOANNE KILBOURN MYSTERY!

"EXCELLENT ..." – *THE NATIONAL POST*

GAIL BOWEN
Author of Deadly Appearances and Murder at the Mendel

BURYING ARIEL

0-7710-1490-2
Hardcover

When university lecturer Ariel Warren is found murdered on campus, her violent death shocks – and divides – Regina's small and fractious academic community. Many students and staff are convinced that Ariel is a victim of male violence. And when Ariel's lover appears to incriminate himself on a popular radio show on the day of the murder, their assumption seems to be dead on. But are they right? Joanne, for one, is not so sure.

" ... nearly flawless plotting, characterization and writing." –*The London Free Press*

"... a ripping good mystery." – *The Calgary Herald*

THE WANDERING SOUL MURDERS

NOW THE MAJOR CTV MOVIE

NOMINATED FOR BEST NOVEL BY THE CRIME WRITERS OF CANADA

GAIL BOWEN
THE WANDERING SOUL MURDERS

0-7710-1494-5
Paperback

Joanne Kilbourn's morning is darkened when her daughter Mieka discovers the corpse of a young woman in an alley near her store. Just twenty-four hours later, Joanne is in for another terrible shock when her son's girlfriend drowns in a lake. The two dead women had each spent time at a drop-in centre for street kids. By the time Joanne realizes the connection, she is deeply embroiled in a twilight world where money can buy anything and there are always people willing to pay.

"Bowen has a fine grasp of characters and setting in this book and she pulls her complicated story together around a shocking and all-too-realistic secret ... Her best book to date."
– *The Globe and Mail*